The Politician

Maze Investigations
Book 4

M. K. Jones

Cover Design: Alison Morgan at www.alicat-design.co.uk

First Edition 2023 published by M. K. Jones

Chapter 1
Newport, December 1896

Adolphus Quinn had just made the worst mistake of his life, but he didn't know it… yet.

Reaching the steps of his house, he paused, looked up at the lights in the parlour window, saw the shadows of his children

His walk had been undertaken in dense fog, uphill, unobserved. Moisture glistened on his heavy coat in the mist-shrouded gaslight. He gave himself a few seconds to get his breathing under control; important to maintain his usual sangfroid and famous bonhomie when he chose that particular façade.

He flexed his gloved hands a few times, stamped his feet once and drew himself up to his full six feet height. Marching up the steps he rang his doorbell three times to ensure that his imminent arrival indoors was anticipated. The door was answered at once by his butler, who kept his gaze down to the floor as he bowed Adolphus into the now hushed house.

Having given his coat and top hat to the silent servant, he checked his reflection in the hallstand, composed his expression and tweaked his moustache into a satisfying shape. A few steps brought him to the door of the parlour. He paused before it, to ensure they knew he was there, then flung it open.

As he had anticipated, the cheerfulness he had glimpsed through the window was gone. His wife sat with her embroidery in her lap, lips pulled into a tight smile. His three children were seated on the settee reading what he knew would be educational tomes. Their upward glances checked his expression, found it stern, mirrored it and looked down again. Adolphus was only interested in one person.

"What are you reading there, Michael?"

Without waiting for an answer, he strode across the room and pulled the book out of the boy's trembling hands.

"The Life of Saint Vincent de Paul," he remarked. "Very good."

The boy's shudder of relief was almost audible.

"Mary, Margaret, you may go to bed."

The two older girls stood up, quickly returned their books to the shelf, said goodnight to their mother and left the room. Before the sound of their footsteps running up the stairs had diminished, Adolphus went to sit next to his wife, who, drawing in a deep breath, kept up her fixed smile. He kissed her cheek and ran a finger down her arm. She understood the gesture, stood and bade him goodnight and left the room for her bedroom, steeling herself for what was to follow.

He turned back to his son. "Come Michael, you and I shall go up and say our prayers together. You will tell me about all the exciting things you have done today."

. This was happiness. This was his dynasty. He would have liked another boy but she had said that this was impossible now after Michael's birth, not that it would stop Adolphus trying. The thought of her impending suffering pleased him. He paused at the bottom of the stairs to shudder at the anticipation of his pleasure and her pain.

He picked up the little boy and hugged him, fleetingly consumed by rage, but deciding to ignore the stiffness of the puny body. The boy put his arms around his father's neck. Tightening his grip and breathing in the perfume of the small head, Adolphus headed towards the door. This was contentment.

As he mounted the stairs his thoughts turned briefly to the future. The two useless girls could be married off; his name meant enough to warrant no lack of suitors in a few years, particularly once he became Mayor. He had already heard of the whispered hints to recommend his elevation to the position of Alderman. He would be one of the youngest ever to be so honoured. The culmination of years of climbing the social ladder, enduring the righteous, bribing the not-so-righteous. Having taken his father-in-law's business to the height of respectability, success and admiration, his plans would soon come to fruition. He had transformed every aspect of himself to become Adolphus Quinn: builder, politician, family man, and philanthropist.

Torturer, rapist, and murderer they would never know. They would all look up to him and he would hide his contempt as he smiled down on them, dolts, fools, dumb oxen. Then the bonus, an Alderman could sit as a magistrate. What a delicious outrage.

At the top of the stairs, from the master bedroom, he heard his wife's prayers of supplication; no mercy. He took Michael into his bedroom where they said their nightly devotions. He put the boy into bed and bade him goodnight. He could barely contain himself.

"Don't you want to hear what I did today, Papa?"

"My apologies, my darling boy, I remember I have some business with your mother."

**

Three days later the fog and gloom had not lifted. It still swirled around the gas lamps outside the Quinn household, causing coughing and chills. Adolphus Quinn had refused to have fires lit during the day, until Michael began to cough.

On the morning of the third day, Adolphus sat at the breakfast table, an unread newspaper beside him. Breakfast was always taken in silence. The children ate and removed themselves. Mrs Bridget Quinn had not appeared at the table for the third day running.

He was about to rise when the insistent ringing of the doorbell interrupted his thoughts. If it were important, he would receive the visitor in the breakfast room. The butler arrived, followed by another man, a small, wiry man in a damp coat and a bowler hat. The man paused in the doorway as the butler stood aside for him. Introductions were not necessary.

"Welcome, Martin. You are up and about early. Leave us, Shore."

The butler bowed and closed the door as the smaller man walked with short quick strides to the table. He threw himself into a chair opposite Adolphus and removed his hat.

"Well?"

"Trouble, brother. Big trouble." Martin Quinn stretched out his hand towards a teacup, but was shaking so much he found he couldn't hold it and pulled his hand back towards his stomach, where he beat it rhythmically. "Have you not yet looked at the newspaper?"

"Clearly not, as I have no idea what you are talking about, Martin. Calm down and explain. And take off your coat – it smells."

Martin Quinn glanced down, realizing he was still wearing the damp overcoat. He pulled it down from his shoulders and let it hang over the back of the chair. He cast his gimlet brown eyes on his brother. "Take a look."

Adolphus picked up the newspaper and perused the local news on page three for several minutes.

"I see nothing here to disturb me. Trouble on a ship at the docks with fever detected, a murder in Cardiff – again. Aah… I see," he paused for a few moments, the newspaper raised; then he put it down and stared at his brother. "As I said, I see nothing to disturb me."

His brother jumped up out of his chair, his coat falling to the floor and paced the length of the dining table. "That is not the end of the story. I have come from the docks where the body was found. By tomorrow it will be even bigger news."

"Hmm. Inconveniently quick, but why should there be concern about the body of a whore?"

"Because this body was not a whore, brother," Martin shouted. "This was a respectable woman, making her way home. She is… was… a well-known medium. She had attended a séance in a house near the South Dock. What they are saying about the state of the body—" He stopped, sweating, and fell into a different chair.

"Yes, yes, calm yourself Martin. There is no danger."

"A man was seen walking near an empty house in which was found… they found… *instruments*."

"Was there a good description of this man?"

"Not that I am aware of but the police are searching seriously this time. They took little notice of the previous cases - now it's different." His voice had sunk to a whisper.

"In that case when I attend the Chamber tomorrow I shall make a speech deploring this horror and calling for more strenuous action from our police, whilst supporting their efforts, of course." He picked up the newspaper again.

For a few moments, his brother seemed to have lost the power of speech. He opened and closed his mouth, sat up, sat back, then put his hands over his face.

"Don't be so dramatic, brother," said the bored voice from behind the newspaper.

"She was a respectable woman," Martin Quinn whispered into his hands.

"There is no such thing," the voice replied. "They are all disgusting, vile creatures, every one. Now," he slammed the paper down onto the table, knocking over a teacup and gaining his brother's attention. "Get control of yourself. This will pass. You will accompany me tomorrow. Today, we must talk business. There are several accounts you and I must examine. I will not condone debt."

"Where is Bridget?"

Adolphus Quinn stood up and rang the bell for the butler. "Vile and disgusting creatures. My wife's whereabouts are none of your business."

**

Adolphus Quinn's speech was well-received in the Chamber, greeted by cheers and shouts of support and encouragement from both sides.

As head of the Watch Committee and a member of the Finance Committee, his support of the local police force was much appreciated, as would be his efforts to give extra funds to the search.

He confirmed that he had conducted an interview with the Head Constable and had been encouraged by the efforts being made. He also remarked that he himself had been in the area on that very evening, but hoped he was not a suspect. Laughter ensued.

In a deep, earnest voice he talked of how much he loved the town, wanted it to be admired for its achievements during its rise to prosperity. He did not want it to become a place of notoriety, like another not too far away. The Councillors nodded gravely at the remark, understanding he was talking about Cardiff. He left the Chamber with handshakes and many good wishes.

Chapter 2
Sicily, Italy. Mid June. Present Day

On the balcony of her room on the fourth floor of the Sicilian seaside hotel, Maggie Gilbert, elbows on the wall, breathed in the spectacular view and the warmth of the early morning sun.

The room being on the corner of the hotel, allowed her a two-way view. Her gaze followed a sparkling trail of sunlight across the azure blue sea, up to the twelfth-century castle on the promontory at the end of the bay. On the hilltop that continued along from the castle, the rays were hitting the village of Savoca which had doubled for the town of Corleone in the first Godfather film. Below and to her right the main street of the provincial seaside town was coming to life, with the sounds of warm raucous Italian and revving scooters. Above the town in the distance were the dark Sicilian Mountains, where remote villages perched on precarious slopes and summits.

She had no idea before coming to Sicily that it was so mountainous. What was the word that she had been searching for since they arrived? Wild? Pretty? Neither; she couldn't decide, but it would come to her, eventually.

It was still early, around 7am and the sun had risen over the sea at the front of the small family run hotel. Bob Pugh had chosen both the hotel and the room. For him it was a familiar place, visited many times and he never tired of it.

She glanced back into the room through the lightly billowing curtains at Bob asleep on his back, snoring gently, the covers pushed back to reveal the red scar that ran the length of his chest.

**

Their relationship had almost failed the previous year,

following an incident with a ruthless family, the relatives of her Maze Investigations colleague, Zelah Trevear. Bob's police training had caused him not to fully inform Maggie about a raid he had set up with the Irish Garda. He and Maggie had travelled to Cork to challenge the family and to get Zelah away from them.

It had turned into a bloodbath. Maggie had feared for her life, not knowing that an army of Gards were standing by. She had been so angry with Bob for not telling her that help was at hand that for months they had barely spoken and she believed their relationship was over. They were both obstinately strong characters, each believing that they had acted appropriately and refusing to apologise; Bob for not telling her everything, and Maggie for insisting that he should have done. That was, until she got the phone call.

Maggie didn't remember much about the ride to the hospital. Zelah was in the office when the call came, and had driven her there at crazy speed. It wasn't until later, when she thought about why the hospital had called her, she discovered Bob had retained her name as his next of kin.

When she burst into Accident and Emergency she was shown to the resuscitation area. She saw the quiet, efficient team working in fierce concentration around him, the discarded blood-soaked swabs, and the machines. Her heart hammered to bursting point. It took every bit of willpower she had to stay on her feet.

There came a moment when the lead Consultant looked up at her and questioned her presence.

"Will he live?" she asked.

"We're doing our best. Are you his wife?"

"His partner." She knew in that moment that she was and always would be.

"It would be better if you waited outside." A nurse took her by the arm and guided her and Zelah to the waiting area. Three policemen in uniform were also in the room. She recognised the Superintendent, Bob's boss, who had called her.

"What happened? Why was he shot?" Zelah asked the questions.

Maggie couldn't speak, her nails dug into the palms of her hands. She wanted to be back in the resuscitation area to see what was happening. She could take it, whatever it was, but she needed to be there. She walked out and went to the Resus door and pushed it open a fraction.

He wasn't there. She burst into the room and yelled, "WHERE IS HE?"

A doctor glanced up and walked over to her. "I was just coming to talk to you, he's gone for a scan. We saw some bubbling in the wound after we applied a dressing, which might have meant a tension pneumothorax, that's air in an area of the lungs. It's potentially life threatening so we needed to put in a chest drain. Our lead cardio thoracic surgeon, Miss Griffiths, was here all the time, in charge. The bleeding slowed, his obs looked OK, so we gave him fluids. As he was stable enough, we did an X-ray and sent him for a CT scan. He won't be long."

"What then?"

"That will depend on the outcome of the scan. We didn't find an exit wound, and the X-ray shows that the bullet is lodged in his lung. Even so, I'll say again, for the time being he's stable. Now, would you like to come with me back to the relatives' room so I can explain to his colleagues?"

Maggie nodded and walked back with the doctor and a nurse.

The policemen and Zelah stood up as they entered the room.

As the doctor began to speak Maggie collapsed into a chair. "Are you OK?" Zelah's voice turned to whisper.

"I've gone all wobbly. My legs don't seem to work," Maggie replied with a sound between a hiccup and a giggle.

The nurse interrupted. "Shock. I'll get her some tea when we're done here."

"You carry on. I'll get it now," said Zelah.

**

After a three-hour operation Bob spent a couple of days in the intensive care unit, then another ten days on a ward, at which point he demanded to be let out, claiming that he was well enough to go home. That was, until he got home – Maggie's home – where he found that away from the rigorous support of the hospital team he was as weak as a new-born baby.

Six more weeks of Maggie's compassionate but disciplined support saw him back on his feet and back in the gym. She complained that he wasn't ready. He insisted he was. This was the watershed moment, if they were going to be a lifelong partnership. She had to accept he was a stubborn man. In this instance nothing she could say would move him. She had to decide if she could accept him as he was, putting the past behind them. If she could, they would be able to work together with a deeper understanding of each other.

That was six months ago and he had already been back at work for two months, on light duties only. When he rebelled at being behind a desk for so long, it was agreed that he could return to active work, but only after a holiday. So, here they were in Sicily.

Deciding what kind of holiday would suit them both had been an interesting discussion. A package holiday on a deserted beach was quickly dismissed. Maggie suggested an historic city like Dubrovnik or Athens but Bob wasn't keen. The discussion had taken place on a Saturday night when they were watching one of her favourite TV programmes, the Italian detective series

Inspector Montalbano.

"What about Sicily?" Bob asked.

"What about it?" she replied. "What's there that would interest both of us?"

"Well, I can climb Mount Etna again and you could see perfect ancient Greek theatres."

The discussion had begun in earnest and they eventually decided to spread the trip out to southern Italy. There was Pompeii and Herculaneum for her, Vesuvius for him; then travelling on to Sicily with Etna for him, Syracusa and Taormina for her.

After a couple of hours of discussion they decided on southern Italy first. Maggie had Pompeii, Bob got Vesuvius. From there they would drive down to Sicily to a hotel on the south coast of the island.

They added a side-trip to Stromboli to see a volcano that spat boiling lava into the air at regular intervals, all of which had sounded fine on paper.

Maggie had realised early on that to climb volcanoes she would need to be fitter. She spent some time in the gym and the swimming pool, and made sure that she took the correct clothes for volcano ascending.

Their first day was spent strolling around Pompeii, ignoring the official guides and breathing in the atmosphere. Maggie paused only to put her hands on the stones and columns where so many ancient Roman fingers had brushed by before her. Bob walked behind her, making the occasional comment of support and showing some interest. The following day they spent at their hotel, for her legs to recover, ready to tackle Vesuvius.

The best Maggie could say was that she made it. If the walk up had been a struggle, the return on the slippery, precipitous gradient was agony. Her legs had given out halfway back and she made the last quarter of a mile on willpower. When they got back to the hotel Bob had made her sit in a bath of cold water.

"I had all of the right gear" she complained.

"But none of the right muscles," he replied with a grin.

The next day they drove down to Sicily. Mount Etna proved easier, being a much bigger volcano. The first part of the ascent was made by cable car, which Maggie found unsettling but fascinating as the car jolted its way upwards. This was followed by a further journey by safari bus across ascending bleak acreages of how she thought a Martian landscape might look. Finally, the crater itself; Maggie made it around the circumference with Bob at one point with both hands on her back pushing her up the steepest part, but she made it, and felt exultant.

Maggie had fallen in love with both volcanoes and Sicily. They had visited Taormina the next morning, taking in the Greek theatre and the main square of the town where they sat to drink strong Italian coffee, in the warmth of the sunshine, overlooking the Mediterranean a hundred feet beneath.

In the afternoon, they moved on to Syracusa, again visiting the Greek theatre and the ancient city ruins, before going into the city.

Her only sadness was that they didn't have time to visit Ragusa, the city where the Montalbano series was filmed, nor the temples of Agrigento as they were leaving later that day for Stromboli. These went onto a bucket list for the not-too-distant future.

She hadn't discussed this with Bob. For him, it was the highlight of the trip, to see an active volcano spitting and belching red hot lava. He had told her that the walk up could only be done with a guided group and it would take around three to four hours. She was dreading it. Not dreading seeing the volcano in action, of course. She feared she wouldn't be able to cope with the walking and that she would let him down by having to turn back. Somehow, she had to raise this with him, today.

A breeze hit the curtains as the sun reached across the bay and warmed up the balcony. Bob opened his eyes.

"How long have you been there?"

"About half an hour," she replied, tipping her face to meet the sun's rays on the pillar. "I could soak up this view forever."

He sat up. "Make it another half an hour. We have to pack and get the car back to the port so we can pick up the ferry. I'm going to hit the shower." He paused for a moment. "You OK?"

"Yes, of course," she replied, "I'm going for a quick swim. Meet you at breakfast."

**

As soon as they helped themselves to breakfast and found a shaded table on the terrace overlooking the beach, Maggie decided that the time had come to speak up.

"Bob, about Stromboli…" was as far as she got.

"I know," he interrupted, pausing with the final piece of croissant in his hand that had been on its way to his mouth. "I'm not stupid, nor do I not notice things. Look, we both know that you probably won't make it to the top and it would be daft of me to try to force you. So, I've made an alternative arrangement."

She drew in a rapid breath and decided there was no point in trying to get him to think about consulting her first. At least by now she knew that if she didn't like whatever his 'alternative arrangements' were she could say so without too much concern about his feelings.

"Which is?"

"OK. It's a four-hour slog to the top. It's steep, stony and slippery. The walk back down in the dark, on shale, is even harder. I don't want you to feel you'd have to give up. If you did I'd likely give up too. Nor, my love, could I watch you

15

struggle and injure yourself." He smiled. "There's an alternative."

"Which is?"

"We arrive there mid-afternoon on the hydrofoil. Instead of having dinner at the hotel, we're going for a walk, around to another side of the volcano. There's a pizzeria that's been built on a promontory, about a quarter of the way up. It's on the side of the slope where the lava runs down into the sea and it's got a great view up to the crater. You can eat pizza and watch the eruptions at the same time; it's not the same as being above the active crater, but still a live show. They give you a lift up and back to the hotel by jeep. Tomorrow I can do the long climb with a group, before we head off for Naples. What do you think?"

"What about you?"

"I'm still going to do the climb the following evening but it would leave you on your own. I guess you could cope with that?"

"You guess correctly." She leaned across and took his croissant-free hand. "This is a big relief -thank you."

"Thought so," he replied, chewing the last piece of his breakfast as he stood up. "Let's get going then."

Maggie stood, turned her face away, shook her head slightly and smiled. This is how he would always be. He had been thinking about her, and about himself, making sure that they each got something out of the experience.

**

Two days later, as they sat in Naples airport, waiting for the early morning flight back to Bristol Maggie's phone rang. It had been agreed that her children Jack and Alice could call her whenever they felt the need. Zelah and Nick, her partners in Maze Investigations, would give her and Bob space and not call about work issues. This was Zelah phoning.

16

"Hi Zelah. We're almost back, just at the airport."

"Something I need to talk to you about, quite urgently. What time are you back at the house?"

"Um, about two-ish, I think. What's up?"

"It can wait, see you later," Zelah replied and ended the call.

"*Have you had a nice holiday? Yes, thanks for asking Zelah,*" Maggie muttered to herself, loudly enough to disturb Bob from his book.

"Typical Zelah," she said in response to his raised eyebrow "Told me it was urgent, then said it could wait."

"Couldn't be that urgent, then." He looked down at his book, but added, "Nothing wrong that you know of? Kids OK?"

"They're fine. I spoke to both of them last night. No, whatever it'll be work. Whatever, it can wait."

"You are OK with work still, aren't you? I caught a bit of frustration there."

"Yes, I'm fine with it. My frustration is with Zelah."

"She's a fixed point in the universe," he grinned. "She's never going to be anything but frustrating. You wouldn't really have her any other way, would you?"

"No, of course not, but it doesn't mean that I can always handle her rudeness."

He went to add something but was interrupted by a muffled public address announcement.

"That's us," Bob said. "Let's go. Whatever it is, you'll find out soon enough."

Chapter 3

They arrived back early in the afternoon at Maggie's house in Cwmbran, shivering under a grey sky.

Bob made lunch whilst Maggie unpacked and started their washing. She was glancing out at the wet and windy garden, when Zelah drove up, let herself in and came to find them in the kitchen. She plonked herself down at the table, poured a cup of coffee from the cafetière that Bob put in front of her, slurped back the whole cup and sat up again.

"I have a friend with a big problem that she wants us to sort out," she said, looking from one to the other. Maggie went to sit at the table and Bob stood next to the cooker, arms folded.

"Then you'd better tell me the story," Maggie said, "and why it's so urgent."

"Her name is Isobel. Isobel Ramona Blackstock. Professionally, she goes by the name of Madame Ramona."

"I think I remember that name," Maggie ruminated. "Wasn't there something in the papers, about a year ago?"

"Thought you might," Zelah replied. "Isobel is a medium. She got herself into trouble last year; she was exposed by a newspaper as a scammer."

"Of course, I remember now. She'd been doing theatre shows for bereaved families and pretending to give them information from loved ones from the 'other side'. The paper showed her up to be a fraud. What does she need us for? Please don't tell me she has news for us."

"There's no need to be like that about it," Zelah said, "she isn't a fraud, Not exactly. It's just that sometimes she speaks… hopefully."

"You mean she makes it up," Bob interjected.

"I wouldn't say that, sometimes she knows things."

"I'm surprised at you, Zelah. Unusual for you to put up with flummery."

"It's not flummery!" Zelah muttered, rounding her shoulders and sitting back into the chair. "Are you prepared to listen, or not?"

Maggie was nonplussed. In all the time she had known Zelah, defensive was rarely her response. She sat back and tapped her fingers on the table. "OK, tell me the story and I won't interrupt—"

"I'm going into the living room," Bob interrupted again before Zelah could begin. "I think it's more than flummery. Giving messages from dead friends and relatives to grieving people for money. 'Far as I'm concerned it's shameful. Should be illegal. I don't want to hear about this." He left the kitchen.

"How is he doing?" Zelah asked.

"He seems to be fine," Maggie replied. "He hasn't said anything about being shot, shared his innermost feelings, if that's what you mean. He's never been one for blurting out his emotions."

"Strong, silent type," Zelah said.

"Maybe, if there is such a type." Maggie paused for a moment, "I'm leaving it up to him to speak if he needs to; he only accepted an invitation from the police psychologist when they wouldn't let him back on active duty. I don't know what he said either." She paused, staring into her teacup, "I think he's a strong man, certainly, and he knows his own mind. I've enough examples of that to last a lifetime. Yes, I do worry that it's a dam waiting to burst. If it does, we'll all have his back, I hope."

Zelah nodded. "Yes, we will. Even Nick."

Maggie grinned. "His relationship with Stella Bell seems to be developing well. I'm pleased for him."

19

"Well at least he looks at her when he talks to her. He's not wearing a glove now he's taking less notice of that stupid birthmark on his hand, so the signs are encouraging," Zelah said.

"And what about you and Rick? Are you going back to Nova Scotia any time soon, or is he paying us another visit?"

Zelah shuffled in her chair and sat up in one of her aggressive poses. "We're friends, that's all. I like my space and he likes his; I may go back out in the autumn."

Maggie knew better than to question further. She had become fond of Rick Mathis, the gruff Canadian widower Zelah had met on a brief research trip to Canada, for a previous case. They seemed to have hit it off at once, Rick being an ideal foil for Zelah's own tight, brusque personality. Each was quietly grieving the loss of a spouse after a long, happy marriage, but neither was the type to talk about it.

"It must look gorgeous as the seasons change out there," she said casually, getting up from her chair and moving to the sink. "Anyway, back to business. When is the meeting with Isobel?"

Zelah looked at her watch. "Fifteen minutes."

Maggie spun around. "Oh, for God's sake, Zelah, you could have given me more warning. Where are we supposed to meet her?" She turned back, and banged her cup down in the sink. There was an ominous cracking sound, which she ignored. I said it was urgent," Zelah replied. "She's coming here." She held up her hands against Maggie's yell of surprise. "Just sit down again, and I'll tell you the story."

"We never have clients here, Zelah, this is my home, you know that," she glared.

"Yes, but I've made this an exception. She's having to keep a low profile at the moment, and can't go anywhere in public until the fuss dies down. You haven't seen the local papers recently."

"Couldn't she disguise herself?"

"Silly idea," Zelah retorted. "There's more to it than that. Let me get on with the story, will you?"

Maggie thumped back down into the kitchen chair, and jerked a nod at Zelah.

"Isobel received a message… no, wait. The bigger picture. First, and this won't seem related yet, but it is OK? Two weeks ago, when you were in Italy, a story came out of a Gwentshire County Council sub-committee meeting. They want to spend money putting up a statue to a Victorian philanthropist, which seemed innocuous enough. Apparently, he was a patron of charities, put money into building the Royal Gwent Hospital, and was one of the first to build social housing. He was an Irish immigrant, made good in the building trade, married well and expanded his father-in-law's small building company into a large-scale enterprise. He built a lot of the houses that are still standing in streets throughout the County."

Maggie shrugged, a 'so what?' but Zelah kept going.

"There was a dispute, Council finances being what they are, money not well spent according to some; it was proposed and lobbied for by a businessman who's a descendant of the great man. He persuaded them to agree this was an important remembrance of Gwentshire history and growth. It goes to a final vote at Gwentshire's full Council meeting, which is just over a week away, but it's expected to get the nod. So, the following day the story appeared in the Argus, just a small piece. On that same day Isobel held a séance at her home. When it had finished, she had another message. A strange one from her great-great-grandmother. A woman called Ada Blackstock who was also a medium, in Cardiff in the 1890s." Zelah paused and took a deep breath.

"And the message was…?" Maggie asked.

"First you need to know about Isobel."

Maggie was about to remonstrate but the doorbell stopped her, ringing, three times, each time for exactly three seconds.

"And here she is," Zelah said. "You can see for yourself." She left the kitchen, followed by Maggie.

Approaching the front door. Maggie could see an odd, immobile shape, distorted by the glass panels; it seemed to be as broad as it was high. When Zelah opened the door, she understood. The woman standing there was around her own height, wearing a flowing robe and a wide turban. The face underneath the turban was broad, with a strong nose and slightly protuberant dark eyes. Beneath the nose was a wide mouth, resplendent with an eye-watering shade of red lipstick. The robe was black with oversized red flowers the same colour as the lipstick and the turban. Around her neck she wore a string of black beads, each the size of an egg and she carried a king-sized black bag across her arm.

The woman swept forward into the hall, causing Maggie to take two steps back. She enveloped Zelah in a theatrical hug, with air kisses at both cheeks, during which Zelah didn't move. Then she turned to Maggie.

"Darling, Zelah has told me so much about you." She moved to hug Maggie, who stepped back two more steps. "I don't do hugs with strangers," she said.

The woman paused, and threw Zelah a surprised look. She opened her mouth to speak but Zelah jumped in. "Isobel, come this way, and just shut up for now." Zelah turned into the office, indicating they follow her, with a flicking finger over her shoulder.

The three sat at the office table, Maggie with her lips pursed, Isobel Blackstock gloweringly offended and Zelah scowling. All three went to speak just as a sudden lashing of rain hammered the window. They paused for a second giving Zelah the opportunity to open the conversation.

"Maggie, as you have realised, this is Isobel. Isobel, I said be discreet; you are not Madame bloody Arcati, nor are you Hermione Gingold. This isn't a séance or a consultation, so drop the act and be yourself, please."

The woman jumped to her feet. "Actually darling, it was Margaret Rutherford and—" she stopped suddenly and dropped back into the chair.

"Oh, all right," she said in a low voice, unlike the previous shrieking tone, and pulled off her turban. Her hair was mousy; short, thin, lank and greasy. Maggie thought it might be the result of continuously covering it with the outlandish headwear.

"Now," Zelah began again, "Isobel, I've hardly had a chance to tell Maggie about you, so it's up to you; but we want the real you, not the act."

Maggie held up her hand. "Wait, I think we need a re-start here. Coffee Isobel?"

She nodded and Maggie thought she saw glistening in the woman's eyes... tears? Coffee was definitely needed. She left the room, which would also give Zelah the chance to restore calm.

She was right. By the time she returned Isobel and Zelah looked more composed and relaxed.

As Maggie poured the coffees and passed them around, Isobel said "Sorry, I'm so used to acting in a certain way with strangers. I've been rather stressed over the past two weeks, so I went into Madame Ramona mode. It helps me.""

"Fair enough," Maggie replied. "Zelah has told me you have an urgent problem, actually beyond urgent."

"Someone is trying to hurt me," Isobel said. "I'm frightened and if I'm not careful they will succeed. I am in hiding at present."

"Why would anyone want to hurt you?"

"Because of a message I received that affects a decision being made by Gwentshire Council next week. They are going to erect a statue to commemorate and honour a man; a man who deserves no such honour or memory."

"Why not?"

"Because he is, rather he was, a degenerate torturer and murderer, and a psychopath who preyed on vulnerable women." She paused for a moment. "One of his victims was my great-great-grandmother, Ada Blackstock."

Chapter 4

"Why is he being honoured?" Maggie asked. "Surely he must have at least come under suspicion at the time?"

Isobel sighed, folded her arms and leant forward on the table. "He was a renowned figure in the town. His name was already being touted for Mayor, and he could even have become a Member of Parliament for the Monmouth Boroughs. So far, I've only been able to read the newspaper reports, but there's no mention of him in relation to the murders. Except for him pledging support to the police force, on behalf of the Council, and offering to divert funds to them for further investigation."

"Then what makes you believe that he was a killer?"

The medium sighed and sat up. "It was two weeks ago. I didn't see the piece in the paper that day about the statue, I was busy with a meeting of people in my studio."

"A séance?" Maggie asked.

"That's what you may choose to call it," Isobel replied with a sniff. "My spirit guide took us through the messages for those who were present. After the messages were all given, my guests departed. I sat back at the table to drink some water. It's emotionally exhausting, you understand."

Maggie raised an eyebrow but didn't interrupt.

"Suddenly, I felt something strange in the room, nothing I had ever felt before. My orb began to tremble and smoke appeared inside it. Then there was a voice, I didn't recognise it, it was struggling as if it hadn't spoken for a long time. I couldn't understand it at first, the words weren't even whole sentences. My spirit guide is eloquent, but this... was different. I asked, *"Who are you?"* The voice replied '*Ada*'. At first it was strung out like two words – Ay-Dar. It took me a few seconds to realise it was saying Ada. I asked, '*Are you Ada Blackstock?*' The voice whispered …'*Yes*'. I jumped up from the table and walked around the room, I didn't know what to do. Honestly, I was terrified. I always get a feeling of happiness from my spirit guide, but this was different, cold and intense."

"I felt compelled to carry on, so I sat down and put my hands on the glass, I felt it shudder. I said, 'Do you need something from me?' The voice said, 'Stop him.' I asked, 'Who, stop who?' It said, 'Man in the black hat; he killed me; father and son; the doll.'

"Then everything changed. The smoke disappeared, and everything felt normal again. It took me a while to get my composure back, I can tell you. I couldn't think what she meant. I knew she had been murdered, it's a family scandal, and for years no-one talked about it, but some of us in the family knew. I'm the first to inherit her special gifts."

She stopped and gave them both a self-satisfied look, then collapsed again into her seat and drew a deep breath. She put her fingers up to her temples, as if she needed to support her head.

"I'd read about the news of her death some time ago; it was a terrible tragedy, back in 1896. I read as much as I could find about her, once I found out that she had passed her gifts on to me." She gazed around the room as she recalled the memory...

"I was only in my teens. When it started, I thought I was going mad. Hearing voices, well to a thirteen-year-old that was crazy, wasn't it? I didn't tell anyone, of course. At that time I didn't know anything about Ada. I was brought up by my mother. I have no idea who my father was, and I doubt she knew either; she was a free spirit, a hippy as they were called back then. Because she left me alone to get on with my life I spent a lot of time with my grandparents. They didn't approve of Susan, my mother, but they were good to me. Ada was

Grandad's grandmother, not that he knew her. When I found some old photo albums, I asked him about the people in them. That was when Grandad Paul told me about Ada."

"You have a photograph of her?" Maggie asked.

"Yes. When Grandad Paul died, he left me the albums."

"What was she like?"

Isobel bristled and brought her gaze directly back to Maggie. "If you are asking me, can you tell what she was like from a photograph, you are very much mistaken. We don't have external marks of the gift."

"I'm just curious," Maggie replied, "Please, carry on with your story." Her tone was neither apologetic nor encouraging, Isobel glanced at Zelah, who shrugged but didn't say anything.

"The photographs were taken in her late teens, before her son, Henry was born. They were a big family, she was the fifth of nine children. She was accepted by the family then. They were comfortably off. Her father, Charles, was a stonemason. I can show you the photographs, if you wish."

"Yes, I'd like to see them," Maggie said.

"I'll give them to Zelah to bring them over. To continue, she was the middle child. The youngest was Owen. He was only about eight when Ada died, but he survived into his eighties. He was the person who told Grandad Paul all about her. Only what he could remember, and from his child's perspective. He said she was different from the rest of them, quieter, more introspective. He said she kept herself to herself. Grandad Paul thought that, with nine children in the house, it would have been busy and noisy, so Ada would have liked her own space. When her gifts began to manifest themselves, the family didn't know what to make of her—"

"The Victorians were fascinated with life after death," Zelah interrupted. "There were lots of psychic societies in South Wales, and they were fascinated by everything about the spirit

27

world and séances, what was on 'the other side'. Even Charles Dickens had an interest. It was a national obsession, back then."

"That's true and all very well," Isobel said. "Except when it's a member of your own family conducting them. I think they saw the publicity as notoriety, not something to be welcomed in a respectable family."

"So, she garnered a following and publicity?" Maggie asked.

"Oh yes, she was well-known locally, though her fame didn't extend beyond South Wales. She was consulted by the police on at least one occasion that I know of, the fatal shooting of a carpenter on the St Fagan's estate."

"And did she enjoy her fame?" Maggie asked.

"I find your questions on the brink of insulting," Isobel said. "Zelah, does your organisation really want to help me?"

"I want Maggie to hear the full story," Zelah replied. "I agree with you that her questioning could be a little more sympathetic, but please carry on." She gave Maggie a glare.

"You can read up for yourselves about her death, her murder. It was horrible. I suspect that much of the detail didn't make the papers. From what I know of the other deaths, before Ada, there was torture and maiming. If you do find out, I don't want to know any details." Her hands went up to her necklace and ran across the egg-like beads as she subconsciously shook her head from side to side.

"We'll check it all out," said Maggie. "However I still can't see how this relates to the statue. What was his name, by the way and how does any of this relate to who is frightening you?"

Isobel sighed. "He was called Adolphus Quinn. He came to South Wales as a young man in his mid-twenties. Last week, when I went onto a newspaper archive site, I typed in 'man in the black hat'. It seemed to me there was something intriguing about the phrase, more than just a simple description. Don't ask me why or how I perceived that." She tossed back her head.

Maggie winced at the theatrics.

"Up came a newspaper article from six months before Ada's death. The headline was *The Man in the Black Hat*, and it was about Adolphus Quinn."

She stopped to delve down into her bag, brought out two sheets of A4 paper and handed one each to Maggie and Zelah.

"Here's the article, read it for yourself."

It was a short piece with a photograph of Adolphus Quinn wearing what had become his customary black top hat. Maggie thought he appeared rather pompous, solemn, and proud. He had a thick nose that looked as if it might have been broken, large oval eyes and a wide mouth. His bushy moustache hid much of his lower face, but it was nevertheless, an alluring, handsome face. Could she detect a touch of cruelty in the eyes, or was she allowing her impression to be led by what she had just learned about him?

The article listed his many successes and achievements then moved to the subject of the hat. He explained that he liked to be recognised, as he walked through the docks area of town, since he was a man of the people and wanted to meet as many working folk as he could. Another of his idiosyncrasies was that he always walked, he never took private transport, although he could easily afford it. He ensured that no-one should ever be afraid to approach him. They could ask him anything, and he would listen with sympathy, even if he was not always able to offer help. He had come from a poor, hopeless existence himself but with the help of God, and his own hard work, had made something of himself. Now he wanted to give back to the poor people of the docks area. After all, that was where he had started his journey.

Maggie could picture him benignly smiling at the interviewer. There was nothing about the photograph that gave him away as being anything other than how he described himself. Nor was there anything glib about his answers. He appeared to be a genteel Victorian philanthropist, possibly a little smug, but honest enough. Certainly nothing to suggest what Isobel was claiming.

"Is there anything else about him?" Maggie asked.

"Only his death," Isobel replied, once again delving in her black bag up to her elbow and producing another folder. "He was murdered; it was thought to be a political killing."

"Wow," Maggie muttered, as she and Zelah read again. This time there was a sheaf of paper. Maggie skimmed through the headlines of each page, deciding to read the detail later. "He was an Irishman against the Republic, not a popular position, especially around Newport Docks."

"They must have felt betrayed," Zelah added.

"The IRA, of course," Isobel said. "They called it a political assassination but it was murder."

"No, there was no IRA at that time," Zelah said, "there was the Irish Republican Brotherhood, also known as the Fenians. Is that why it's taken so long to get the statue agreed?"

Isobel shrugged, "I don't know. It doesn't matter much to people now, does it? It's his philanthropy that's being recognised, and it's being organised by his heirs." She sat back, her expression glum.

"Who are…?" Maggie asked.

"Rufus Quinn, you may have heard of him. He's a business man, started as a developer, retired now. He's the Chairman of Joint Business Ventures throughout the County, heads up lots of charities, works closely with Gwentshire Council on a load of projects, etcetera, etcetera."

"I've heard that name," Maggie said. "Has he been in the news?"

"Oh yes," Zelah replied, "a lot of people have heard of him, and wish they hadn't. He's has a property empire now; owns about a hundred properties in and around the Gwent area. There are rumours that he's not the best of landlords. He doesn't like people who complain."

"So why has he been in the news?"

"Not about his property empire," Zelah replied. "He's become a big name in the area."

"Have you met him?"

"A couple of times, at Council events, charity receptions, that kind of thing. I dislike the bloody things, but sometimes I have to go."

"What's he like in person?" Maggie asked.

"Full of himself," Zelah replied, "doesn't like people who disagree with him."

"As I did," Isobel interjected. They turned to look at her.

"I presume this is part of your story?" Maggie asked.

"Rufus Quinn is the great-grandson of Adolphus Quinn. He's been lobbying for this statue to honour his ancestor for the past twelve months," Isobel explained, "and he's finally made it happen."

"I am guessing you marched up to him and told him that his revered ancestor was a vicious murderer?" Maggie asked her.

Isobel ran her fingers over her beads again. "Sort of. He asked for my evidence. When I told him, he laughed at me, and had me escorted out of the reception."

"You did that in front of his friends and colleagues?" Maggie asked, "and you're surprised that he didn't take it well?"

"I thought he might have at least given me a hearing," Isobel replied, flushing and pulling at the beads. "I was embarrassed but prepared to try talking to him again. That night, a rag soaked in petrol was pushed through my letterbox followed by a lit match. Later that day a note appeared saying I should shut up and go away, if I know what's good for me." Her hands were shaking so much, she let go of the beads, and clasped them together in her lap.

"You think it was Rufus Quinn?" Maggie asked. "Is a supposedly well respected business man capable of such a thing? Perhaps it could have been a disgruntled customer?"

Isobel bristled. "They are clients and friends, though possibly I suppose. I'm sure it's Rufus Quinn, not in person, of course, but on his behalf; or it was that son of his."

"Do you have any concrete reason to believe that?"

Isobel paused for a moment, then shook her head, "No, just instinct, there was something about the look in his eyes when I told him about Ada. I thought he recognised her name, then he roared with laughter, and told the group he was with that I was a local nut job, and had me escorted out. As I looked back he was watching me, and it wasn't the look of someone who was laughing. It was malicious and it shook me, so, when the burning rag set my hall on fire, I knew it was him."

"I'm sorry," Maggie said, "truly I am. That's a horrible thing to have happened, but for me it's not clear cut. What about you, Zelah?"

If Maggie had been expecting support, she didn't get it.

"I agree with Isobel," Zelah replied decisively. "I've met him, I don't like him and there is something about him that rings an alarm bell, don't ask me what; it's instinct, like Isobel said."

"OK, what do you want us to do, Isobel?"

"Well, as I said, I got the feeling that he recognised Ada's name. It was a solid feeling and when I get such feelings they are usually right. He knows something that might harm his plan for the statue. That can only mean he knows something he isn't telling, about his so-called virtuous ancestor." She finished with a decisive nod.

"What you do you want us to do?" Maggie repeated.

"Oh, find the proof, of course, find out the truth about

Adolphus Quinn and Ada Blackstock. Then we can stop that statue being approved."

"And how long do we have?"

"Until Thursday week. That's the date of the full County meeting at the Headquarters over in Red Bridge. Now, I must go, I've promised to meet with a client at her home, and I can't let her down." She stood up, re-positioned her turban around her head and picked up her voluminous bag.

"Isobel, you're supposed to be keeping a low profile," Zelah said.

"It's just one client," Isobel replied as she headed for the door. "Ciao, darlings," and she blew them a kiss.

"Whoa, hang on a minute," Maggie said, following Isobel to the door. "What about the rest of the message, the bit about the father and son and the doll?"

"Sorry darling, I have no idea what that means, I presume that the father and son are the Quinns. I have no idea what the doll means, I'm hoping you'll be able to tell me." With that, Isobel opened the front door, produced a large umbrella from her bag and flounced off down the path.

Chapter 5

"Back in Madame Ramona mode," Zelah muttered to Maggie.

"Where is she staying while this is going on?" Maggie asked.

"At my flat," Zelah replied, "I'm not happy, but she is frightened. She has to stay somewhere, she can't afford a hotel."

"The spooky business not paying too well?"

"Don't be facetious, it doesn't suit you," Zelah replied. "She's not a bad person, and sometimes she knows extraordinary things. She once helped Martin."

"Was it something genuine?" Maggie asked, trying to disguise a yawn.

"Yes it was, but I can see it's time for me to go. I'll see you tomorrow."

She let herself out, as Bob put his head around the office door. "All gone?"

"Yep," Maggie replied, as the front door banged again. This time it was Jack coming home. He rushed up to Maggie and gave her a crushing hug. "You're home, mum!"

"Yes, and it's lovely to see you too, but please let me breathe. That's better," she said as he let go, "how's college been?"

"Excellent," he replied. "Tomorrow's our last day. I'm really looking forward to this weekend," he added, his eyes lighting up.

For a moment Maggie froze, trying to remember. Then it came to her. "Yes, I bet you are, we all are. How many are coming?"

"All except Lucy, she has a family thing. Their parents are dropping them here, on Saturday morning at about ten. That's OK, isn't it, Then collecting them again after lunch on Sunday?"

"No problem at all," Maggie replied, with a smile. Then something occurred to her, "I think that this time, we may have a live case for you all to work on."

"Brilliant, what is it?"

"I'll tell you over dinner. Go and get changed. Dinner at six."

He kissed her on the cheek and ran off up the stairs, having discarded his sopping wet bags in the hall.

Bob took her by the hand, led her into the sitting room and guided her into an armchair. "You are exhausted," he said, "I'll cook something, you have a rest." He kissed her quickly on the top of her head and went back to the kitchen.

The sound of rain lashing on the windows made Maggie feel instantly sleepy, but she wanted to process everything that Isobel had told them. Her first thought was: did she want to take on this case at all? This was Zelah's friend and, despite her overblown presentation, Maggie did believe the woman was upset. What had upset her? Was it the message, the man's reaction, or the arson attack? She understood why Rufus Quinn had reacted the way he had. Nevertheless he could have ushered her into a quieter space, listened to what she had to say, before rejecting her. That didn't sound likely from what Zelah knew. If humiliating her in front of others pleased him that made him a nasty man. But was there any more to it that than that? Had Isobel imagined the way he looked at her? She shuffled herself into a more comfortable position, resting her head on the cushion, and yawned. And then there was…

"Wake up, dinner's ready," Bob was shaking her arm. She had fallen into such a deep sleep for a moment she struggled to remember where she was. *Were they in Italy?* It was probably only seconds, but it felt much longer, as she forced her brain to think. *What's the day, what's the time? Where on earth am I?*

Bob shook her again. "You've slept for almost two hours

35

Come on, Jack's in the kitchen." She gave him a groggy nod. The kitchen, yes, they'd come home. She had been thinking about Isobel Blackstock. They had to take the case. This was Zelah's friend and Maggie hoped Zelah would do the same, if the roles were reversed. She tried to pull herself up, but had to cling on to Bob, who pulled her out of the chair.

"All that uphill walking has knackered you out," he said as they walked into the kitchen "but you've come home fitter than when you left. You'll need to keep it up."

"We'll see," she muttered, as she flopped down into a chair at the table in the conservatory.

"You OK, mum?"

"I walked to the top of two volcanoes, up and down some long, precipitous, uneven paths that made my leg muscles think they were under attack from a jellylegs curse."

"But it was good?"

She smiled, leaned her elbows on the table and cupped her chin with both hands. "It was beyond good. It was amazing. On Etna there was a lot of activity, not that we could get close to the crater that's currently active. There are four craters, but they aren't all active. There were smoking vents and the smoke coming out was actually poisonous gases, which meant we couldn't get close but it was stunning to watch.

We walked around the rim of one of the inactive craters. I imagine it's what the surface of the moon looks like, black and barren and covered in rocks and dust, as far as you can see. The crater on Vesuvius is deeper and quieter and it's steam not smoke coming out from the vents. The view of the Bay of Naples from the top was awesome."

"And we climbed hundreds of steps up and down ancient Greek theatres," Bob added as he dished out the food.

"What was Pompeii like?" Jack asked through a spoonful of spaghetti and sauce.

"My favourite place, as you know," Maggie replied. "There's so much there. You can really feel you're walking in the steps of people who were there when Vesuvius erupted. There are the casts of the people who didn't survive. They get to you a bit. They're curled up with hands covering their faces." She paused. "But I loved the cobbled streets. You can see the marks of cart tracks and there are crossing stones, and, oh, so much else. I'll take you and Alice there, she'd love it too."

Jack nodded enthusiastically, "More interesting than what we've been studying in history this year. The Russian and German monarchies and how they shaped Europe; not that fascinating."

"What about your new client?" Bob asked.

"Isobel, I'm not sure she is yet," Maggie replied. "I was thinking about what she said when I fell asleep. I think we'll have to pursue it as she's Zelah's friend. You know, she's a medium?"

Bob scowled.

"Yes, I know what you think, but the story of the spirit message she received is interesting. It involves an unsolved crime from the late 1890s. She's the descendant of another medium, a Victorian woman called Ada Blackstock. According to Isobel, Ada has given her a message about the man who killed her, and several prostitutes, in Newport Docks. She said that the man who killed her was a local dignitary and philanthropist and she wants us to find the evidence."

"Who wants you to find it, this woman or her ancestor?"

"Both, I think, and as soon as possible."

"Why does it matter when you find it?"

"Because a descendant of this man, a County bigwig, has been lobbying for a statue to be put up in his ancestor's honour in the centre of one of the County towns, which would be a horrible travesty, if the man is a psychopathic killer, wouldn't it?"

"Wouldn't look good if the story came out *after* they put the statue up," Bob grinned. "I presume your short deadline is to stop it happening?"

"Yes, the Council meeting to approve the statue and its financing is next Thursday."

"That is quick. Can you do it?"

"I was thinking that, as Jack has his groupies here at the weekend, they can help with the research. We'll look for Ada and see what we can find."

"That's great," Jack said, "we'll be doing some real investigating." He beamed at his mother, "Thanks mum, and we're a youth online family history research group. Please don't call them groupies, just because they're all girls."

"I'll try to remember, just that the name has stuck. Anyway, Zelah and I will get started tomorrow. As soon as the girls arrive I can brief you and you can get started too."

He jumped up from the table. "I'm going to let them know. That's so cool. They'll be excited to get stuck into some real research."

Maggie went to pick up a plate to stack it but Bob stopped her. "I'll do it, you sit and tell me about this philanthropic slaughterer."

"His name was Adolphus Quinn and Isobel's great-great-grandmother Ada was killed, according to her, by him in 1896 and—" She stopped as Bob turned to face her. "What's the matter?" His face had drained of colour and he was standing still.

"You said the ancestor is a local business man. Is he by any chance Rufus Quinn, the landlord?"

"Yes, that's right. How did you know?"

Bob put the plates down, returned to the table and sat opposite her, his hands palm down on the table.

"Because we believe that his son, Kennet Quinn, is the man who had me shot."

Chapter 6

"Not that he did it himself," Bob continued, "but Kennet Quinn makes Rufus look like a fluffy bunny." He folded his arms and sat back in the chair. "Mind you, if you met Kennet, you'd wonder what the fuss was about. He's always smartly dressed; tall, round-shouldered, wears glasses with thick lenses and looks a bit pathetic. Then you see his eyes, and it's like looking at that glassy fixed gaze of dead fish. That's when you realise, you are being assessed by him, for your level of threat."

He stopped and took a deep breath as Maggie waited. "Kennet is an accountant. Rufus has stepped back now and Kennet looks after the Quinn property empire. At the lower end of their portfolio the environmental health issues are shocking. Kennet's the enforcer, or rather he runs a group of enforcers who carry out the orders. He sits in the background and calls them his property managers. They're dangerous people and I would prefer it if you had nothing to do with them." He stared unblinking at Maggie, waiting for her reply.

The silence persisted as Maggie weighed up her options. There was clear water here between Zelah and Bob. If Kennet Quinn had tried to kill him, how could she refuse to do as Bob asked? But if they were also the people who tried to burn down Isobel's home, how could she ignore that?

"Did you know that someone put a petrol-soaked rag through Isobel Blackstock's letterbox followed by a lit match?"

"No, I hadn't heard. Has she reported it to the police?"

"I'm not sure; she's convinced it was the Quinns."

"Why?"

She told him the story of Isobel's approach to Rufus Quinn, how she was treated and what she saw as she left him, followed later that night by the arson attack. She finished with "Can you tell me what you know, and why you believe that he ordered the attack on you?"

"Not all of it, but I can tell you that Kennet Quinn is a feared landlord in certain parts of their property empire. He uses the Section 21 notice to get rid of anyone who complains; not too often, mind, as that might attract unwanted attention. Some complainants get a lesser version of what Zelah's friend experienced, to make sure they know that complaining is not a good idea."

"Why would that interest you? Surely it's the Council's job to investigate environmental health complaints from tenants, not the police?"

"It should be, but they're stretched by years of budget cuts, and Kennet has a way of finding out what complaints have been made if they are about public health.. He does some repairs. If people persist, Kennet's team sometimes have a quiet word with them about the health and welfare of their children, or they meet with an unfortunate accident, those kind of things."

"That's disgusting. You hear about this, but I've never been close to it. Still, what's your involvement?"

"A couple of times Kennet's enforcers have gone too far. A few tenants ended up seriously hurt in hospital, one in intensive care. Last year, they really went too far, and a man died from a beating. He had been complaining loudly and publicly about the state of his family's flat: damp, cockroaches, rats and mould. Kennet had him beaten, to death as it turned out.

"Our investigation led us to a couple of brave men who were prepared to work with us to try to catch him. I was outside one of their homes, waiting for Kennet's men to turn up, when I was shot. Needless to say, the potential informants have withdrawn, and we're back to square one in the murder enquiry."

Maggie heard his frustration, even though his face hadn't moved a muscle whilst he was speaking.

"This isn't a decision I can take alone, Bob, I have to talk to Zelah. Can I tell her what you've just told me?"

"Yes, but I won't be saying any more."

"I'll call her this evening and ask her to come over tomorrow morning."

"These are dangerous people, Maggie. If Rufus Quinn has put his reputation on the line, in regard to this statue, he's not going to take it well if someone is investigating Madame Ramona's claims."

"I understand. Let's leave it here so Zelah and I will talk tomorrow. Can you find out if Isobel reported her arson attack to the police in Newport? She's not really called Madame Ramona, that's her professional name."

He nodded and stood up from the table. He seemed steady enough but was still pale.

Maggie sat for a while. She was surprised that he hadn't tried to ban her from the case. Perhaps he had learned something, from their time together on holiday. If he was right though, they were facing a formidable task, if she agreed to help Isobel. Did she want to, it was intriguing, even she had to admit that?

If she went ahead, she would be involving Jack and the girls in the investigation. They were all aged sixteen and seventeen and were enthusiastically researching their own family's ancestry. This would be their second 'training' weekend. The first time Maggie, Zelah and Nick had set them a series of exercises, which they had dived into with enthusiasm. It had been a successful weekend, Maggie, Zelah and Nick enjoyed themselves too. Until now the timing had not been a problem, but what should Maggie do now? She pulled out her phone and called Zelah.

For once, Zelah listened quietly. "That's a problem," was all she said. "I'm sorry I dragged you into this."

"Don't be sorry. What should we do?"

"There is no we. I promised Isobel that I'd help her, and I will. You don't have to be involved. Leave this one to me."

"Absolutely not," Maggie said. "You couldn't wait for me to get home and even called me in Italy. Now I've heard her story, well, I don't like what these people are doing. I was going to say that we should proceed carefully, and stay in the background, as much as we can. Zelah, do not go it alone. We're a team and we need to tell Nick."

"We're not the three bloody musketeers. We may take joint responsibility, but this wouldn't be the first time we've done research separately."

"I think we should talk about it in the morning. I need time to think. What time can you get here?"

"See you at nine," Zelah replied, and ended the call.

Maggie went back to the kitchen, realising that she had talked about 'how' not 'if'. She shrugged. The die was cast.

Chapter 7
Newport, 1896

The death of Ada Blackstock had become national news, accompanied by anger rising to outrage, at the inability of the police to discover her killer. Somehow - some whispered due to a substantial bribe to someone in the constabulary - details of the injuries done to the women before being killed had been leaked to the newspapers, who led the righteous indignation whilst revelling in the abhorrent details…

In the following seven days, after the discovery of Ada's mutilated body, the police had questioned over one hundred people. They had no interest in stories from the working or workless poor, until a beggar reported seeing a 'man in a tall black hat' stalking the streets in the docks area. The story spread quickly, and the police found themselves under pressure to find and arrest this man. Their problem was, according to the various stories that subsequently emerged, the descriptions of this potential suspect. He was anywhere between five and six feet tall, upright or bent, with a long, hooked nose and claw-like fingers, or featureless with gloved hands.

But in every story, there was one consistency: the tall black hat. There was one man in Newport who was known for his walks around the docks wearing such a hot: Councillor Adolphus Quinn.

At first Inspector Stanley Freeman, in charge of the case, refused point blank to speak to the politician. As the stories multiplied, and came to the attention of his Head Constable, his hand was forced. The Head Constable understood Freeman's position etc., etc., but he had to clear Quinn from the investigation; on the basis that such an important member of the community could not be subjected to such malicious rumour and suspicion.

Adolphus Quinn had seen this coming. Therefore, on the morning Inspector Freeman had politely asked to speak with him at home, he knew exactly what was impending and was prepared.

Just before eleven in the morning Adolphus Quinn was seated behind the desk in his study. He had decided that his brother should be present, but was now regretting that decision, as he watched Martin put his hands up to neck yet again.

"For God's sake, Martin, stop scratching. You'll give yourself away."

Martin Quinn's neck was raw and lined with visible nail marks. He pulled his hands away onto his lap. Adolphus opened his mouth to add a further rebuke, but the sound of the doorbell stopped him. "They are here. Pull yourself together and put a smile on your face. Follow my lead." He settled himself comfortably back in his chair.

He called 'enter' to the discreet knock and the butler opened the door to two men. One was a uniformed constable who was gazing around in admiration. The second, dressed in a suit and ill-fitting jacket barely covering his extended belly, held out his hand. Adolphus Quinn rose to shake the hand and felt its sweaty palm. *Good*, he thought, *very good*.

He indicated two chairs next to his brother, introduced Martin who smiled but didn't offer a handshake, and sat back in his chair behind the desk.

"I am at your disposal, Inspector Freeman," Adolphus said. "I have asked my brother to attend, in case there is anything he can add that might help your enquiries, I hope you don't mind?"

"Of course not, Mr Quinn. We welcome any assistance with this dreadful case."

Adolphus was in his element now. The supplication in the man's voice told him the Inspector was here under duress which would allow him to manipulate the interrogation any way he chose. He put up his fingers, joined them together under his chin in a prayer gesture and said, "Let me perhaps forestall what you are about to ask me. You are enquiring about 'the man in the black hat' and you know that one of my… what shall we say - peculiarities… is that I always wear a top hat when I walks around the docks. Another is that I always walk and never take transport." He smiled at them.

The Inspector let out the breath he had been holding. "Yes, Mr Quinn. There have been several reports of a man of your general description, wearing a tall hat, walking around the streets of the Pillgwenlly docks area on the night that Miss Ada Blackstock was brutally murdered. And on other nights, when at least two of the–" he hesitated and flushed, "women of the streets were also killed."

"I understand, Inspector." Quinn smiled benignly. "I don't deny that I was walking along Commercial Street on the night the unfortunate girl was murdered, at around nine. I had been visiting Father Delaney at the church in Clarence Street. We had discussed one of our ongoing projects – the new school we have built next to the church. Please, feel free to check with him."

"I'm sure that won't be necessary," the Inspector replied, "but there were other nights…" His voice trailed off and he looked down at his hands.

"Inspector." This time the voice was commanding and the detective looked up, which was what Adolphus wanted. He needed this man's full attention. Adolophus Quinn's stare was one of his most effective weapons. It was direct and unblinking, a trick he had taught himself years earlier, that he used on political opponents to great effect.

"If you know anything about me, you will know that I visit the church and the community I represent, at least twice a week. I may now live in a grand home," he waved an elegant arm around at the room, "but my beginnings were humble. I came to Newport no more than a lad, with nothing. Me and my brother here," he nodded towards Martin, his accent becoming more pronouncedly Irish. "We were hard workers and I had good fortune. However I will never, I repeat never, forget how the community took us in and gave two poor Irish boys a home. They are great people, dignified although they are poor, and they help their own. Now that I have all of this, I want to do as much as I can for my community. I work with the priest and local people to build, not just houses, but structures wherein the common man can benefit. I am proud of this and I do not deny my past."

"Indeed, Mr Quinn, indeed. I hope you understand, I have to ask," Freeman stuttered.

"Of course you do, certainly I understand. Unfortunately, I saw nothing suspicious that night of. I often leave meetings with my head full of thoughts and ideas and plans. I probably wouldn't have noticed if a wild bull had crossed my path!"

He had altered his tone to match that of the Inspector and he had put his hands palm up on the desk. By the time he finished speaking, the Inspector was nodding vehemently. Out of the corner of his eye Martin Quinn noticed that the constable was not.

"So, you saw nothing of note, Mr Quinn?" the constable asked.

"I remember the evening of the murder well enough. I recall there was a thick fog that made the atmosphere leaden and it was difficult to see anything. It came as a great shock to me, that I could have been so close to such an event, at the time it happened. No, as I said, I was thinking about the plans I had discussed with Father Delaney. There were few other people on the streets around the time she was killed; I cannot recall anything further of note." He shook his head and turned to his brother. "Have you anything to add, Martin?"

"Nothing, indeed, nothing," Martin said, his voice low but firm. "I was at my own home all evening."

"Do you recall any other evenings when the street women were killed, Sir?" the Inspector asked Martin Quinn.

"I don't know which evenings those were," Martin replied. "I don't attend the church meetings with my brother. I am an accountant and if there are financial dealings involved my brother informs me. I cannot help you, I'm afraid."

"We didn't expect so," Inspector Freeman replied, standing up and bowing to each brother. "I will bid you good day, Mr Quinn, and Mr Quinn. Thank you for being so forthcoming with me. Come, constable."

"You are doing your duty, Inspector. We the people can expect no more than that. Let me see you out," said Adolphus.

He left the room with them, leaving Martin in his seat. When he returned, he took his brother by the arm and pulled him out of his chair. "Do not look away when you are asked a direct question, you fool."

Martin shook off his brother's arm. "I have done enough for you, you must stop, now. I beg you, brother. A visit from the police will not go unnoticed."

Adolphus laughed, "Those two? Easily dealt with." He flicked his fingers at the door as if the policemen had been no more than a couple of pesky flies.

"I'm not so sure," Martin replied. "The Inspector, yes, he was a nervous fool. The constable picked up on something, I don't know what, but I saw him frown."

"Imagination," Adolphus replied, "From another nervous fool. Now get out of here, I've had enough of your nerves today."

Without a word Martin left the room, took his greatcoat and hat, and went out into the street. To his relief there were no signs of the two policemen.

From the bedroom window Bridget Quinn watched him go. Neither of them knew she had been outside the office door, listening to both the interview and the conversation between the brothers.

**

As they walked down Stow Hill towards the police station, Inspector Freeman noticed that the constable was quiet.

"Well, that's the end of that, thank the Good Lord."

"Is it?" the constable replied. "I'm not so sure, Sir."

Freeman stopped walking. "What do you mean?"

"I'm not sure. There was something not right. I don't like Mr Adolphus Quinn, and his brother was awfully nervous. Did you see his neck?"

"No, I did not see his neck. Even the innocent would be nervous, being interviewed by a detective about a gruesome murder. Councillor Adolphus Quinn gave a good account of himself and that's the end of it, as I shall report back to the Head Constable."

He began to walk again at a brisk pace, ahead of the constable, his chest sticking out and arms swinging. The constable trailed behind, thinking. Something had been wrong but he couldn't put his finger on it.

Chapter 8

Zelah arrived promptly at nine and joined Maggie, Nick and Bob in the office.

Maggie had decided the previous evening to tell Bob that she wanted to take on the case, although she understood his fears and would tread carefully. It hadn't been an easy conversation, but Bob was resigned to it. He made Maggie agree that there would be no direct approach to the Quinns, just research.

As Nick had arrived early Maggie used the time to fill him in on the new case, and to ask him what he thought.

"I think you're going to take it on regardless of what I say," he replied. "If it's true, there are multiple historic injustices, and the probability of another now. I can't see you letting that go. How are you going to start?"

Maggie smiled. "Thanks for the vote of confidence."

"Do you need any input from me?"

"Not sure yet, Nick. We may ask you to come with us, should we need to get face-to-face with Rufus Quinn, at some point. Don't tell Bob I said that please. I've promised I won't go near either Quinn, and I'm going to try not to. Your particular insights could be helpful, if you have time this morning."

"Fine. Mind if I get on with my project whilst you're all talking?"

"Go for it. Keep an ear open, in case you have anything to add."

**

"I've told Nick the story already Zelah, so we're all up to date. Bob is going to find out today about Isobel's arson attack. Did she report it?"

"She said so," Zelah replied. "Although, come to think of it, she's supposed to have told them where she's staying and we haven't had any visits from the police, so I'll check again when I get back." She frowned, "If she hasn't, I can't think why she would lie to me."

"They threatened her to shut up and go away," Maggie mused. "Perhaps the note also said do not speak to the police. Did you see it?"

"No, but if it did, she should have told me, I don't like being lied to."

"Try to keep an open mind for now, about whether or not she's lying. Right, where do we start? We have Jack and the girls here this weekend, I think it will be safe enough to let them research the history of the case, as we're keeping a low profile. Zelah, you and I can make a start today, I thought perhaps we could make a timeline for the Quinn family back to Adolphus Quinn. We can get some names and dates down to help us understand the basic family line. We can look at the newspaper reports too. Bob is going to follow up on the arson. Is there anything else we can do for now?"

"There is something, but I'm not sure if you'll agree to it. I wasn't going to tell you, but as it seems Isobel might be lying to me, it's hypocritical of me to withhold something from you." She paused, looked at them both, and turned to Bob. "I have a soiree to attend tomorrow evening, at the Council HQ in Red Bridge, an award ceremony for young artists. I'm giving a joint grant, together with the Arts Committee. Rufus Quinn will be there in his capacity of Chairman of a South Wales Arts charity and I was thinking I might approach him." She said this last sentence with her usual aggressive look, which made clear this was for information only, she didn't require anyone's opinion.

"Why?" Maggie said. "I've promised Bob we'd keep under their radar. We can investigate quietly, to see if this story has legs. If Kennet Quinn is as dangerous as Bob says, then surely the best thing is to keep as far away from him as possible, at least until we have some evidence?"

Bob sat up in his chair, looking daggers at Zelah and Maggie.

"I haven't promised Bob and Kennet won't be there," Zelah countered. "This gives us until tomorrow evening to get something solid, doesn't it? I think we should get started now." She stood up and moved to her desk.

"I can't stop you, Zelah," Bob said as she walked past him. "No-one can, once you've made up your mind, but putting other people in danger, is that what you want? I am going to hold you responsible, as this affects me as much as all of you. Possibly more so."

Zelah turned and walked back towards him, "You're referring to what happened in Ireland. You chose to follow me there, I did not put either of you in danger. I am proposing to see Rufus Quinn in a room full of people. I will tell him that Isobel is my friend, and I have an interest in her story. I want to see if I get the same look, she claims to have seen."

"And if you do?"

"Then I will know for certain this case is worth pursuing." Uncharacteristically, she put a hand on his arm and lowered her tone. "Bob, I understand what you're saying about who Kennet is, and what he has done to you, and I am going to be extremely careful."

"What if he finds out about Maze, which he is likely to? *You* may not be the target?"

Maggie decided it was time to intervene. "We'll have to play this carefully. We don't want to put anyone in danger, do we Zelah?"

"As a rhetorical question, that's a cracker," Zelah replied huffily, sitting down at her screen.

When Bob left shortly after, Maggie went with him to the door. It was time...

"There's something I need to explain to you about Zelah. Is tonight OK?"

"Sure, if you think it's important."

"It's beyond important."

For a few seconds he looked like he was about to comment, but shook his head and said, "OK see you later."

Back in the office, Maggie walked up to Zelah's side, "I'm going to tell him."

"If you think it's the right time. You said you'd wait for the right moment. What about Nick?"

"If you mean what I think you mean, I already know," Nick said, not looking away from his screen. "I'm not sure you can keep everyone safe all of the time, Zelah, no matter what extraordinary things you can do."

Maggie jumped in, before Zelah could ask. "I told Nick after we got back from Ireland; he was already suspicious. Remember, he has a gift too. He can read you far better than other people can."

"Fair enough," Zelah replied, not looking at Nick. "Can we please get on now? We have a lot to cover before tomorrow evening."

"I agree. Let's start with the online reports we can get from the newspapers of the time. You take the Welsh ones, I'll do the national, OK? We'll look for the murder, for Ada, and for Adolphus Quinn. Then we'll do the timeline... but please remember, Zelah, I am walking a personal tightrope here."

**

Three hours later they stopped for a stretch, a break and lunch. The weather had improved, so they ventured into the garden, with drinks and plates of sandwiches.

"Who wants to go first?" Nick asked.

"I have a question before that," Maggie said, "Zelah, if Rufus Quinn is such a nightmare, how did he get into so many positions of responsibility?"

"He's rich and very good at marketing himself. He makes sure to be seen with the right people, does just enough good works and charity now he's retired. He's managed his personal brand very well and kept the not-so-good stuff well hidden, thanks to some powerful allies, including the local media."

Maggie shrugged, but didn't ask anything more.

"Let's get on, then. I'll go first," Zelah said. "I've been looking at Ada. She was twenty-one when she died, and living alone in Cardiff."

"Not with her family?" Maggie asked. "Why not?"

"Think about it, Maggie, consider the obvious. How did Isobel get to be her great-granddaughter?"

"Oh. She wasn't a married woman?"

"Nope."

"Who was the father?"

"There's no information. We could get the birth certificate. I'm guessing Isobel has checked already and the space for name of father is blank."

"How old was the child when Ada died?"

"Six months. He was born in the second quarter of 1896, named Henry George Blackstock."

"Was there a christening? Might give us more information. I wonder if the police tried to follow up on the father."

"There's no record of a christening online, I've tried all of the available sites. We can narrow it down if I can get my hands on the birth certificate to get her address at the time, which means we can look for the nearest church. We'll also need to check the archives to see if any police records are available and whether or not they tried to find the father when she died."

"Any idea what happened to the boy after Ada died?"

"No idea. The family might have stepped in, it's worth finding out. Before we go back inside, I'll give Isobel a call to check if she knows any of this."

"Anything else?" Maggie asked.

"Well, there's quite a bit in the papers about her death, and the other deaths. It was revolting. Ada's murder and mutilation took place on a foggy evening in November. She'd attended a séance at the home of a client and was heading to the home of another medium, only a few streets away. There were no witnesses in the fifteen minutes between leaving the client, and when she disappeared. She must have been grabbed off the street.

"Now, an interesting thing was, as well as no-one seeing her, nobody heard anything either. It's a built-up area, with hundreds of people living there. Many houses were in multiple occupation, with people squashed together in an overcrowded urban area. Yet nobody heard a thing, which suggests to me, as it did to the papers at the time, that she may have known the assailant. Perhaps it was a client or a member of a local spiritualist society, not necessarily Adolphus Quinn."

"Where was her body found?"

"The séance took place in Potter Street, off Commercial Road. The papers said she was found twenty-four hours after she disappeared, in a derelict house in Alma Street, which is also off Commercial Road."

"Who found her?"

"A vagrant looking for somewhere sheltered to sleep. For a few nights around the time of her death it was raining and after a while he noticed the smell."

"Ugh, isn't Commercial Road the long, straight one that runs from the bottom end of High Street down to the docks?"

"Yes, you can see the Transporter Bridge from the top end. Did they interview the vagrant?"

"Yes," Zelah replied. "He'd been in a different place the previous evening, with other vagrants. It was fortunate he even called for the police. The only other clue the police found was a man who claimed he had seen a man in a tall black hat walking along Commercial Road, in the same direction that Ada walked. An artist did a sketch and the story took off. That was when it became a national story."

"Yes, I found it in newspapers as far away as Scotland," Maggie said.

"The press ran with it as the major clue," Zelah continued, "but it turned out that the man was, in fact …"

"Adolphus Quinn," Nick butted in.

"How the hell did you know that?" Zelah demanded.

"Had to be, if the message from Ada to Isobel is real, then Quinn must have been in the area at the same time as Ada. If it was him, he took a huge risk."

"You're right," Maggie said. "Did that ever get into the papers?"

"Oh yes," Zelah said, "it was announced by Quinn himself in the Council Chamber. He insisted that additional funds be made available to the police, told them to spare no expense in finding the villain who had carried out such monstrous crimes. Then he said he had himself been on Commercial Road that same night, a road he walked many times when he had been at the church and had been identified by his hat. Apparently, the hat was his foible. He always wore it outdoors. He said he wished he had been a better witness, but that he had been deep in thought as he walked and sadly hadn't seen anything. He made a joke of it, a tasteful one, naturally, that he could be attacked at any time, when he walked along lost in thought, and he wouldn't even notice."

"That was clever," Maggie remarked. "I'm assuming the police interviewed him."

"They'd have had to," Nick said, "He must have been a convincing liar. Are you going to research the police reports?"

"They're archived up at the County Archives in Ebbw Vale. Could we go tomorrow?" Zelah asked, looking at Maggie.

"Don't see why not," Maggie replied, "If there's nothing else, would you like to hear what I've found out?"

"Go for it," Zelah said.

Chapter 9

"First, I have a question," Maggie said. "Why was wearing a top hat such an identifying mark? Wasn't it standard dress in his class of business man in the 1890s?"

"Good question," Nick replied. "Perhaps it was the combination of walking everywhere when he was rich enough to take transport and in particular visiting the docks area. He would definitely have stood out amongst the throng there. He must have been a narcissist; if he was attacking women, why make himself so easily identifiable?"

"As you said, Nick, it was standard dress in those days," Zelah replied. "If he let himself become known as 'the man in the black hat' he managed to both stand out and at the same time wear something that anyone else could have worn. Clever, perhaps, and egotistical." She sat back in her chair and put her hands behind her head. "Think about his history. He had arrived as a poor labourer. If he wore headwear, it would have been the labourer's cloth cap. His rise out of poverty meant that he could afford better. He dressed in a way that demonstrated his wealth, but he still wanted to be known as a 'man of the people'. I think the top hat was part of the character he created for himself. He would have been recognised and accepted and he wanted to be approachable. It was ego."

"Possibly," Nick replied, "but he was taking a risk. If the hat identified him, why would he wear it when he was going to kill?"

"It suggests to me that he had made a rod for his own back," Maggie said. "He identified himself publicly in this way. If he stopped wearing the hat, it would have attracted more notice than when he did wear it. He must have taken a calculated risk, and decided that he could get away with it."

"Like most narcissists and psychopaths," Zelah said, "he didn't believe he could be caught. He thought he was too clever."

"Well, it looks as if he was too clever," Nick replied.

"Anyway, going back to Ada," Maggie continued, "there's nothing much else about her. She had an obituary in the Western Daily Press, which was unusual, both for her age, and profession and as she was also a single mother. It was probably the notoriety of her death that made her sufficiently respectable. "

"It said that she discovered her gifts as a young girl, she attended séances regularly, and was renowned for the accuracy of her information from the spirit world. She had many people speak highly of her gift. She assisted the police in Cardiff, on a particularly difficult murder case, one that was never solved. Her name wasn't mentioned in that case, at her own request. She was an unassuming young lady; quiet, humble, and modest. Her death was deeply mourned-in public at least by her family and by the spiritualist community in South Wales. Unlike Isobel," she added. "Quiet, humble and modest she is not."

She expected a riposte from Zelah but none came. Zelah felt the question hanging over Isobel's honesty more than Maggie might have expected. She knew that people, even the most trustworthy, could be economical with their information, usually to protect themselves. Zelah was no stranger to such behaviour herself.

"Well, let me add the little I've found about Adolphus Quinn," Maggie said. "I'll come back to his line of descent. I've concentrated on what we know about the time he arrived in Newport, mostly from his own information. He did not shun publicity, that's for certain. There are a good number of interviews in the papers. He loved to talk about himself, but there are inconsistencies in his stories, only small ones. But for me, they point to a man who was trying to re-invent himself."

"Tell us the story, do," said Zelah.

"He seems to have arrived in Newport during his early twenties, with his brother Martin, who was a couple of years younger. He said they had come from Dublin, where they were brought up in a poor family, and were looking for work. Nothing unusual about that, Newport was a magnet for Irish immigrants looking for work. Then, a few years later, in a different interview, he said that he arrived in Liverpool, then moved around the country for a few years before coming to Newport."

"Nothing in that," Zelah interjected, "he could have done both."

"Yes, he could, but later again, he says he went 'abroad' for a while before coming to Newport."

"OK, that's inconsistent."

"They're only small inconsistencies, but why? The next thing people remarked on was his looks, and the fact that he had a broken nose and part of an ear missing. He gave three different accounts for those injuries too: fighting, an accident on a building site, and being attacked by thieves. Again, the interviews were years apart, but still it's strange."

"Two lies and a truth," Nick said. "Which is true?"

"That's what we need to find out. Anyway, he went to work for a man called Michael Kelly. Adolphus was a good worker, and a clever man, as was his brother. They both worked on building sites, until Adolphus paid for Martin to study as an accountant, at which he apparently excelled.

"Michael Kelly promoted Adolphus to Foreman, and he was so good at it he soon became Manager.

"Kelly had a daughter, Bridget, who was five years older than Adolphus. He was handsome, apart from his broken nose, and charming. Within a couple of years of joining the firm, he married Bridget, They had three children, two girls and a boy.

"When Kelly died Adolphus inherited the firm. He wasn't an architect, but he could see Newport was up-and-coming. There was an opportunity to build houses for the new gentry, and he did so, successfully.

"As a Catholic, he was an active member of St Michael's on Clarence Street. He had lived in the same street, in digs, when he and Martin first arrived in Newport. He always supported the docks community, saying he wanted to give something back to the people who had supported him. He branched out later to building houses in Pontypool, Abergavenny, Monmouth and so on.

"He was elected to the Council, proved himself to be a gifted orator, and was being touted for a future Mayor. Then disaster struck in 1897, just one year after Ada's death; he was murdered."

"He can't have been very old," Zelah said.

"He was in his early thirties, savagely beaten and robbed, on one of his walks through the town, near to the church. Ironic, given his 'joke' in the Council Chamber."

"Did the police find the murderer?" Nick asked.

"No they didn't," Maggie replied, "Isobel put forward the idea it was political, but there's no mention of that, even though he was against Irish Republicanism."

"That's odd," Nick said.

"Why?" Maggie asked.

"Because of the joke he made, and it happening in the same area. Tell me, were there any other similar murders of women, before or after he died?"

"Just one before he died," Maggie said, "though nothing in the intervening year. It was an attempted abduction, but the woman broke free. She mentioned the top hat and a scarf worn above the nose but couldn't add any more details. There was an actual murder was about two months after Adolphus died. There was public outcry again, but the culprit was never caught."

"If I were you, I'd read up the details of that one then compare it to the others," said Nick.

"Is something occurring to you Nick?" Zelah asked.

"Possibly, I think it's worth checking." He stood up. "I'm going to get a biscuit."

"Did anyone else get looked at for Ada's murder?" Zelah asked Maggie.

"Yes, there was a sailor who came under suspicion. The police looked at the ships in port, at the time of each murder. There was only one docked consistently. They interviewed the crew, one of whom was a suspect. The prostitutes who worked the docks said he had a vicious streak. He beat one of the girls for refusing to do what he wanted. In the end nothing came of it. He denied it and it turned out he had an alibi for two of the murders. The police were so sure that all of the murders were the work of one man, they dropped him as a suspect," said Maggie. "What I cannot understand," she continued, "is why Adolphus Quinn would have killed anyone? He was a self-made, successful man, a supporter of his community, a philanthropist and a family man."

"The most successful serial killers are those who are able to avoid both suspicion and justice. They create a façade of respectability. There's plenty of historical and contemporary evidence where male killers succeeded in keeping the police at bay for years. Whoever killed those women had to be a seriously disturbed man. Our job isn't to find out who did it, we just have to prove whether or not it was Adolphus Quinn. If Isobel's message was wrong and it wasn't him, then a good man gets a statue erected in his honour," said Zelah.

"I agree," Maggie replied. "But if it was him I can't think of anything worse than people unknowingly admiring a monument to an unhinged serial killer."

"Nor anything more embarrassing for the County Council, if the statue goes up before proof of his crimes then come to light," Zelah said. "Let's get back to work."

"I've only have another hour or so, as Jack's finishing early today. I've promised we'll go for a meal, to celebrate the end of his first year at college; just the two of us."

"Fair enough. When is Alice back?"

"She finishes next Friday afternoon. She and a few friends are spending this last weekend together, at her friend Matthew's house. They have a pool and a tennis court."

"I didn't think such fripperies would attract Alice," Zelah said.

"You'd be surprised. Thing is, she likes her friends and won't be seeing much of them for a while."

"Are you going away for a holiday this year?" Zelah asked.

"Nothing planned yet. Last time Alice was home for the weekend I suggested camping for the three of us. You should have seen the looks on their faces. You'd have thought I'd suggested boot camp. Your friend's house in Cornwall was an introduction to luxury, and now there's no returning to my preferred holiday accommodation," Maggie said as they cleared up the remains of the lunch and went back to the office.

Maggie returned to her newspaper search for information about Adolphus Quinn. Zelah concentrated on Ada Blackstock and the spiritualist societies of South Wales in the 1890s.

**

"I've found a couple of things here. Nothing direct, but it's building up a picture," Maggie said an hour later. "I'm just going to print this out I'd be grateful if both of you could take a look, and tell me what you see." She took the papers off the printer and spread them out on the table. Zelah and Nick gathered around, to look at a set of articles and photographs.

After a few minutes Nick said, "Yes, I see."

"Explain," Zelah replied. "All I see is his wife doesn't smile much."

Nick pointed to a report, a year after Adolphus Quinn's death. "No pictures in this one, but this is an account from the Council, wishing to honour him. Bridget flatly refuses. She says she is sure he would not have wanted such an honour. From the little we know, I think he would have wanted it very much.

"Now look at this," Maggie continued. "When photographs begin to appear in the newspapers, here she is at a ceremony representing the firm. She's accompanied by his brother Martin. Look at the expression on her face."

Zelah leaned in. "Hmm, she looks like she has a bad smell under her nose."

"That's disgust," Nick said. "She can't help herself."

"The camera has captured the moment," Maggie said.

"What was the ceremony for?" Zelah asked.

"The dedication of a building built by Kelly & Quinn Construction, in the names of her father, Michael Kelly and Adolphus Quinn,"" Maggie replied. "It's an orphanage, so why on earth does she look disgusted, at an event like that?"

"Agreed," Nick said. "Now these final photographs. This was in 1909, twelve years after he died. I assume this is the wedding of one of Bridget's daughters?"

"Yes, Mary, the elder of the two. She was walked down the aisle by her Uncle Martin. The caption under Bridget's photograph says she is the widow of '… local hero Adolphus Quinn'. I don't know where the 'hero' came from. Again her expression is not what you'd expect from the mother of the bride. I don't know what to say it is, anger, disgust? Something must have been said to her before the photograph was taken, something about the 'hero' perhaps?"

"Speculation, she looks OK in the family group," Zelah replied. "Of course, none of them smiled. Nobody did back then, because the exposure times were so long, a smile would end up looking like a grimace. Photographs were usually a serious business, whatever the circumstance or occasion, but at a wedding they didn't usually look as if they were chewing a wasp."

Nick shrugged, "Altogether it says enough for me to guess there's a story here."

"And finally these." Maggie grabbed three more pieces of paper off the printer and put them on the table.

"The 1901 census," she said. "Look who's now living in the family home, and again in 1911." She pointed to the name of Martin Quinn on each document.

"Still doesn't mean anything," Zelah said. "So, he moved in to support his sister-in-law, it was a big house. I know that road, the houses are enormous; seven bedrooms on three floors, and servants' quarters in the attic.

"And the last one." Maggie put the third newspaper article on the table. "In the family notices it announces the marriage of Bridget Quinn to Mr Martin Quinn in 1910."

"So what? I can't see that any of this adds to the suspicion that Adolphus Quinn wasn't legit?"

"I think you're being a bit black and-white, Zelah," Nick said. "What we're trying to do is create a 3D picture of the man. I agree it doesn't prove anything at this stage, but you don't know what details, however small, may have significance later. You know this; this isn't like you."

"OK, yes I know. I've been developing a bad feeling about Isobel. It's not often I put my trust in another person; there's only you two, Bob and Rick. And the Irish boys. I've been thinking about Isobel's reaction to that fire. She was genuinely frightened, so why didn't she report it? How can she expect to complete an insurance claim, if she hasn't reported it to the police? I've seen the damage, it's not huge, but it's taken a sizeable area of her hallway. Fire damage is distressing and it's going to need professional repair. The smell is terrible and the water damage, from where she used her pressure hose to put it out, is going to take weeks to dry out. As she was so distressed, I accepted her story one hundred percent, but now I've got a feeling that she hasn't told me everything."

"Not everyone says exactly what they are thinking," Maggie replied. "Give her time, it's only been a couple of days." Then she added, "We thought perhaps Kennet Quinn might have threatened her, about not going to the police?"

"I'm going to ask her. We need the information from the birth certificate. We also want to find out what happened to little Henry, after Ada died."

"Be gentle."

In response, Maggie received a snort.

A banging on the front door announced the arrival of Jack. He came straight into the office.

"That's it," he announced, punching the air, "year one done and six weeks off. Hi guys, what are you up to?"

"The project I told you about," Maggie replied, "the one you and the girls are going to help with at the weekend."

"Sick," he replied.

"That means 'great'," Nick explained to Zelah's puzzlement.

"Anyway," Jack said, "I'll be in my room for a couple of hours, what time we going out mum?"

"About half-six."

"Time for me to go," Zelah said. "I'm going to talk to Isobel directly, rather than phone her. She's going to a reading tonight. I'll call you later to let you know what she says. What time are we going to the archives tomorrow?"

"Let's go first thing," Maggie replied. "We need time to get the info and decide on your approach to Rufus Quinn."

Jack and Zelah left the office together.

"Maggie be careful with this one. The little I know about the Quinn family, Kennet especially, is not good," said Nick.

"You're not the first person to say that, Nick, and in almost the same words. I'm anxious about Zelah approaching Rufus Quinn. I think we should do this without him knowing, but you know Zelah."

"That's what worries me, she'd be the first to stop you and me, but she has no constraints on her own behaviour."

Chapter 10
Newport, December 1896

Constable David Bale made his way back to Pillgwenlly Police Headquarters at a slow pace.

Adolphus Quinn had put his back up, and his brother looked as nervous as a cat amongst a pack of snarling dogs. To be fair, just because he didn't like a man with such arrogance, nor his quivering brother, it was no basis for suspicion. Yet suspect Adolphus Quinn he did. There was something about the way the man acted... no, not the way he acted. It was the way he oozed, what he felt, was something he could only describe as 'badness'. His Inspector hadn't felt it at all. And who was Martin Quinn so nervous of? The Inspector? His own brother? It was altogether exceedingly strange and unsettling.

He ignored the groups of children on the pavements as he passed, who called out to him but didn't get the usual good-natured insult in response. They looked at him, waiting, then shrugged and went back to their game. It was the same for the men standing outside the King of Prussia pub.

In the coming weeks both groups would have cause to remember David Bale's out-of-the-ordinary unresponsiveness that day. He spoke to no-one, whilst walking from one end of the town to the other.

He went over every aspect of the interview as he walked. What were the exact words that Adolphus Quinn had used? He was sure something had been said, misspoken by accident, as so often happened when arrogant criminals let their guard down. Criminals: was he so sure that Quinn was a criminal? He stopped for a moment, outside St Paul's Church, and took out his notebook and read through it as he continued his walk.

At the top of Cardiff Road, he stopped, staring at the words he had written and the question mark he had added. That was it. That's what was… not wrong, but something that he wasn't certain how Adolphus Quinn could have known. Only one way to find out. Head up now, his pace quickened back to the station.

On arrival he asked for the Inspector but found that he had not yet returned. He assumed that Stanley Freeman had gone to the other, main Newport station.

He went into the back office. Checking he wasn't being watched, he took out the file on the murders that Freeman had put in the drawer of his desk before they left that morning. He needed to work quickly. Freeman wasn't going to be sympathetic to anything more Bale had to say, on the matter of Adolphus Quinn. He opened the file on the desktop, and went through the notes, until he came to the murder of Ada Blackstock. The note he wanted was about the time of death. He was right, it was around or shortly after nine in the evening, the same time that Adolphus Quinn had been on Commercial Road. Nothing wrong with that, but what Adolphus Quinn didn't know, was that the information about the time of Ada Blackstock's death had not been made public. For all he knew it could have been hours later, or earlier. So why did he say that it had been at nine? Could someone else have told him? But why would they, whoever they were, give him such a detailed piece of information? It couldn't be of any interest to Quinn at what time the woman died.

He stood up straight, closed the file, and put it back in the desk exactly the way it had been placed there. No need to alert Freeman that he'd been looking at it, without permission. He sauntered into the front office looking casual. His brain was whirring. What to do now? If he alerted the Inspector he expected that he would be told to leave well alone. Freeman would say it was insignificant. For Constable Bale it nevertheless posed an unanswered question. What were the alternatives? This would not leave him alone. It was like a bee buzzing around his head. No matter how hard he tried to swat it away, he knew it would keep coming back, attracted to the sour odour of his suspicions.

The only other course of action open to him was to approach Adolphus Quinn himself. Risky. Possibly dangerous. On the other hand, alerting the man to his suspicions might make him give up something further. Criminals could be agitated in such a way, and after all, he was a policeman. The man could not attack him whilst he was in uniform, but when and where? During the daytime and somewhere public? Approach Quinn in a friendly way, remind him how they met, and ask him straight out how he knew? No. Mention the co-incidence that Quinn was walking at that time. He noticed that Councillor Quinn knew what time Ada Blackstock had disappeared. Don't make it a question, just a comment. That was it. He would tell Inspector Freeman afterwards, when he was certain.

There was a Council meeting two days later, and by beneficial chance, Constable Bale found himself on duty at the Chamber in the High Street.

As the Councillors left the Chamber Bale took a deep breath and putting a smile on his face he strode over to Adolphus Quinn, the minute he spotted him alone. It went exactly as he had planned. Quinn looked stunned for just a moment. Then he matched Bale's smile, and agreed with the Constable, this was just such a co-incidence his being out there at the exact time of Ada's disappearance. Bale couldn't help himself. If he had walked away at that point all would probably have ended well. He knew he should, but excitement prodded his inner detective.

"Yes Sir, funny that. The police didn't release the information about the exact time of Miss Blackstock's death because we wanted to know about anyone who had been around throughout the entire evening."

The flash in Quinn's eyes confirmed Constable Bale's worst fears, but again the man was too quick for him.

"Ah Constable, I'm not just anyone, am I? Of course I knew. I have sources at the highest level, don't you know?" He gave Bale a meaningful look.

"I am sure you do Sir, well I'll bid you good day." He walked away, feeling sick, knowing that he had given himself away for nothing. What to do next…? Another slow walk back to the station, by which time he decided he had run out of options. No point talking to Freeman, who would be furious. Furthermore, he could only hope that Adolphus Quinn wouldn't say anything about his approach. The sick feeling turned to nausea, together with a flutter of fear; he truly didn't like that man. He considered approaching Martin Quinn, but decided against it. If there was any chance that Adolphus Quinn was going to let it go, approaching his brother would only alert and anger him, which could be perilous. He believed now, with nausea rising from his stomach into his throat, that Adolphus Quinn was undeniably involved in the death of Ada Blackstock.

A walk in the fresh air helped, it gave him time to think hard. By the time he reached the station, he decided there was only one course of action. He found paper, pen and ink and wrote a full note of his concerns, his actions and his suspicions. He put the note in an envelope and tucked it into the back of the file, where it stayed unopened and undetected. When the case was finally closed, without being solved, it was locked away with the rest of the file.

**

One month later there had been no further news of the

death of Ada Blackstock. When berating the police had failed to sell more newspapers, the town was again shocked by the headline story of another death. This time, it was unclear whether it was an accident, or something more sinister. A young man was drowned in the river, and when his body was recovered, it was found to have a head wound. The coroner, however, could not say if this was a deliberate wound, or brought about by the victim falling from a bridge or other structure into the water. There was suspicion, but when the presence of alcohol was discovered an accident became a more likely possibility. At first, the victim could not be identified, as he had nothing on him apart from a soggy notebook that was too water-damaged to give up anything useful. Then the next day a young woman came forward, and identified the young man as her husband, Police Constable David Bale.

Immediately an enquiry was set up, Mrs Bale confirmed that her husband had been worried lately. He believed he had discovered something significant in the death of the medium, Ada Blackstock. He was off duty at the time of his death and was known to have taken a small drink earlier in the evening, at The Murringer public house. The landlord reported that the constable was not drunk, but 'had taken a small glass of beer' and was had been asking questions about the women who had been murdered.

At once the newspapers were ignited, and the hunt was on for a man who might have killed the constable. Unfortunately, no-one was able to confirm his whereabouts at the time of his death. Nothing was found to confirm any suspicions he might have had. The enquiry closed and the news dropped from the headlines.

The inquest recorded a verdict of 'death by accidental drowning' and the newspapers mourned the loss of a devoted public servant.

Then they lost interest and moved onto the next scandal.

Chapter 11

Zelah was quiet on the drive up to the Gwent Archives. Maggie had expected to hear about the discussion with Isobel, the previous evening. When nothing was forthcoming she decided to wade in.

"Did you speak to Isobel about the police report?"

At first Zelah didn't answer.

"Zelah, did you hear me?"

"I'm concentrating on the traffic."

"There isn't any to speak of, Zelah, what's going on?"

Zelah hunched forward over the steering wheel. "She's prevaricating. She says she spoke to them, but wasn't sure if it constituted a formal report."

"What does she have to say about the insurance claim?"

"She says there wasn't really much damage, she's going to take care of it herself. No point in going through her insurers."

"Do you believe her?"

Again, a short pause, before Zelah said, "No I don't, something's not right and I don't like it."

"Anything solid to go on?"

"There was a phone call last night for Isobel, after she had gone out. I was annoyed because I told her that no-one should know she's staying with me; for both our sakes. Anyway, this was a member of her local society, anxious and concerned and asking how she was. I said she was OK and they asked to pass on their regards, and to tell her that Claire asked if the information was useful. When I told Isobel later, she went white, stuttered and stumbled, before saying she would call Claire herself. Then she said goodnight and disappeared up to bed."

"Doesn't sound like much," Maggie considered, "but given where we are, who knows? What did you say to her about telling people she was staying with you?"

"I said she'd put both of us at risk and she might as well go back to her own place."

Maggie decided not to comment. Instead she asked, "Did you ask her about Ada's son's birth certificate?"

"Yes, as we suspected the father's name is blank. I have a copy with me. She didn't know where the christening took place, if there was one. The certificate records her address at the time of the birth, so we can look for it on a map and find the closest church. She also said Henry was taken in by Ada's family after her death."

"I finished the Quinn timeline last night," Maggie said. "Adolphus' son Michael took over the firm from his mother, when he was old enough. He was followed by his own son, Gerard, then came Rufus, Gerard's only son. Rufus has three children, Kennet being the youngest. Kennet is married, his wife is called Michelle. Kennet and Michelle have two children, a girl named Mischa and a boy named Gerard."

"Good, pretty straightforward, Adolphus to Michael to Gerard to Rufus to Kennet." She paused then went on. "So did you tell him? How did he react?"

"You mean Bob, yes I told him. He didn't say much, it's a lot to take in. He's a policeman, remember. He deals in facts."

"I hope he didn't ask for a demo. I'm not going to make things fly around the room just to convince him it's not a party trick."

"Of course not, but he's sceptical, most people would be. He agreed with Nick though, you can't keep everyone safe all of the time"

"I know, but I can use it efficaciously."

"What does that mean?"

In reply, Zelah grinned. "We're here, we'll have to park down the road in the carpark, and walk back. Isobel gave me a photograph of Ada Blackstock; we'll look at it in the archive room."

Zelah had called ahead and ordered the documents they wanted to look at. These were waiting for them when they checked in, held by a friendly young man called Ben with whom Zelah was on first name terms. She was well known at the archives and highly thought of. Maggie not so much, but they accorded her the same respect, being Zelah's colleague and friend.

Before they started on the pile of documents and files, they checked the birth certificate.

"See," Zelah said pointing to the address, "it's Windsor Place. A respectable street, close to the centre of Cardiff. This tells us that she was doing OK. I wonder who she was living with? In 1891 she was only sixteen so would most likely have been at home, and she was dead by the time of the 1901 census. She registered the birth herself, from the same address, so no clues there."

"Let's take a look at trade directories or street directories for Cardiff, if they have any here. See if the property's listed in any of them."

Zelah went to find out and order what was available, but discovered that if there were any, they would be in the Glamorgan Archives in Cardiff.

"Another trip," she said to Maggie. "We'll have to go to Glamorgan Archives anyway, to look for the baptismal record."

"OK, we've got enough to get on with here for now. I've just checked the census returns, Ada was with her family in 1891. In 1901 Henry George, who was five, was with his maternal aunt in Cardiff. From the 1881 census I found this was the eldest daughter, Caroline Blackstock. She married a man called Thomas Watson and by 1901 they had three children of their own as well as Henry George. He's described as a 'nephew', born in Cardiff. I haven't looked at the 1911 census yet, but he'd have been fifteen so probably still with them. Just a minute, which street did you say was given on the birth cert?"

Zelah repeated it.

"That's Caroline and Thomas's house in 1901. Just a minute." She flipped a page on her laptop, "Yes! They were there in 1891 and they had no children so would probably have not long been married. Thomas Watson is also a stonemason, like Caroline and Ada's father."

"So her sister took her in, at some point. She wasn't living alone. They kept her with them, after she had her baby; perhaps they were going to claim it as theirs. Or say that her husband was in the navy or something like that."

"Or maybe Thomas Watson was the father," Zelah mused. "Wouldn't have been the first time something like that happened, and kept within the family."

"We'll never know. Let's get cracking on the files, see if there's reference to the possible father in the police records."

She collected the records from the desk, and they worked in silence for the next few hours. They divided the files in half, pausing now and then to compare notes. Zelah arranged for them to have copies made of documents that couldn't give them a clear digital image.

"I think we should stop for lunch," Maggie said, just after twelve thirty. "We need to talk over the implications of what we've found, and I need to stop reading these reports for a while. My stomach is churning."

"Hungry?" Zelah asked.

"Not really, more disgusted at what I'm reading. Did you know that the monster had started to bite their flesh?"

Zelah's head shot up. "How many times?"

"Just Ada and the one before that. It seems to me that he was accelerating his viciousness. The earlier women were tortured with fire, just a hand or a foot. Later he started burning other body parts."

"That news never came out," Zelah said. "The papers gave some graphic detail about beatings, but none of that."

"I suspect the police kept it quiet, too much for the public stomach. Like it's too much for mine. Come on, let's get a cup of tea and a quick walk outside, I need some air. The images are going to stay in my head for a while."

"You are a bit pale," Zelah said. "We've done enough for today."

"No," Maggie replied. "If you're still planning to approach Rufus Quinn tonight, we need all the evidence we can get from this visit."

Sitting on a bench on the small pedestrian area outside the building, Zelah produced the photograph of Ada. It was a portrait with the usual Victorian solemn expression, at an angle to the camera, staring off into the distance. She had no particularly interesting features, just a simple girl dressed in the fashion of her time, who would be unremarkable in a crowd.

"Interesting to know what she looked like," Zelah remarked. "Adds to the reality of the situation."

Back inside, an hour later, Maggie called for Zelah's attention. She had been going through the police report details of interviews with potential witnesses, in the death of Ada Blackstock.

"I can't find anything about the baby's father, but this is interesting. An Inspector called Freeman went to interview Adolphus Quinn, and Quinn confirmed that he was the 'man in the black hat' who had been seen on Commercial Road."

"We knew that already," Zelah replied, not looking up from

her file.

"Yes, but there's more." Zelah looked up. "He was accompanied by a constable called David Bale. Later that week Bale wrote a note which he put in an envelope in the back of the file."

"What does it say?"

"It's not there anymore, just the empty envelope, which says 'see Animus'.

"What the hell does that mean?"

"No idea," Maggie said. "There's nothing else in the file that refers to 'Animus', I've checked."

"It must mean something." Zelah glanced at her watch. "We have to go, I need to get ready for the event tonight. Have to look my best for the great and mighty." She collected up the files and returned them to the Ben at the front desk, spending a few minutes chatting to him.

"That was interesting," Zelah said to Maggie as they left the building, "Two interesting things, actually. First, someone else has been in to read the files before us. A couple of months ago, a Mr Smith, as if! They can't be sure if Bale's envelope had been sealed or not, before that. The second thing, I asked Ben if he knew what 'Animus' meant, and he laughed. Apparently there was another police constable who wasn't the sharpest tool in the box and couldn't spell; 'Animus' was how he spelled 'anonymous'. Ben's seen it before in a different police file."

"Can he remember which one?"

"He thinks he can, so I've arranged to pay him to do the research for us. He'll do it tomorrow and email the results through to me."

"Very good, and did Mr Smith...?"

"No, he didn't follow it up, never came back," Zelah interrupted. "Which should put us ahead of Mr Smith, whoever he might be."

"An associate of the Quinns?" Maggie murmured.

"Something else. I took a look at what Nick suggested, the murder after Adolphus Quinn's death," Zelah began. "He's right, there was something about it. I think it might have been a copycat. It's exactly the same *modus operandi*, but without the depth of savagery."

"If it's exactly the same, how did the killer know the details?" Maggie asked. "If the worst of it was never released to the public, how could he have exactly replicated it?"

"Good point. It could have been a member of the constabulary."

"Nick was expecting something like this, he has some sort of theory. Let's get back and finish off. We're going to need time at the office, to talk over what you can say to Rufus Quinn tonight."

**

If Zelah had been apprehensive about a pretext to make her approach to Rufus Quinn, she need not have worried. She had dressed to both stand out and impress in a red two-piece Armani dress and jacket, with her best matching jewellery. Diamond pins shone in her hair and she had put on her highest, stiletto-heeled, most expensive red shoes. Although the Mayor was going to announce the award winners, Zelah was an honoured guest, it being her money that made the event possible.

She had barely walked through the door before the Mayor spotted her. She had been hovering near the entrance on the look-out and didn't want anyone else collaring Zelah ahead of her. She seized Zelah's arm and guided her over to her colleagues. Usually Zelah would have shrugged this off, but as the group included Rufus Quinn, she let herself be led to them. At six foot four, he towered over her, but what Zelah lacked in height she made up for in formidable presence. On being introduced, Quinn took both her hands in his but she pulled them back, asserting her control. He leaned back in surprise, a fleeting glimpse of irritation on his face, replaced with a wide, false smile that didn't rise beyond his upper lip. He leaned in again.

"Delighted to meet you Mrs Fitzgerald."

Zelah steeled herself against the unctuousness, giving him an equally false, tight smile before turning away to be introduced by the Mayor to the others in the group. The Mayor was about to walk her on again, when Zelah stopped and turned back to Quinn.

"We have a friend in common, Mr Quinn."

"Oh, really? Who could that be?"

"Isobel Blackstock."

This time, he didn't attempt to check the shock. "That does astonish me Mrs Fitzgerald. You may know that *your* friend, made something of a fool of herself here last week. I had to have her removed from the reception I was attending."

Out of the corner of her eye, Zelah spotted the Mayor now standing stock still, face paling by the second. She saw the twitching noses of interest in the rest of the group.

"Yes she told me. Thought-provoking story, wasn't it? About your ancestor, Adolphus Quinn? It piqued my interest, as a genealogy researcher," she replied with a smile. Turning back to the Mayor, Zelah took her elbow, saying politely, "Let's meet the recipients shall we?"

Throughout the presentations, as Zelah smiled, clapped and handed over plaques and cheques, she never lost sight of Rufus Quinn. She was satisfied to see that he stayed throughout, never taking his eyes off her.

After the formal part of the evening was finished, the recipients and their families, the Councillors and their guests moved on to the buffet. Zelah found herself standing alone.

Rufus Quinn chose his opportunity to approach her again. *'He needs to make the next move,'* she thought, *'Good'*.

"You will no doubt know, Mrs Fitzgerald," he said, waving around his glass of wine, not noticing that he had slopped a little over the side of the glass, "that Gwentshire has agreed to erect a statue to my ancestor Adolphus Quinn."

"I am aware, Mr Quinn."

"I don't understand why you're taking an interest in this personal affair of mine?"

"As it's public money paying for the statue, it's not entirely personal, is it?"

"I am myself making a sizeable contribution to the cost. What's it got to do with you, as a so-called genealogist?" He was slurring his words, and moved close enough for Zelah to feel sour breath on her face.

"I am interested in the story of Adolphus Quinn and what my friend Isobel says about him."

"Your friend is an idiot," he replied, loudly enough for several people to stop talking and look at them. "My ancestor was an honour–, honourable man." He would have continued but a man, who appeared to have just entered the Chamber, was walking rapidly in their direction.

As he reached them, he whispered, "come away please; I'll deal with this."

Although done discreetly, the words were delivered with sufficient menace to stop Rufus, who, at first, had looked belligerently at the newcomer. When he squinted and saw who it was, he turned to Zelah and said in a muffled tone, "You should mind your own business." He turned away, put his glass down on the first table he passed, and walked out of the room. Zelah and the newcomer watched his departure in silence.

"Good evening Mr Quinn," Zelah said.

"Mrs Trevear," Kennet Quinn replied. "I apologise for my

father."

"No need. You've only just arrived?"

"No, I have been here all evening, I would like to invite you to visit us at home, tomorrow morning at ten."

Zelah bristled. She didn't like being manipulated, but this was to her advantage. "Be delighted," she replied.

"Why not bring Mrs Gilbert with you, I should like to meet her too."

Alarm bells rang, but it was too late to retract her acceptance. Zelah tilted her head, walked around him, and headed for the exit. It was only when she reached her car, she realised she hadn't asked for his address. He hadn't offered it to her, but she knew the house, and he knew that.

Chapter 12
Newport, December 1896

The story of Ada Blackstock's murder was all but gone from the newspapers. An article in the latest edition of the South Wales Argus, tried to revive interest, but had not been covered elsewhere. The story had been overtaken by the discovery of the body of Constable David Bale in the River Usk, half a mile from Town Bridge. This proved to be a short-lived item, once it was discovered that Constable Bale had been drinking in several public houses in the docks area shortly before his death, not only that night but on previous nights too. This suggested he might have been a heavy drinker so any possibility of a suspicious death was quashed.

What didn't make the news was that Bale had been asking questions in each of the pubs, about events surrounding the night of Ada Blackstock's death, and the murders of the prostitutes.

He had discovered over the course of three nights, and jotted in a notebook he carried, that there had been other disappearances, over five years prior to the first of the murders. All were female, and all were prostitutes. Someone was murdering street women and, until recently, had successfully disposed of their bodies.

Why had no-one reported the disappearances? He got the answer from one of the women he had spoken to, Annabel. Unlikely to be her real name, not that it mattered.

The women who disappeared were single girls who had no-one to miss them. They kept themselves to themselves. No family, no children, no friends, only customers who didn't care. Of course, it might be they had moved away, but Annabel didn't think so. They barely earned enough to keep themselves alive, living in a single room in vile conditions, and would not have had the wherewithal to move on.

Of those whose bodies had not been found – five that Annabel knew by name – all had simply disappeared overnight without a word to anyone. No-one cared enough to notice, never mind enquire, and not one of them had taken any of their meagre possessions with them. That was strange, Annabel told him.

Annabel had, for the price of several glasses of gin, told Bale everything she could remember; not that she would remember anything the next day. He left her sleeping on a bench and was sure that, as soon as he was gone, the landlord would throw her out.

One fact came through so repeatedly that he was no longer in any doubt: the 'man in the black hat' had been in the area every time a girl disappeared. They were all girls, no older than seventeen or eighteen. The girls felt a sense of unease around this man. They didn't like the way he looked at them, as he passed them in the street. One said it was 'like being considered a juicy joint for tomorrow's dinner, but of course, no-one had asked them for an opinion – not an official one.

Late on that night, PC David Bale made his way home after the pubs closed. He had heard nothing of interest that particular night, and had no reason to get out his notebook and pencil. He reached Town Bridge and crossed it. He was shivering, but almost home to his wife at their lodgings in Maindee. He glanced over the iron railings of the bridge, into the black waters of high tide, swirling around the central pillars below.

As he quickened his pace he heard footsteps approaching from behind and became immediately alert. As they reached him, he flicked his head around to see if it was anyone he knew.

His first, and last, feeling was amazement as he was picked up and thrown over the railings into the water. He hit it with a crash, flailing, failing to keep himself above water as his heavy overcoat dragged him down.

He cried out for help but there was no response. He struggled for breath, as the freezing water overwhelmed him and he lost control as the fast tide reached out and dragged down his head. His last thought, before the water burst into his lungs, was of his lovely wife waiting close by, at their fireside.

Two days later his body was discovered, near Pillgwenlly, in the mud at low tide.

Chapter 13

Zelah called Maggie as soon as she arrived home from the prize giving. Eventually, Maggie agreed to the visit. They arranged to meet at eight thirty the following morning to talk over likely scenarios at the Quinn home.

Maggie also agreed, reluctantly, not to tell Bob that she was going. She reasoned that if Kennet Quinn already knew who she was, he would also know about her connection to Bob. What else did he know? Bob would be furious with her, she knew, but she needed to find out.

Isobel had already gone to bed when Zelah arrived home. She wrote a note with the questions they still had that Isobel might be able to answer and pushed it under her door, telling her she would pick up with her at lunchtime the next day.

The following morning, before she left, Zelah popped her head around the spare bedroom door, to find that the room was empty; Isobel had gone. She must have packed her things during the day, and left as soon as Zelah had gone out the previous evening. The note was unread.

"She didn't leave a message, a note, nothing," Zelah told Maggie in the café across the road from St Woolos Cathedral. "What a bitch she's turned out to be."

"Don't use that word," Maggie frowned at her. "I agree she's behaved badly, but that's not the way to talk about another woman."

"Last thing I care about right now," Zelah grumped.

"Did she give you any indication she wanted to go home?"

"No, I saw her briefly after we got back from the archives office. I told her we'd found some interesting information, but she didn't seem to want to hear."

"Let's go to her house after we're finished at the Quinns, see what we can get from her."

"OK. Now we'd best discuss what we are about to walk into."

Just before ten they got up to leave, having discussed what they would say and what they might encounter. It took just a few minutes to walk around to the Quinns' house in Stow Road, an imposing red-brick house with gothic features, built over four storeys. As they walked up the steps to the double front door, Maggie sensed movement down in the lower basement, where she glimpsed a modern kitchen. She tugged on the antiquated bellpull, heard a resounding clang from inside, and waited. No-one came to answer.

After standing for a couple of minutes Zelah tried again, still no response.

"Perhaps this is his idea of a joke," Maggie said.

"Can't understand why," Zelah replied. "I thought he wanted to hear what we know. Whatever; come on, let's go. I'm not standing around waiting for this jerk."

They turned away and had descended the first two steps, when the door opened, and a voice shouted, "Stop!"

Zelah stopped and turned back to look at a young girl dressed in the full black regalia of a Goth. "Why should we?"

The Goth grinned, her black rimmed eyes wide with amusement. "Because my Pa is trying to annoy you. He knows you're waiting." She stood aside and swept an arm at them. "Come on in."

"So, it is going to be a face-off," Maggie whispered.

"Looks like it," Zelah replied, as they stepped into the inner hall.

They could see that the house had retained many of its Victorian features, and was tastefully decorated. There wasn't time for a good look around, as a door at the far end of the hallway opened, and Rufus Quinn appeared. The girl, who was wearing a tight black skirt, thigh-high boots and a black crop top, stopped in front of him and made a theatrical bow.

"In here," he said brusquely and walked into the room. With a quick glance at each other they followed him. The girl followed too but was stopped in the doorway by another voice from inside the room. "Not you. Get back upstairs, clean up your face and change your clothes."

"I wasn't upstairs," she pouted, but retreated, poking her tongue out in her father's direction, once she was sure he couldn't see her.

Rufus had positioned himself behind a desk that stood in front of the bay window, where Kennet was waiting.

Maggie and Zelah were left standing in the middle of a room lined with bookshelves floor to ceiling that were perfectly synchronised, so much so Maggie thought they were there for show, not for interest in their subject matter.

One wall had a substantial fireplace with an impressive mantle and shelf over. It featured just a ticking clock and a miniature, indeterminable object, which looked like a lump of wood. Two armchairs, either side of the hearth, faced at an angle to the fire. Maggie took her time looking around. What stood out was the lack of homely feeling in the room. There were no personal items, no mementos, no photographs. It should have been a comfortable space, but it was impersonal. This was a room in which to show off and impress.

In their pre-emptive discussion they had agreed that, whatever Rufus or Kennet said, they would not react. Both now had to grit their teeth at this treatment. Maggie wondered who would be the first to move. It turned out to be Zelah, Who walked past the desk to the bay window and leaned forward to peer out. "Very nice garden," she said. "Do you do it yourselves? No, probably not, can't see either of you getting your hands dirty. Not your style is it?"

They both looked up but neither reacted. Maggie decided it was her turn. "Can you please stop this childish behaviour? You invited us here, what do you want?"

Kennet walked around the desk and started towards her but diverted to one of the armchairs. He sat, crossed his legs, and flicked imaginary pieces of fluff from his three-piece suit. He straightened his tie, a final check of the knife edge creases in his trouser legs, and he looked up at her. Zelah was still standing at the window.

"How nice to meet you, Mrs Gilbert." His face was impassive, and she understood what Bob had said about the eyes of a dead fish. He was making eye contact, but his face was expressionless. Zelah walked back around the desk to stand next to Maggie.

"I do hope your family are all well," he said, fixing his stare on Maggie. "Jack and Alice, isn't it? Seventeen and thirteen. How is Alice enjoying school in Hereford? Your business partner, Mr Howell and his rather pleasant girlfriend Miss Bell, I do hope they are well and healthy. Inspector Bob Pugh, of course. How well is he recovering?"

Maggie's throat had closed up. She swallowed and was about to speak but Zelah got in first. "They are all fine and are going to stay that way. How's your wife, Mr Quinn, Michelle I believe is her name? I gather she doesn't live here now. Your daughter must favour her. She certainly doesn't look anything like you, does she?"

He opened his mouth, but they were all momentarily distracted by a snort from outside the door which had been left ajar.

"I told you to get upstairs, and close the door," Kennet had spoken softly, but the tone didn't brook opposition.

"Allow me," Zelah said. She turned her head and flicked it

in the direction of the door. It slammed shut. For the first time Kennet's eyes showed expression. He turned his head to Zelah, who was looking at him in amusement in response to his puzzlement, her eyebrows raised. His expression struck Maggie as odd, but she couldn't think how better to describe it. She glanced across at Rufus, who was staring open-mouthed.

"Now then," Zelah continued as if nothing had happened, "how is your wife, Kennet? I can call you Kennet, can't I? I feel like we're starting to get to know each other quite nicely. How is Michelle, whom we both know is not dead, contrary to your assertions."

He didn't reply.

"Nothing more to say on the subject of family?" she continued, "Good. You made such an excellent start, telling us what you know but I know things too, Kennet. I will repeat my colleague's question: why did you ask us here and what do you want?"

"What the hell are you doing?" This time it was Rufus. "How dare you investigate my great-grandfather?"

"I will investigate whoever I want to investigate," Zelah said without turning. Her eyes were still fixed on Kennet. "Would you like the door open again? It's getting a little warm, isn't it? Shall we let some air in to cool us down?" In response to another flick of her head the handle turned and the door sprang open.

They all turned to stare, except Maggie, who was used to Zelah's ability, inherited from her Cornish witch ancestor, to make objects move. She had been looking at Kennet. What she saw astonished her but Zelah was already talking again.

"My investigation into your ancestor, Rufus, tells me that something isn't right. Whoever you sent to the archives office has already told you that. Not nice to have stolen that document, by the way." Rufus swallowed. "Not that we need it.

We have plenty to be going on with. Now, Kennet, I already knew what you are capable of; now you know what I can do. If your words were meant to frighten us, then believe me, I can bring hell's fury down on you and yours whenever I feel like it. If I am in the room or a hundred miles away; opening and closing doors is just a party trick." She turned to Maggie. "I think we should go now." She marched to the door. Maggie who had been momentarily stunned, ran to catch up.

They kept up a reasonable pace until they reached Zelah's car. Maggie stood in silence, holding onto the bonnet, taking deep breaths. It took a moment before she felt she could move her legs, without falling over. She yanked the car door open and slid into the passenger seat.

"That was horrible," she began, but before she could continue, a loud bang on the car window made them both jump. To their relief it was the Goth, still in full black makeup and costume. Maggie's heart hammered and, for a split second she had expected to see one of the male Quinns. The girl, who was grinning at them, signalled to wind down the window.

She stuck her head inside and, looking across at Zelah, she said, "That was fucking awesome... with the door. Did you see my Pa's face when it opened again? I thought he was going to have a stroke."

"He might do before I'm finished," Zelah muttered but Maggie signalled to her to be quiet.

"I presume you're Kennet's daughter, Mischa isn't it?"

"That's me," the girl said. "Look, can I squeeze in, I need to talk to you?" A quick glance at Zelah confirmed she was OK with it. Maggie got out, moved her seat forward as far as it would go, and the girl slid herself through the tiny gap in the space between the front seat and the back of the car.

"This is fucking awesome, too, what is it?" she said, her eyes sweeping every aspect of the car.

"It's an Audi R8 Spyder convertible."

"This year's model?"

"Of course."

"Why isn't it red?"

"Last year's colour."

"Does anyone else ever get to drive it?"

"Maggie's son," Zelah replied. "Now, how can we help you? I am assuming that's why you're here?"

"Um, yeah, well, I heard what you were saying. Great that you stood up to Pa, by the way. He likes to intimidate people and humiliate them. Great that you didn't fall for it. By the way how did you do that door thing?"

"Party trick," Zelah replied. Despite herself, she couldn't help a slight smile at the girl's unrelenting cheerfulness. "I presume you were hiding somewhere in the hall, not upstairs. What do you want?"

"I want you to help me find my mum," the girl said. "I was listening through the keyhole after you shut the door. I heard you say she's not dead. That's what I think too, never mind what Pa has always told us."

"Us?" Maggie asked. "There's more than one of you?"

"Brother, Gerard. Saint Gerry I call him. He's a year younger than me. He's Grandpa's favourite, not that I care. Anyway, I want to find my mum. She paused and bit her bottom lip. "Will you help me?"

Moved by the appeal in her voice, and before Zelah could speak, Maggie said "Possibly. We'll need to talk more, in a more suitable place. You're going to get cramp if you kneel there much longer. Do you get out of the house on your own?"

Mischa shook her head, causing her hair to bounce around her face. "Pa usually makes me take a minder, but I know how to do it without any of them knowing. Where and when?"

Zelah reached over and took a card from the glovebox.

"Here's our office phone number, I presume he doesn't body search you? We'll be back there later. Give us half an hour or so then call us, and we'll arrange something. Now, you'd better get back home."

Maggie got out and the girl jumped through from the back of the car onto the road. "Great, speak later," she said, and waved to them as she ran off.

"Not sure if this is wise," Zelah mused. "She seems like a nice kid, but… I hope Kennet didn't send her after us. He's a devious weasel. What do you think?"

"I think I want to go home, consider what we know and mull over all of this. First, we should try to find Isobel and check she's OK."

Chapter 14

It was after midday when they reached Maggie's house. Their visit to Isobel had proved fruitless. Maggie had looked in through the letterbox and told Zelah there was no sign of anyone being at home but the smell of burning was still strong and bitter.

Nick was already in the office and they brought him up to speed on what had happened.

"Does Bob know you went there?" he asked.

Maggie pursed her lips. "Not precisely."

"That's 'no' then. Are you going to tell him?"

"Yes, this evening. He's supposed to be back at about five. Now I'm seriously wondering if we should cancel Jack's visitors."

"Absolutely not," Zelah said. "He's been looking forward to this. Think about it: they aren't going out of the house, are they? They'll be safe here, we can watch over them all weekend. The one you do have to think about is Alice, at her friend's house. How are you going to explain to her hosts they'll have to keep an eye out for someone trying to get near her?"

Maggie frowned. "I'll have to tell them and give them the option of saying 'no' to her staying there. She'll be upset, but I have to do it. I'll call them now."

Fifteen minutes later she returned to the office. "That wasn't as bad as I expected," she said, sitting at the table. "I've met the family a couple of times and they didn't strike me as being different. It seems they are seriously wealthy, to the point where they have high-level personal security, which I think may be something to do with his job, but I didn't ask, not my business. There are four kids staying there and they won't be leaving the house. They'll be taken back to school on Sunday evening. I agreed to tell the school right away too, and Alice."

"I'm seriously wealthy," Zelah said, "do I strike you as being *different?*"

"From the day we first met in the library," Maggie replied, "but I'm used to you."

"How did Alice take it?" Nick intervened before Zelah could get argumentative.

"She was fine about it." She shook her head. "The girl has no sense of danger. She promised me that she'd stay with the others and wouldn't attempt to go out. Anyway, sounds like there's enough there to keep them interested. She sends her love and says she never realised genealogy was so dangerous. She reminded me that I was kicked in the back once, in my previous corporate role, and had to go to hospital; and I thought that was as bad as it could get. The school head was concerned, but I think OK."

"Never a dull moment," Zelah replied. "I just tried calling Isobel. No answer, so I left a message."

"OK, what are the significant bits of what we've found out yesterday and today? Plus what are we going to do about Mischa Quinn?"

"Why are you talking about Mischa Quinn?" barked a harsh voice.

"Oh, hi Bob, I didn't know you were coming home for lunch." One look at his face gave full meaning to 'incandescent with rage'.

"Don't change the subject. What about Mischa Quinn?"

"We met her this morning and she's asked to talk to us. She wants us to help her find her mother." She rushed the words out, hoping Bob wouldn't ask more questions but knowing that there was little chance.

"Where did you meet her?" His narrowed eyes and

96

reddening face suggested that he knew the answer already, but he was going to make her tell him. Well, that wasn't going to work.

She folded her arms across her chest and moved closer to stare eyeball to eyeball. "Are you having me followed now?"

In a low voice he replied, "Not you."

Zelah was about to comment that the heat blazing from his face was going to melt the varnish on the table, when she realised the significance of what he said.

"Blame me, not her," she intervened. "I poked Kennet's father with a stick last night at the prize giving. Kennet sent Rufus away and invited me to go to his house to meet them."

"Which of course you couldn't resist," he snarled before looking back at Maggie, "You decided to go with her?"

"He invited Zelah to bring me along. He knows who we all are, where we all live. He seemed to think it would frighten us. It's too late to hide from him," she replied.

Bob, standing upright with folded arms, said, "You could be right, but trying to face it out with him is just about your stupidest idea yet. My officers wasted valuable time trying to work out who you were. Imagine my surprise when they came to me with your names."

"Sarcasm does not help," Maggie retorted.

"Anyway, I think we came out better from the exchange. Zelah showed him what she could do and I saw him cross himself with shaking hands. He quickly kissed a cross hanging around his neck, when he thought no-one was looking. Kennet Quinn is a surprisingly superstitious man, which can only be good for us."

Bob turned away and rubbed his head with his hands. He turned back and sat at the table, "Right, sit, all of you, and tell me what you know about Michelle and Kennet's children."

"And will you tell us what you know?" Zelah asked, still

standing with arms crossed.

"I can tell you some things, now, sit down; you're going to need to."

"I know that Michelle Quinn is not dead," Zelah began. "Kennet has been lying to his children. Mischa has now realised this too. She was listening when I told Kennet that we knew. She wants our help to find her mother. She followed us out to the car after we left. She told us that her brother Gerard is the apple of both his grandfather's and father's eye, she called him 'Saint Gerry'. I've given her the office phone number, and I'm waiting for her to call. That's it."

"We did wonder if Kennet had sent her after us," Maggie added, "but I think not. He keeps control of her as far as possible, but she enjoys the game of getting one up on him. I don't think she has any respect for either her father or her grandfather."

Bob nodded and rubbed his chin. "Anything else?" He shrugged. "At least you got into the house. We've never been able to achieve that." Maggie sensed a slight cooling off.

"It's a lovely house inside, traditional, plush, but…" Maggie stopped and thought for a second, "It felt impersonal, cold, no family photos, no mementos of any kind."

"That's because they are impersonal and cold," Bob said. "Kennet doesn't value relationships. Everything is business, just business. He keeps close control over his children because to him they are property."

"How old are they now?" Maggie asked. She thought Mischa had seemed young.

"The girl is nineteen and the boy eighteen."

"What do you know about his, presumably, ex-wife?" Zelah asked.

"I know that they've never divorced, I suspect because she was too afraid of him finding out where she was. She left him when Mischa was four and Gerard three on Christmas Day."

"She walked out on Christmas Day, with two young children?" Maggie asked, amazed.

"She didn't walk," Bob replied. "She was taken by a friend to the Royal Gwent Hospital. Kennet had poured boiling water over her hands. Apparently he didn't think she was doing a good job of preparing Christmas lunch."

Maggie put a hand over her mouth and muttered, "Oh, my God."

"What happened next?" Zelah asked.

"When she was discharged from the hospital she went to a refuge in Cardiff. She refused to press charges against him and no-one has seen her since. She's made no contact with any of her own family, we think she did a runner."

"So he got away with it?"

"Yes, he did, he gets away with it. He's clever, don't think he's anything else. He'll be planning ways to stop your investigation."

"Then perhaps I should give him another reminder of what I can do," Zelah said. "Get my retaliation in first."

"If you hurt anyone, you'll get yourself and all of us into trouble," Nick said. "It won't help Bob's official investigation." He turned to Bob. "Is what we're doing getting in your way?"

After a few seconds Bob said "No, not entirely. If Mischa gets in touch I want you to tell me everything she tells you about her family. This might just turn out to be the best lead we've had in a long time. Don't think about arguing with me," he aimed at Maggie. "I'm going to have to think about how to protect all of you, now. Mischa Quinn is payback."

"Seems fair," Nick said.

"I don't like it, but I agree," Zelah added.

Maggie didn't speak.

"If you still need persuading," Bob said to her, "I can tell you this, 'Saint Gerry' is probably the man who shot me. He'll not be 'child of the month' with his dad and granddad, because he didn't kill me. This must have been his chance to prove himself. They like a job well done and I'm guessing so as far as Kennet's concerned, Gerry failed. Yesterday, we found the missing complaining tenant in A&E. He'd had two fingernails pulled out. He's claiming it was an accident, and won't even speak to us now, he's too traumatised."

Maggie sighed and closed her eyes, "OK, if she calls – if – we'll let you know."

Bob jumped to his feet. "I'll get back to work then, see *you* later."

Maggie knew that this was addressed to her and meant that it wasn't the end of it by a long shot. He just wasn't going to say any more in front of Zelah and Nick.

"Don't let him bully you," Zelah said when he had left the house.

Maggie stopped her. "He's not a bully, Zelah. I know him better now, he's scared for all of us, and he thinks I still don't take it all seriously enough after what happened in Ireland. Of course I take it seriously. Can we talk about Adolphus Quinn now? What have we got so far?"

"Yes, but can we please take a break? You two are giving off enough energy to power the national grid and I have a headache. I'm going to take a walk in the garden," Nick said, as he stood and walked out.

"Let him go," Zelah said, taking Maggie's arm to restrain her, "give him a bit of space."

She nodded and went out to the kitchen.

By the time Nick came back, Maggie and Zelah were sitting at the kitchen table with tea and biscuits.

"Excellent," Nick said, helping himself to a handful of biscuits. "That's better."

As he crunched away, Maggie kicked off the discussion. "From the visit to the archives yesterday and from the information we picked up online, I'm thinking that Adolphus Quinn is a good candidate for the murder of Ada and the prostitutes. He was in the area at the time of Ada's murder and identified independently. His background is unclear. He changed his life story three times."

"And his wife didn't like him, despised him going by the photographs and news stories," Zelah said.

"What about the later murders?" Nick asked, "the one just before, and the one after his death?"

"The one before wasn't a murder, the woman got away. You're fixated on the one after, aren't you?" Zelah said to him, "Why?"

"Just a thought. Did you check them out?" Nick asked.

"We did," Maggie replied, "and there was a difference in the one after his death. It was almost the same method, but not nearly so violent. There was also a man in a black hat seen again in the area on that evening." She paused for a second. "Do you think the one after his death was a copycat?"

"That was my thought," Nick said to the ceiling.

"Was someone trying to prove that it couldn't have been Adolphus Quinn?" Zelah mused.

"Perhaps," Nick said, "I wondered if it was someone in authority, who knew it might have been Quinn. The publicity would have been terrible for the town and the Council if it was him. So, maybe someone committed another unsolvable murder, but they couldn't bring themselves to do what the original murderer did."

"Interesting theory," Zelah said.

"Did he leave a will?" Nick asked.

"Haven't checked yet," Maggie replied. "Given how little time we've got, is it worth checking?"

"He was young when he died, so I doubt he did, but we can check the probate register," Nick said.

"Zelah, anything to add?" Maggie asked.

"It's not much to go on. Do we have anything to prove he didn't commit murder?"

"No, but what we have is circumstantial. What do we do next?" Maggie asked.

"I can ring the archives, see if Ben has come up with anything about 'animus'."

"OK, I'm thinking that we'll ask Jack's groupies to work on Adolphus Quinn's history. To see if they can identify where he came from, it will be useful to know."

"You said that someone could help me out," Nick interrupted. "I have this Lincolnshire project to follow up on. There's precious little on the main websites, so we're going to have to see what's available elsewhere on the net. Some lateral thinking will be good for them."

"How about they swap over halfway? Jack and one girl concentrate on Adolphus tomorrow afternoon, whilst the other pair work with you. Then they can swap on Sunday morning, which will give us some summing-up time, before their parents pick them up after lunch."

"Good," Nick said, "that way they get the experience of both the direct and indirect research on live cases."

As he finished speaking the office phone rang and Zelah reached over to take the call. As soon as it began, she signalled to Maggie and Nick and put the caller on speaker.

"Hello," said Mischa Quinn. "Is this a good time?"

"None better," Zelah replied.

"Can we meet up? Two things, I've got some information about my mother and some other information, about my DNA result. It came in the post this morning and I don't understand it."

"OK, when?"

"Are you free this afternoon?"

"We might have some time, but not much. How long do we need?"

"About half an hour, I suppose."

"What transport do you have?"

"None, really."

"OK, we'll come and pick you up in the same place, the parking spaces at the bottom end of the cathedral, in about…" she looked at Maggie and mouthed 'thirty minutes?' Maggie nodded. "In about half an hour. Don't be late."

"I won't," the girl replied, sounding relieved. "Are you bringing the Spyder?"

"No, it's a two-seater. We'll be in Maggie's car – a black Peugeot 207."

"Oh, never mind. See you in half an hour."

"That sorts out what we're doing next," Maggie said. She turned to Nick. "Can you hold the fort? Jack should be up soon. Tell him what we have in mind for the weekend, and ask him to make sure that the girls bring their own laptops this time?"

"Will do, Maggie, Zelah…" He put down his biscuits. "Please be careful. I believe Kennet Quinn to be a violent, disturbed man. If he thinks you are speaking to his daughter..." His voice trailed off for a moment. He shook his head, then added "We'll all have to watch out for ways that Kennet Quinn can stop us finding out about Adolphus. They may not all involve brute force; his is a cunning cleverness."

"I know," Maggie replied, patting his arm, "I'm going to call Bob now and tell him what we're doing."

Chapter 15

They waited for Mischa until they thought she wasn't coming. Then, suddenly, a smart young woman in a business suit, high-heeled shoes, expertly made up, wearing dark framed glasses and carrying a brief case strode up to the car and climbed into the back seat.

"Hello," she said brightly. "Sorry, took me a bit longer than I expected to get away. Had to wait for Grandpa to fall asleep."

"We didn't recognise you, you look much older," Maggie said, pulling away as Zelah, grinning widely looking around at Mischa.

"One of my many disguises."

"Why?"

"Pa thinks I'm a hopeless Goth. I really jam it up for him and his friends. When I want to go out I can put on my real clothes. He probably wouldn't recognise me either."

"And the piercings?"

"Fake, they just clip –on. Clever, isn't it?"

"I'm not sure," Maggie replied. "If one fell off and your father saw it, he'd know you were faking it."

They headed out of Newport towards Caerleon, where they parked in front of the Roman Baths and walked through the small walled town to a vegan café. Inside the café was full, but the long, tapered courtyard garden had only one other occupied table. It was a pretty place decorated in Mediterranean style with waist-high, Ali-baba-type pots of red geraniums around the walls and white cotton sail shades over the tables. They took a place at the far end, up against the medieval town wall under a potted olive tree, where they couldn't be overheard.

After they had ordered drinks, which had taken Zelah some

time and questioning (and a lot of nose wrinkling at the answers to her questions), they began their discussion. Bob had told Maggie to take as many notes as she could and, although she felt deceitful, she explained to Mischa that this was necessary to ensure she didn't miss any important facts.

The first question Mischa asked was how Zelah knew that her mother had not died.

"A brick wall, but not too difficult knock down," Zelah replied. "I couldn't find any evidence that she died. I did take a gamble when I faced your father but his lack of denial told me I was right. I've looked for her death from the time she left you, under both her married and single names. There hasn't been one that fitted her date of birth. When someone dies they should be buried under their own name, although if they have changed it legally that can be difficult to trace. I don't have absolute proof that she's alive, but there's no evidence that she died. Think about it, if she had died there was no reason for your father not to formally acknowledge that she was dead. It tells me that he had no proof either, should you or your brother ever ask for any. I haven't been able to trace her yet, but I know that she has never divorced your father. I can't find her on any public electoral register as a Quinn, or as a Morgan, which was her maiden name. It could mean that he was probably not registered to vote. She could be on a Council Tax register, but under another name, and has withheld the details. There's more we can find out, but we haven't had enough time yet."

"Why a brick wall?" the girl asked.

"It's a genealogical term for when you just can't find anything about a person you know to exist, but about whom there seems to be no recorded information. Sometimes the search goes on for years. People just keep looking, being as creative as they can. Our colleague, Nick, has a case at the moment. He's been looking for a client into the death of an ancestor who died at about thirty-nine. He can't find anything, either online or in archive material. It's been going on for about six months, which is a long time for us. He hasn't found anything at all, other than lots of dead ends. Pardon the pun," Maggie replied.

Mischa nodded, thought for a few moments then said, "Why did you come to see Pa?"

"Do you know about the statue to your ancestor, Adolphus Quinn?"

"Fucking hell, Grandpa never talks about anything else! He thinks he could get to be "Sir Rufus" – fat chance if you ask me - and he wants the thing to celebrate his grand ancestors, to look good. He's even putting in some of his own money."

"Well, we have information that says Adolphus wasn't so grand," Maggie said. "We're trying to find out if it's true."

The girl's eyes lit up. "Spectacular. Is it really bad?"

"Yes," Maggie replied, "the worst."

"Did he kill someone?"

"If our information is correct he killed several people, all women."

The smile disappeared. "Oh, that's bad - bastard."

"We're still trying to determine if it's true," Maggie said.

"When will you find out?"

"Hopefully, before next Thursday, when the Committee meeting takes place to ratify the expenditure. After that, it's too late and a done deal."

"Can I do anything to help?"

Maggie saw an opportunity, but she had to tread carefully. "Possibly. We were at the Gwent Archives yesterday, and found a file that might have held some answers. Unfortunately, someone had been there before us. We can't think why anyone else would be interested…"

"Except my Pa and Grandpa."

"Whoever it was took something from the file that might help us. Could you listen out for anything they might say about it? The person signed in as 'Mr Smith'".

Mischa nodded. "I can search the office. What if I find it?"

"Do not, under any circumstances, put yourself at risk. No, better not to search. It would be helpful if we knew it was them, but we do have another potential source for the information."

Maggie had to stop there, as the waitress brought their drinks.

Zelah gave her glass of thick green liquid a dubious look and took a tentative sip. "Not much better than it looks," she said, pushing the glass away. "Now, what's your DNA information?"

"I had it done to see if I could find anyone related to mum, who might know where she could be," Mischa said. She bent down to retrieve papers from her briefcase. "But it didn't say what I expected." She spread the two sheets of paper out on the table and Maggie and Zelah leaned in.

After a couple of minutes studying, Maggie said, "I see what you mean, there are some Morgans here but there's no-one called Quinn. That's odd, there should be a couple at least."

"Look, there are lots of these." She pointed to the name Ryan. "Look at the connections."

"Second cousin, that's a close connection. Does it mean anything to you?"

"No, nothing. I've never heard the name at home."

"We'll check out the history of these families at the weekend and let you know what we find. Let's go back to your mother. How did you come to believe she's still alive?"

"Because for the last three months Pa's been looking for her. She has something he needs back."

Zelah sat back. "Well that's a corker. What is it?" Zelah asked.

"Not a clue. What I heard was '*she may still have it. We must get it back. The bitch was wearing it when she left. I'll find her somehow'.* Then Grandpa said about not having any idea where she was, maybe she's not even in the country. Then Pa said *'I'll find her, whatever it takes. I'm thinking she won't be far away.'* I wondered why he thought that."

Maggie put her hand on the girl's arm and gave it a gentle squeeze. As a mother she could understand why he might have thought that. "He knew how much she loved you. I think your mother may have left to protect you but couldn't leave you completely. She may have been close by all this time, watching you from a short distance."

The girl's eyes widened. "Do you think I might know her? I mean, I might have spoken to her, or something, but not know who she really is?"

"It's a possibility, I think," Maggie replied. She looked at her watch. "We're going to have to get back. We have a lot of work to do." She stood up.

"I can't take any more of this sludge," Zelah said, glaring at the almost untouched glass. "I don't know how you both drank that stuff."

"Ignore her, Mischa. She's free with her opinions but it's not personal."

"What happens now?" Mischa asked as they walked to the car.

"You let us know anything you hear about Adolphus Quinn and the statue and anything about the paper taken from the archives file. Send Zelah a text and we'll arrange a call. We'll be trying to figure out how we find your mother. Mischa…," The girl looked intently at Maggie. "Do not, I repeat do not, do anything risky. Is that clear?"

Mischa nodded.

They drove back into Newport and dropped the girl at the back of the cathedral.

On their way to the house Zelah and Maggie started on some ideas about what they could do that afternoon.

"I wonder if we missed anything in the files," Zelah said. "Whatever it is they want to find has high significance and they probably want to destroy it."

"Which means danger for Michelle Quinn. We're going to have to find her, without alerting Kennet or Rufus Quinn."

Zelah looked at her watch. "No time to go back to the archives now and they're closed 'til Tuesday. Bugger. I'll phone Ben as soon as I get back. What else can we do?"

"I'm going to have a word with Bob tonight about Michelle Quinn. If he thinks it's a valid enough lead for the police to get involved, maybe he can use some of his resources. If Kennet Quinn is prepared to harm his wife to get back whatever it is, then someone needs to find her. Fast."

Chapter 16

As they walked through the door of Maggie's house Zelah's phone rang. She told Maggie and Nick that it was Ben from the archives, and disappeared into the kitchen.

Thinking about their situation, Maggie's concerns were growing about the weekend. Could she let the girls come, knowing what she now knew about Kennet Quinn? Jack would be horrified if she were to cancel it so late in the day.

"Are you thinking about the weekend?"

"How well you know me, Nick."

"I can see that you're worried, have you talked to Jack about it?"

"Talked to me about what?" Jack said as he sauntered into the room.

"Sit down," Maggie said.

"I think I need to stand," Jack replied. "Tell me, please."

"OK," Maggie took a deep breath, "I told you that we have a live case for you and the girls to work on. Well, something happened this morning, that's giving me concerns about the girls being here at the weekend." His look of horror was exactly what she had expected and she began to talk again to stop his remonstrations. "Please listen to what I have to say". He sat down.

Before she could begin Zelah walked back into the room. "He's found some really useful information," she said before looking at the three faces. "What's wrong? What's happened?"

"Mum wants to cancel the weekend," Jack said, glaring at his mother.

"I didn't say that, although… I think I do." She looked up at Zelah in the doorway. "It's too dangerous. We're right in the thick of it. I've already had to warn Alice's friend's family. We cannot put the girls in the same situation. How would I explain to their parents if anything happened here?

"We can keep them safe here, we've already discussed that," Zelah said, "You're being over-protective."

"When they leave here, what happens then? And what should I tell their parents?" Maggie turned back to Jack, "I'm not prepared to lie to them. Look, I know this is disappointing, more than that, gutting. But, if anyone were to put you in a potentially dangerous situation without telling me, I'd be beyond furious. If we go ahead and anything happens, I will never forgive myself, and they will never forgive me, or you. It would be the end of your group."

"But Zelah said she can keep us safe, and their parents have already booked overnight rooms for themselves for tomorrow night."

"OK, how would you feel if something bad happened to any of them, as a result of being here?" It was a brutal question, but she had to get through to him.

Jack was close to tears. "I see that, but what am I going to say that won't make them angry with me? Make it the end of the group anyway?"

"The truth," Zelah said. "Tell them that we've run into a serious situation that we don't want to expose any of you to. It need only be a couple of weeks and they can come again, once it's all over. Tell them I'll cover the cost of their parents' accommodation." She walked over to Jack and put an arm around him. "Come on, let's go for a drive, we can talk about it."

He pushed back the chair, "I'll have to send them all a message first."

"I'll help." Zelah took his arm and they walked out of the office. He didn't look at Maggie.

"He'll come round," Nick said quietly, "You've done the right thing."

Five minutes later Zelah and Jack came back downstairs. Jack went straight out but Zelah put her head around the office door.

"He'll be OK," she said. "I get what you're saying. Needless to say, they are all mad with disappointment and agog with curiosity, but he hasn't given them any details. I'll keep him out for a couple of hours."

"Thanks, I hate to do this. We'll have to talk over what they were going to do. What did Ben have to say?"

"Tell you when I get back," Zelah replied.

**

Maggie went online to try to begin the research but couldn't concentrate. After an hour had passed, she gave up and went out into the garden, leaving Nick in the office.

She hadn't given it much attention since coming home from Italy and as she wandered around, realised that the flowerbeds had a scruffy, neglected look. Knowing that she wasn't going to get much research done until Jack came home, she unlocked the tool shed, took out some gardening tools and started to attack the plants.

She hadn't noticed how much time had passed when a voice behind her said, "There's pruning, and then there's plant assassination. Probably time to stop before there isn't a flower head left."

Looking up she saw Zelah standing on the patio, grinning at her. "All's well," she said. "He's just gone up to his room, then he'll be back down to talk to you. He gets it, more or less. Of course, I had to make a few expensive gestures."

Maggie wiped her hand on her brow, "I'll pay you back, whatever it is."

"No," Zelah said, "I've said I'll re-imburse them for this

weekend. Then pay for them to stay somewhere swanky when they come back, when this is all over." She held up her hand to stop Maggie's protest. "Don't thank me."

Maggie smiled ruefully. "Thankyou."

"Jack is OK, that's what matters. Come back in before you kill any more of those nice plants."

"They're not dead," Maggie said as she walked past Zelah.

"No, luckily I came back just in time."

They found Nick still at work in the office. "Glad you're back," he said to Zelah. "Maggie's been beheading her prize plants, whether they deserved it or not."

Maggie grinned at them. "Thank you, thank you, that's enough now. Ah, there you are." Jack shuffled into the office.

He shrugged and mumbled "sorry."

"Nothing to apologise for. Do you want to do some of the work with us, or has the enthusiasm gone?"

"I want to help," he replied. "Zelah told me what you're facing. If Nick needs the help, I'll do that, too."

This time she had to suppress the grin. "If it's OK with Nick, we'll use you to see if we can get a handle on Adolphus Quinn's history."

"Fine with me," Nick said without looking up. "You're up against a deadline, mine is slightly less urgent."

"OK, let's get going. First of all what are we looking for?"

"How about I tell you what Ben found out in the archives?"

Maggie and Jack looked at Zelah and nodded.

"Two things. One, police constable David Bale died two weeks after he accompanied Inspector Freeman to visit Adolphus Quinn. He drowned, after falling into the water, whilst walking across Town Bridge. It was high tide and the current took him downstream, so it took a couple of days for his body to be found."

"Was it an accident?" Maggie asked.

"Not sure. The reports say that he had been drinking in a few pubs that evening and on previous evenings. The cause of death was recorded as accidental. When Ben read through more thoroughly he noted Bale's wife said that he wasn't a habitual drinker. It turned out he had been talking to prostitutes in the pubs. One of them came forward to say he had been asking about the girls who had died and others who had disappeared."

"What came of it?"

"Nothing," Zelah said. "Despite the wife telling them that Bale thought he had a significant lead in the murders, the police don't seem to have followed up on any of it. There were no witnesses. They accepted the verdict of accidental death, but I'm not convinced."

"Is there information about what questions he was asking in the pubs?"

"No, just one report that said he was asking about the ubiquitous 'man in the black hat'. The good news is, we have the information about 'Animus'."

"So Ben found it; is it significant?" Maggie asked.

"It certainly confirms that Bale suspected Adolphus Quinn and that he had some evidence. What Ben found was a notebook, that of Constable Herbert Clarence Wilkins, aka 'Animus'. There's one relevant entry, illiterate but just about legible; an account of a conversation between Wilkins and Bale on the subject of the murders. Wilkins wasn't specifically assigned to work on any of the murders and I got the impression from Ben that Wilkins was not highly regarded for his intelligence. The notes confirm that Bale had not only suspicions but had discovered that, whoever committed the murders, took pieces of clothing from each of the women."

"You mean, like trophies that serial killers take from their victims?" Jack asked. "I've seen it on TV programmes."

"Yes, probably," Zelah replied, "he took their

114

undergarments in a couple of cases, a hat in another and a scarf from one more."

"What did he take from Ada? Could it have been something personal to her" Maggie asked. "Is there any chance this could tie in with Kennet saying that he needed to get something back from Michelle?"

"That's the odd thing, Ben checked the file and no clothing was missing. He must have taken something, perhaps we missed it when we looked through the file. We weren't looking for anything like that, were we?"

"No," Maggie mused, "even so I'm surprised that we missed it. How are we going to find out?"

"As luck would have it, Ben pointed out that the archives are open for a half day one Saturday a month and tomorrow is the day. We can go up there first thing. We've got until midday to find out if anything was reported missing from her body."

"Can I come?" Jack asked.

"How about you and Jack go," Maggie said to Zelah and I'll stay here and work on the Adolphus Quinn back history. I'll use the Irish national registration records and we have our subscription to Roots Ireland. There's the BNA too, they have a few good Irish newspapers available now and I can check the probate register."

"What's the BNA?" Jack asked.

"British Newspaper Archive," Maggie replied. "You go with Zelah. You haven't been to an archive before, it'll be a good experience for you."

"Excellent," he grinned and turned to Zelah. "What time?"

"They open at nine thirty, so be ready at half eight."

"Is there any news from Isobel?" Maggie asked.

"No, nothing. I've started asking around her colleagues. I'm getting worried."

"Would you like Bob to get involved?"

"No, not yet. I've put feelers out. Let's give her tonight and tomorrow. If she still hasn't shown up, we'll ask him what he might do."

"Right," Maggie said, "we've missed the Glamorgan archives today. We'll have to go there on Monday or Tuesday. That just leaves us to talk about Mischa Quinn."

"Yes, we'll see what Bob has to say. If he can help us locate her mother that would be useful."

"For us, yes, but if the woman has managed to hide herself close by for so many years she's unlikely to agree to being outed now, that's if we can find her."

"She might do it for her daughter," Nick said.

"We set off an idea in Mischa's head about people she knows who might be around the same age as her mother. We can ask her to think about who they might be, see if we can build a profile. How about asking her if she has a photograph of her mother?"

"Worth a try," Zelah replied. "It doesn't matter if Michelle refuses to be identified, better she's found by us than by Kennet."

Maggie nodded, reluctantly. "I'm going to see what I can find about the history and background of Adolphus Quinn." As she turned to her screen her phone pinged.

"A text from Bob. He wants to talk to us all later, over dinner." She looked up. "Can you both stay?"

Zelah agreed but Nick said, "If it's something about security, I'd like Stella to be here too. Would that be OK with you?"

"Fine with me," Maggie replied. "How much does she know about this, Nick?"

"Everything," he replied.

Chapter 17

Bob appeared at the same time as Stella.

"Sorry we're not meeting in better circumstances," he said. "I need to share information with you all, and it can't wait."

As much as she liked Stella, Maggie always felt untidy when standing next to her. Stella, as usual, was the epitome of effortless elegance. She was a couple of inches so taller than Maggie, towering over Zelah. Today she was dressed in designer jeans and a light t-shirt in grey which highlighted her shoulder length white-blonde hair and lightly, but perfectly made-up face. Maggie couldn't remember the last time she had worn makeup. She greeted Stella warmly nonetheless and received a gentle hug in return.

Dinner was a quiet affair, during which they discussed the information they had on the Quinn family history. Maggie decided that since Stella knew everything there was no need to hold back, including their meetings with Mischa Quinn.

"What chance do you think you have of finding her mother?" Stella asked.

"That depends on any help that Bob can give us," Zelah said. "What about it Bob?"

He shook his head. "Unlikely I can help much. I've already spoken to the refuge where she went immediately after the 'accident', but they couldn't help. They did say a friend came to take her away after a couple of weeks but they didn't have their name."

"If you can't find her, what chance does Kennet Quinn have?" Stella asked.

"Good question." Maggie replied. "It would help if we had a photo. We can use technology to 'age' her to get an idea of what she might look like now. I thought about whether she has any relatives in the area we can talk to, but I guess that's where Kennet Quinn will go first. We don't want to alert him to a search on our part."

"If you can get a photo, I can use a face ageing app, they're really good," Jack said.

"Where can we get a photo?" Maggie asked. "There were no family photos on display in the Quinn house."

"That's something we can ask Mischa. I'll try calling her again now." Zelah rose from the table. "She didn't answer earlier."

"When you're done we should go to the office, I have information I want to show you," Bob said.

Maggie and Bob sent Nick, Stella and Jack into the office whilst they cleared away the remnants of dinner.

"How worried are you?" Maggie asked.

"You'll see," he replied.

Back in the office they found Stella, Nick and Jack talking technology.

"This is an impressive setup," Stella said. "You have a lovely home."

"Thanks," Maggie replied, "it isn't easy to combine home and work, but most of the time it works well. Ah, here's Zelah."

"No photos," she said, taking her seat as Bob set up his laptop. "She's never seen one. I asked her what she knew about her mother's family and background. Michelle went to Newport High School. If they have past year books, or online photos of former pupils it's possible she might be in there somewhere. We can check."

"Right," Bob interrupted, "here we go. I'm going to show you pictures of Kennet Quinn's team. They're supposed to be Property Assistant Managers. They mainly assist in making sure no-one complains too loudly about the property."

The first picture appeared, a head and shoulders shot of a bald headed man, small eyes, a large broken nose and with spider tattoos around his neck. "This is Stephen Dawes, a local man who has worked for Kennet for about five years. Previously in prison for GBH, twice, - take a good look." He followed with another two pictures, one of Dawes full length, showing he was around six feet tall and heavily muscled. The other was of Dawes with Kennet Quinn.

Then came a head and shoulders of another man, shorter, squat and running to fat, with a clipped beard and shoulder length wispy hair.

"This is Damyan Kostov, Bulgarian, thirty-five, worked for Kennet for about seven years." Again there were two further pictures, one full length and one standing with Kennet Quinn.

The third and final man was nothing like the first two. The photo was a full length pose of what looked like a model's photoshoot, of a young man who looked to be in his early twenties, fair haired, blue eyed, fit and well built, well dressed, and pictured with a genuine, warm smile.

"This is Timothy Redland, known as 'Tiny Tim.'" Don't be fooled by either the nickname or the baby face. He's one of the most vicious men I've ever come across. He has neither compassion nor compunction about what he does. He's the fingernail ripper and probably the one who bludgeoned last year's complainant to death with an iron bar."

There was a collective 'Oh' around the room.

"He doesn't look old enough," Maggie said.

"He started young, spent most of his youth in custody. If you see him near you, get away as quickly as you can. Call 999and tell them you have reason to believe that Redland is targeting you." He stopped and looked around, "Jack, are you OK?"

"Not really," the boy replied unsteadily, "I've seen him."

119

Maggie jumped up. "Where?"

"He was in the carpark at college on Wednesday."

"What was he doing?" Bob asked.

"Nothing, really, just standing and smoking. One of the girls wondered who he was because he looked really fit."

"Right, none of you is to go anywhere alone, until this is over. Understand?" No-one argued. "Keep their pictures on the wall and their faces in your mind when you're out."

"I'll print them out," Maggie said. "Is it safe for Jack to go with Zelah to Ebbw Vale tomorrow morning?"

"I'll follow you up there, make sure Redland isn't about," Bob replied. "I know you didn't know about any of this when you took the case on, but you are getting into treacherous territory. I have to be careful too. They could decide to turn their attention back to me at any point."

Chapter 18

The following morning Bob set out behind Zelah and Jack. When they reached the archives building he told them to call him when they were finished. He was sure they hadn't been followed but wasn't willing to let them drive home alone.

When he arrived back at the house Maggie was already at her desk. On the table was the beginning of a sketched out family tree for the Quinn family. She had traced his daughters' marriages and added the husbands, wives and children of the descendant Quinns back to Adolphus.

"This looks complicated," Bob remarked, bending over the chart and pointing to some of the names. "Some of these people have been abroad for a long time."

"Not that complicated," Maggie replied. "I found some of it in charts already on the 'net'. One of his daughter's ancestors put the information on. It all stops with Adolphus, though. There's nothing about parents or siblings; it's all 'unknown'." She leaned her elbows on the table, hands cupping her chin, staring up close at the chart. "It's disappointing. I thought we might have been able to pick something up."

"Does it matter much?" he asked.

"In a case like this every little bit of information helps," she said over her shoulder. "You never know what's going to turn up, so you look at everything. My next job is to find out more about Adolphus' own history, from the information in the old newspapers and from his death certificate. I have an approximate year of birth, but I can't find anything more detailed."

"Is the information there to be found? I thought that Irish records aren't as available as the British ones?"

"Irish civil registration of births began in 1864," Maggie replied. "That was approximately the year Adolphus was born, so he may not have been registered. Irish church records do go back further, which means we may be able to find his baptism, although these are notoriously random. They depend on the individual parish and the willingness of its priest to record correctly. I've been searching in Roots Ireland. It's a good site, but it's only as good as the records they can find and put online."

"What about that Griffiths… something or other?"

"The Griffith Valuation? That was much earlier, from the late 1840s to around 1864 and it's had some updates. It's good, but you have to be clear about who you're looking for and where they were when their area or property was valued. We'd have to know Adolphus' father's name to make use of it. All we know about Adolphus is that he was supposedly born around 1864 in the Dublin area and had a brother called Martin, who was five or six years younger than him, so born around 1870. Martin should have been registered at birth, but there's no information for him, either."

"Could they have come from another part of the country?"

She stood up and rubbed her elbows. "Doesn't look like it. I've checked the whole of Ireland for Martin. The Irish site allows you to do this, and within a 5-year period; there's nothing."

"What are you going to do next?"

"I'll try every boy called Adolphus in each year around the five years of his presumed year of birth, without putting a surname in the search box and see what that gives me."

"I'll leave you to it," he replied, "I'm going back up in an hour or so to meet Zelah and Jack. Let's hope they found something useful."

He took a book and went to sit in the garden. The

unreliable weather had at last delivered some sunshine and warmth and an hour later Maggie found Bob snoozing on a recliner on the patio, the book unopened on his chest. She watched him for a few moments, realising that she'd rarely seen him fall asleep in the daytime, only after a night shift, thinking *I've forgotten how close he came to dying. Maybe he needs more rest than he lets on.*

"Time to go," she said, nudging his arm.

**

She was back at her computer when Bob returned with Zelah and Jack.

"That was awesome," Jack said, bouncing into the office. "There's so much there, you don't know where to start, but we found it!"

Maggie looked around. "That sounds like good news. We could do with some." She swung her chair around as Zelah and Bob came in and sat at the table.

"You haven't had much success?" Zelah asked. Maggie shook her head.

"Then let's tell you our interesting news. We looked over the information in the copies Ben left for us and we went through the Ada Blackstock file again. There was no report of anything missing, but in a separate part of the file, we found a letter from her family to the police. It was asking for return of an item that wasn't with her clothing; a brooch."

"They gave a good description too," Jack added, reading from a copy of the letter he had photographed on his phone. "Gold filigree interspersed with small amber gems, rectangular in shape. Her sister wrote the letter," he said looking up, "and the police replied that they didn't find any such item. Her sister wrote again to say they must have it, because Ada always wore it when she went to a séance as she was particularly fond of it. We think," here he nodded to Zelah, "it might have been given to

123

her by the father of her baby, from something that her sister hinted about. It had sentimental value and was to be passed on to her son, because of its connection to his father."

"That makes sense," Maggie said. "If Adolphus took a brooch from her and it remained in his family – he died only a year later and so suddenly, he wouldn't have thought he needed to get rid of it – then it could have been innocently passed down and ended up with Michelle Quinn."

"Which would explain why she was wearing it on the day she left home," Zelah said, "and why they need it now. This means they must know. The description is so clear it's enough to verify against the actual piece of jewellery."

"If the woman still has it, and if you can find her," Bob reminded them.

"Lucky for us that 'Mr Smith' didn't take that letter," Maggie said to Nick when she called to update him, "He must have reported back on it. How else would Kennet have recognised the description and realised that he needed to find Michelle to get it back?"

"Whoever 'Mr Smith' was, he wasn't much of a researcher. It sounds like he didn't even try the 'Animus' lead," Nick replied. Fortuitous for us."

**

It was time to take a break and review what to do next, which they did over sandwiches and cake at the end of the garden next to the canal. Maggie had put up a sail shade over the table and chairs to allow them to dine protected from the increasing heat.

"I'd like to continue searching for Adolphus and Martin Quinn's birth," she began. "Jack, could you look at the Newport High School website and see if there are any old photos from about twenty-five years ago. Remember she was Michelle Morgan then, Zelah, what about you?"

"I'm going to look into this Ryan family Mischa seems to be related to. It might give us something, you never know."

"OK, if you think it might be helpful," Maggie said.

"Don't you think so? What else do you think we can do? We're almost out of online options."

"I don't know, Zelah. I agree there has to be a reason for her being related to them. I'm just asking, is it the best use of our time?"

Zelah huffed. "God knows, I don't. I want to talk to Mischa again, get her focused on women that she comes across regularly, that might be about the same age as her mother, and I'd like to know if she's found out about what progress the Quinns are making."

"Take care, Zelah," Bob warned. "She's just a kid. If Kennet finds out or even suspects, well… we know what he did to her mother."

"Yes, yes, I get it. I'll see if I can arrange to meet her somewhere tomorrow." She stopped for a moment. "Could I bring her back here?" She held up her hand and spoke again as Maggie rose from her chair. "No, not a good idea. Don't want to give the Quinns any clue that she knows us. Was there any sign of them this morning?"

"No," Bob replied, "I didn't spot anything but we're not going to take any chances. If you're going to meet the girl again, let me know the time and place. We can make sure we know where Rufus and Kennet Quinn are, and where the other three are and I can let you know it's safe before you start to speak to her."

Maggie sighed. "This is getting mega complicated."

Judging by his expression, Bob was about to say something she wouldn't like, when his phone rang. He listened for a few minutes, nodding occasionally. Then he said, "Well, I can't say I'm sorry. What are his chances?"

After another minute of listening and nodding he ended the call with "let me know any developments."

"Anything concerning us?" Zelah asked.

"Yes," he replied, to Maggie's surprise. "There's been an accident. Timothy Redland was on a building site this morning. Seems he was trying to collect rent from one of Kennet's tenants who was in arrears and doing some 'cash-in-hand' work. Against the Foreman's advice, he refused to wear a safety helmet. He was about to drag the man away when a brick fell on his head. He's in the Royal Gwent A&E now. He has a fractured skull."

"Will he die?" Maggie asked.

"Don't know, yet. There'll be an enquiry. There wasn't a brickie anywhere near where he was standing, so no-one can figure out how it happened. Anyway, they'll let me know the extent of his injuries."

"That's one less to follow us around," Zelah said. She made her way back up to the house, humming a tune under her breath.

After lunch Nick left them and Bob went for a walk then sat on the patio with his book. Maggie, Zelah and Jack worked in the office, occasionally commenting to each other. At around six, Maggie said they should stop, but both Jack and Zelah wanted to go on, which turned out to be a good decision, as ten minutes later came the first breakthrough.

"I've got her," Jack shouted, "come and look."

Maggie and Zelah went over to his computer. On the screen was a group photo taken from the South Wales Argus of the Newport High School 6th Form choir, all named. Michelle Morgan sat in the front row. It was a good portrait picture of her face.

"But is it clear enough to use the ageing app?" Maggie asked.

"I'm not sure, I think it needs some work. Let me send it to my friend Alex. He's a good photographer and he's got a lot of professional equipment. He may be able to isolate her and do something with it. Can I do that?"

"Yes," Zelah said, "go for it."

Whilst Jack got in touch with his friend, Maggie and Zelah talked about what they had found.

"You first," Zelah said.

"OK, well I haven't made any progress. I can't find any mention of an Adolphus Quinn or an Adolphus Anyone born five years either side 1864, in the Dublin area. Neither is there any reference to a Martin Quinn."

"Did you find any Adolphus Quinn, or Adolphus Anyone, anywhere else?"

"Adolphus wasn't a well-used name. I found half a dozen called Adolphus, but only one Adolphus Quinn and he was born in County Clare in 1874, so about ten years too young. I also took a quick look at newspapers for any mention of an Adolphus Quinn during his adult years from 1880 to 1885. We don't know exactly when he came to the UK mainland, but we do know that he was in Newport by 1888. That was when he married Bridget Kelly and if he were there a few years before that, he would have arrived around 1885. There's nothing mentioning his name in any of the Irish papers that are online; I'm stumped."

"This is just a wild supposition, but could it mean that Adolphus Quinn wasn't his real name?" Zelah mused.

"I suppose it could, possibly, yes, but if we don't know who he really was, there's little we can do about finding out why he might have left Ireland."

"Was there an Adolphus Ryan?" Zelah asked.

Maggie consulted her list. "No."

"Try Martin Ryan, born around 1870, you said?"

"That's right." Maggie turned back to her laptop and re-entered the Roots Ireland site. She put in the details with two years allowance either side of 1870 and the site returned three possibilities. When she read the third one, she gasped, "Yes, there is, Martin Ryan, born 6 January 1870. Baptised 19 January 1870, parents Michael Ryan and Margaret Dillon, in Ennis, County Clare." She turned to look at Zelah. "Is it possible?"

Zelah thought for a few minutes, then said "What year did Martin Quinn die?"

"I haven't looked at that, why… yes, of course, I'll check."

Jack turned around and asked what was going on.

Zelah replied, "If Martin Quinn was alive in 1939 he would have had to enter his date of birth on the war register. If we can find that he was still alive, then we can check the register to see what date he entered. If it's the same as Martin Ryan's date of birth, then we may have found an interesting lead."

Maggie began with the 'Free BMD' site and gave it a wide set of parameters for a potential death. This time there were seventeen returns over a period of ten years. "Three of them are in Newport and two are after 1939. How are we going to figure out which one is him?"

"Let's go straight to the 1939 register," Zelah replied, "see if he's still living with Bridget."

Maggie switched to that site, with both Jack and Zelah now hanging over her shoulder. She entered his name and his place of abode as Newport, Wales. Nothing came up.

"Organise it by date of birth," Zelah suggested. Now there was just one Martin Quinn, living in Whitchurch in Cardiff whose date of birth was 6 January 1870. She went onto the record, to discover that he had listed himself as a 'Widower'. In the space for profession, he had given his information as 'Accountant, Retired'.

"This has to be him," Maggie said, "but to be absolutely

certain, I'll check the Martin Quinns again on the Irish sites for this date of birth, just in case it's a co-incidence."

As she did so, Zelah and Jack waited in silence until Jack's phone pinged an incoming message.

"It's Alex," he said. "He says he can do it no problem but he's out tomorrow all day with his family. He'll start tomorrow night and should have it ready for us by Monday lunchtime, is that OK?"

"Perfect," Zelah replied.

"That's it, then," Maggie said, "there's no Martin Quinn born or baptised on or around this date in 1870, or within five years."

"So Martin Quinn was very possibly Martin Ryan. What were the parents called, remind me again?"

"Michael Ryan and Margaret Dillon," Maggie replied.

"That's interesting"

"Why?" Jack asked.

"In Ireland at that time, like in many traditional communities, there were naming conventions. First son named after the father's father, first daughter after the mother's mother and so on. It was a strict convention. Adolphus Quinn called his first son Michael, but that would have worked for both fathers. Bridget's father was also a Michael. Was Bridget Quinn's mother called Mary?" Zelah asked. "Because if she was, it's likely they were following the naming conventions."

Maggie called up the 1871 census, found Michael Kelly and his family, including Bridget.

"Correct, here's the family: Michael Kelly is a builder, his wife is Mary and they only have one child, Bridget, who was twelve at the time. First son, father's father - Michael. First daughter mother's mother - Mary. Second daughter father's mother - Margaret. Martin Ryan's mother was called Margaret. In this, at least Adolphus kept to the script."

"Careless of him," Zelah said. "We should be able to find out his real name, now. Maggie, check for the other children of Michael and Margaret Ryan."

Back on the Irish Roots site Maggie entered the names. "What time span should we give it? Adolphus was older than Martin and if Martin was born in 1870 and Adolphus around 1864, then he should be about five years older, that's if the 1891 census information for Newport is correct"

"Why wouldn't it be?" Jack asked.

"Depends on who gave the information to the census enumerator. A lot of people didn't know their date of birth, just how old they were, more or less. Anyone trying to disguise themselves, which Adolphus might have been trying to do, could say anything and no-one would know it was wrong. Census information can be misleading, not often, but sometimes. We know that he was supposed to have been born around 1864. Give it a ten year span Maggie. That should account for most of the Ryan children, there would probably been quite a few. Here we go."

The site had given them eleven entries, which turned out to be double records of baptisms as well as births of some of the same children.

Maggie noted them and removed the duplicates. "There are only two possibilities. There were two girls, born in 1860 and 1862. The first boy is Thomas, born 1864, followed by Daniel in 1866, then Martin in 1870. The next one is Sean, but he wasn't born until 1875, which would make him too young to be Adolphus Quinn. It could only be Daniel or Thomas."

"Check the deaths," Zelah said. "After 1864 they should have registered a death at any age."

Maggie entered the data and there was just one result.

"Daniel Ryan, died in 1867 aged one, father recorded as Michael Ryan. Is it possible then that Adolphus Quinn might really have been Thomas Ryan?"

Before Zelah could reply her phone buzzed. She checked it. "Well fancy that. It's from Isobel, who says she's on her way round; in fact, she's outside, right now."

Before Maggie could reply the doorbell rang. Maggie went to leave the room to answer it, but Zelah caught her arm and said, "Maggie, if this is her trying to jump us, we'll just hear what she has to say. Don't tell her anything we've found out, I have an increasingly bad feeling about this woman."

Chapter 19

Isobel breezed past Maggie and launched herself into the office with arms flung out ready to embrace Zelah.

"Darlings! So sorry I've been out of touch, so many interesting things happening," she announced, smiling widely. Zelah stepped away from her. A frown flashed across Isobel's face as she sat herself down on the settee, clutching her bag to her chest. No-one spoke.

"Well, do tell me what you have been doing, darlings."

Zelah was the first to reply. "If you think you can disappear for days without a word, abuse my hospitality, come swanning back in here pretending nothing has happened, then you have maggots in your head."

"Well that's not a nice welcome," Isobel pouted. "As a matter of fact I've been staying with friends from my community."

"You didn't bother to tell me, or any of us, because…?"

Isobel ignored her.

"What do you want, Isobel?" Maggie asked.

"Want? Nothing really, I came to tell you that I'm not concerned about the Ada thing anymore. I can't see there's anything to be gained by following it any further. Let it go, dears, let it go, let the man have his statue. It's simply all too long ago to be bothered about." She paused for a moment. "Though do tell me what you have found out."

"No," Zelah said, "I don't think we will."

"Well, I think I deserve to know. This was my relative after all."

"You just said you're not bothered. You came to my home, desperate, crying, frightened and begging for my help, our help.

Now, this complete about-face. Something is going on and you're going to tell us what it is."

"Oh, just drop it all, then," Isobel muttered, though her flickering eyes told a different story.

"OK."

Maggie looked at Zelah, who gave her a quick, barely noticeable wink.

"We've got better things to do," Maggie said, picking up the hint. "You can go, now. We have work to get on with and I don't want you in my house. Please don't come here again."

"Oh, please, I would like to know if you found anything. I am interested in Ada, just generally." Isobel had recovered herself. She gave them what she thought was a winning smile, and settled herself down in the settee.

Zelah gave her back an equally false smile. "OK, if you've decided that you don't have a serious problem after all, then you can become a client. We'll send out a contract for you to sign and you owe us about five hundred pounds so far. Pay up and we'll carry on," Zelah walked towards her. "If you aren't willing to pay, then please leave, as Maggie has politely requested. I'm not going to be so polite in just a minute from now."

Zelah's smile had become wolf-like. Isobel shuffled forward on the settee.

"You've seen what they can do," she hissed. "If you carry on, then on your heads be it."

"We've just said we'll give it up," Maggie replied. "Now, again, please leave, I don't expect to ever see you again."

Isobel stood up, laughed and said "Fools." She marched to the door but before she could leave Zelah called her. "Isobel, by the way, Claire says to say hello." Isobel stopped so abruptly she had to hold herself upright. Her face had paled. She looked as if she wanted to say something, but thought better of it, tossed

133

her head and continued to walk. Nick, who was letting himself in after a quick visit to make sure Stella was OK, passed her in the hallway. She opened and then slammed closed the door without looking at him.

Maggie, having followed her into the hall, locked the door and returned to the office, followed by Nick, where Zelah and Jack waited in silence.

"What did I miss?" Nick asked

"Isobel had a tantrum trying to get information of us, but I don't understand why" Maggie said.

"This might be something to do with it," Jack replied, handing her his mobile phone.

Maggie read quickly. "So, Madame Arcati has a national tour, starting in Swansea, in two weeks' time. Is she just trying to maintain her reputation? Perhaps if people found out that she had challenged Rufus Quinn and been thrown out of a Council reception that wouldn't be good. Zelah, what was that about 'Claire'?"

"I'm not sure," Zelah replied. "The last time Claire was mentioned she reacted the same way. It may be nothing, but I'm going to find out, out of curiosity."

"Zelah, we don't have time to waste being side-tracked on trivialities."

"Whatever. Let's get back to where we were."

"Before we carry on, I just want us to pause for a moment and ask ourselves a question. Do we want to carry on now? I mean, this isn't a client or a friend anymore, is it? It's putting us all in jeopardy. Why *are* we doing this?"

"I've been wondering that, too." Bob had wandered in from the garden, attracted by the raised voices.

Zelah leapt to her feet, but before she could Bob said, "Maggie is right to ask the question. This has now moved on well away from where it started. You could stop now, and get the Quinns off your backs."

"What about Mischa Quinn and her mother?" Zelah remonstrated, "don't they count? What about the fact that Gwentshire Council might just be about to vote to honour a serial killer? Are we going to stand by and let that happen?"

"What about the people around us, Zelah? My kids, Nick's Stella. How do you know they won't target Rick?" She sat down at the table and waved at all of them to do the same. "I'm just not sure I want to carry on. There's nothing in it for us."

"You were the one who said there was a wrong to be put right," Zelah argued.

"Not at any cost," Maggie remonstrated.

Nick stepped up to the table brought his hand down with a crash, which stopped them both. "I think Maggie is right to ask the question. None of us can go out alone for fear of physical attack, and I suspect it's causing Bob a massive headache, right?"

Bob nodded.

"It's right we think this through. If we stop this statue being commissioned, where does that leave us all with the Quinn family? They won't like being bested. If Adolphus Quinn did kill women in the way that we now view as a serial killer, then the statue should not be put up. On the other hand, Mischa Quinn has been promised help. Uniting her with her mother, an outcome we may not achieve easily, if at all, seems like a worthwhile thing to try to do. Lots of aspects to consider."

"Are you going to get around to giving us your opinion?" Zelah asked.

"Not yet," He paused for a moment, standing back and staring at the wall. "It's true that as a company there's nothing in this for Maze. We'll never be able to advertise what we've done here, but does that mean we shouldn't do it? Is there a bigger moral reason for us to carry on?"

"Does my opinion count?" Jack interrupted. He stood up in front of his mother, looking down at her. "Never thought you were a wuss." He folded his arms.

"I am not a wuss, don't you dare say that" Maggie hit back. "I'll admit, I'm worried. They could do any of us harm and it scares me."

"Well I don't think we can stop now," Jack replied. "I agree with Zelah. What about this Mischa and her mother? You've given her an expectation that you'll help her. You can't just back out. If it were me, I'd be really pissed off with you."

"How pissed off would you be if we decided to carry on and either Alice or I were seriously hurt?"

His eyes widened, he shrugged and sat down again. There was a brief silence and then he said, "I get that, but I think we've come too far to stop. I don't think it will make any difference if we do or don't carry on, anyway."

"I agree," Zelah jumped in.

"How about this then?" Nick said. "We carry on, cautiously, very cautiously. We do *not*," he emphasised the word, "*not* confront the Quinns again. We do what we can to help Mischa. Here's my suggestion: if we are able to find the definitive proof that Adolphus Quinn carried out all of those terrible murders, then we, probably you, Zelah, quietly inform Gwentshire Council. You have a good relationship with the Mayor. The Committee has been deliberately deceived and mislead. Once they know they can drop the idea for whatever reason they choose, financial, whatever. We do not make our involvement in any way public."

They all gave it a few moments thought, then each nodded and said in turn "Agreed."

"How about this then?" Nick said. "We carry on, cautiously, very cautiously. We do *not*," he emphasised the word, "*not* confront the Quinns again. We do what we can to help Mischa.

Here's my suggestion: if we are able to find the definitive proof that Adolphus Quinn carried out all of those terrible murders, then we, probably you, Zelah, quietly inform Gwentshire Council. You have a good relationship with the Mayor. "If my opinion counts, I think you should stop, but I can't stop you. That woman's a charlatan, by the way" Bob said. "I told you, you're better off without her. I checked again, she definitely hasn't made a formal report about the fire."

"We're all on the same page with that one," Maggie said. "You were right, I have to admit."

He made a mock bow.

"Right, so where are we?" Jack perked up.

"We've just found out that Adolphus Quinn was possibly Thomas Ryan, born in County Clare in 1864." Zelah glanced at her watch. "It's getting late and I don't know about you, but I've had enough for today."

"Me too," Nick added "and I've only just got here."

"I'm off," Zelah said. "Do you want to work here tomorrow?"

"Yes, definitely," Maggie replied, "we need to work more on the Ryan and Quinn families. I think we're onto something and tomorrow will bring us a step closer to finding out who Adolphus Quinn really was."

"And what he was," Zelah replied. "Leopards don't change their spots."

Chapter 20

Bob followed Zelah home and emphasised that she must lock herself in and call immediately if she suspected anything threatening. He also insisted she call him before setting off in the morning. Ignoring her snort of derision, he returned home.

Awaiting his return Maggie called Alice and was relieved she had nothing to report except she was having a lot of fun. They had spent the day in the pool and on the tennis court and were planning a maths competition for their evening's entertainment.

Bob grinned when he heard. "Most kids their age would be attempting to watch an 18-rated gory film or acting as judge and jury on Britain's Got Talent."

"They aren't most kids their age," Maggie replied.

Despite feeling worn out and going to bed shortly after nine, Maggie had not slept well. She fell into a deep sleep, which was soon punctuated by vivid dreams, in which people screamed and protected their nails. Pans of boiling water were being waved around her head. She awoke in a sweat several times and after dreaming she was watching someone have their stomach ripped open and chewed, she couldn't stand it any longer and got up. It was a little before six in the morning and already light outside.

She crept downstairs and took a quick look at the garden. It was quiet and soothing and she spent ten minutes sitting on the patio in a meditative pose, listening to the birdsong, trying to calm herself. Then she made tea and took her cup into the office.

Thomas Ryan, she felt that this had to be the key. But where to start? Go back to the birth, marriage and death records, scrutinise them again, more thoroughly, in case they had missed something last night. On Roots Ireland she confirmed the parents, Michael and Margaret. This time she checked all their children born over a fifteen year period. This confirmed that there had been a total of ten children in the family, six girls and four boys. She already knew about the four boys, Daniel, Thomas, Martin and Sean. As they now suspected that Adolphus Quinn was really Thomas Ryan, this meant Sean Ryan was the only remaining ancestor of traceable descent with the Ryan name. Next step then, trace his family, see where it led. If the second and third cousins named in Mischa's DNA result were the descendants of Sean Ryan, it was further proof of Adolophus Quinn being Thomas Ryan. Still only a secondary source, but an important one.

Before starting she checked online to see if Louisa Ryan, the one name she remembered from the DNA matches, had entered a public record of her family tree on Ancestry. Thankfully she had, but there were few names on the Ryan side and the immediate family was 'private', which meant that they were living relatives. Louisa's concentration had been on her mother's side. Her mother, Maggie saw, had died a year ago, probably the reason for the interest in the genealogy and the DNA. She wondered about sending a message to the woman but decided to wait and talk it over with Zelah

Next she tried a painstaking search of births, marriages and deaths, the available Irish census records not being immediately useful. Unlike the UK, there were few Irish census returns to check. Almost everything before 1901 had been destroyed, either by fire or deliberately after they were recorded. For so many people around the world searching for their Irish Roots, it was a massive gap and each time it came up she felt sad.

**

A couple of hours later, when Bob had set off to Zelah's flat outside Newport and returned driving behind her, Maggie had made good progress. She immediately updated Zelah and Nick, who had turned up unexpectedly with one of Bob's team following him.

"Stella has a busy day today, an outdoor event at the Manor, hectic all day. Thought I'd come in and get on with some work."

"Here's what I've found," Maggie began. "First, Mischa's closest DNA match, Louisa Ryan, has a public tree, although there's not much on it, mainly her mother's ancestry. Secondly and luckily for us, available BMD records and census returns show that Sean Ryan, the youngest of Michael Ryan's four sons, stayed in County Clare. In 1900 he married a girl called Sarah Cassidy. They had eight children, three of which were boys. I'm trying to trace those three boys and their families.

"We need to join the dots, to be sure that Louisa and Thomas Ryan have a connection. At one end we have Sean Ryan, youngest son of Michael and Margaret. At the other end we have Louisa Ryan. We need the connecting generations between one of Sean's sons and Louisa. There will be at least two, possibly three generations. We know that they will be male, in order for Louisa to still have the family name. I suggest that we take each of the sons of Sean Ryan and trace his family, to see if we can find Louisa at the end of the line."

"I'll start on one. What were their names and what are we hoping to find?" Zelah asked.

"Sean's sons were called Michael, Edward and Eamonn. I'm just working on Michael now. Can you take Edward? After I've finished with Michael, if I don't get a result, I'll move on to Eamonn. What we are looking for is any son of a son, for now, that connects to Louisa in Ennis

"Have you checked Irish births or baptisms for Louisa? There's a chance her father's name might be mentioned."

"Can we get information like from the 1990s?" Maggie

asked "Surely it's private information? I'd struggle to get that here in the UK."

"Let me have a go. How about you make coffee and I'll do a search."

Maggie came back in ten minutes later to find Zelah sitting back and grinning. "Her father's name is Liam Ryan," she said.

"Where did you get that?" Maggie asked.

"Facebook profiles."

"Really, wow. Well, that's one generation accounted for. Will he be the son of one of Sean Ryan's sons, do you think?"

"He could be, but I think that, given the years involved, there are likely to be four generations from Sean to Louisa; that's Sean, one of his sons, maybe one more, then Liam and then Louisa."

"Have you tried just entering Sean Ryan and his birth date, in another tree search?" Nick asked. "He might come up somewhere else."

"Not yet, I just started with Louisa's.

"I'll do it," he replied and turned back to his screen.

"We can assume," Maggie went on, "that as Louisa Ryan is still in County Clare, that her ancestors also remained there. Let's keep our search to that area, for now."

When Bob re-joined them half an hour later the only sound in the room was of clicking keyboards, interspersed by pens scratching out notes on paper. He held a tray of drinks and they all helped themselves. "Found anything useful?" he said.

"No," they answered in unison. "I've searched a number of trees, nothing matching yet. There's still a list to do," Nick said, pausing to drink coffee. "Give me another half hour."

"It looks like Michael Ryan is a dead end," Maggie added. No marriage or offspring that I can find in Ennis or in the County. He died, potentially, without children. I'm just about to look for a death or burial record. Anything for Edward,

141

Zelah?"

"Edward was born in 1919, married in 1949 and his wife was Esmerelda Flynn; unusual name. So far I have two daughters."

"If you do the maths, Sean would have been forty-four when Edward was born. That's old, isn't it?" Bob began. They all looked around but before he could say any more his phone pinged - an incoming message. He took it out of his pocket, read it and jumped up.

"I have to go. Timothy Redland just died of his injuries." He paused for a moment. "There'll be an enquiry. I'll have to tell everything I know about your research involving Rufus and Kennet Quinn, no choice now."

He turned to go, but Maggie called him, "Bob, can you leave out anything about Michelle and Mischa Quinn, for now?"

"No promises," he replied as he turned to go. "Don't go out alone. I'll arrange something."

"Well at least he didn't say no," Zelah said. "This ups the ante. Let's get on."

They all turned back to their screens, deep in a range of thoughts. The main one being that Kennet Quinn wasn't going to like this at all and they were likely to be even higher on his list of targets.

Chapter 21

Fifteen minutes later Zelah clapped her hands together and shouted, "I've got him." They all stopped and looked around. "Liam Ryan, son of Edward Ryan, born 1955, in Ennis, County Clare. It's a good match."

"And I've found a tree with the early Ryan family," Nick added. Putting it on the screen."

Maggie and Zelah turned to look at the white board, where a few seconds later a public tree appeared. Nick used an infrared pointer to highlight the names on the board.

"This tree was put on by one of Edward's siblings, who's added a good amount of detail. Edward's parents are Sean and Sarah, plus their parents, Michael and Margaret Ryan."

"Fingers crossed we can join the dots. The line starts with Michael, then Sean, then his son Edward, then Liam, then Louisa," Zelah said, scribbling on her notepad. "Bob was right, Sean would have been about forty-four or five when Edward was born." She paused for a few seconds. "The only way we can find out for sure is to ask Louisa Ryan. We've got enough to approach her, now"

"Can we get Mischa to make contact with her?" Maggie asked.

"How about we just go ahead and do it?"

"No, Zelah, you have to ask her, it's her DNA report. I expect she'll agree, but you have to ask her."

"Alright, alright, I'll text her now."

"Presuming she agrees, what are we going to say to Louisa Ryan?" Nick asked Maggie, as Zelah texted.

"Before we decide that, just go back to that chart again Nick."

He put it back up on the whiteboard.

"Martin Ryan is there, look, born in 1870, but no Thomas. All the others are exactly as I found in the birth records, including Daniel who died. Even dates, where we have them, are matching. So, where's Thomas Ryan? Why isn't he there?"

Zelah looked up from her phone. "She's replied right away and says fine, can't wait to hear what this Louisa has to say."

Maggie pointed to the Ryan family tree with Thomas Ryan missing.

"That's odd," Zelah said. "It's too close a match to be a different family. Time to ask Louisa Ryan if she'll correspond with us."

It took some time to agree the content of the message. In the end they went with simple but hopefully intriguing enough to pique Louisa Ryan's interest and allow her to reply to them quickly. They added that speed was important, but not why. They decided not to name Mischa.

It was time for a break during which Zelah disappeared with her phone. When she came back into the room she said "I've just been talking to Mischa. Last night I asked her to think about women she knows, who might be around her mother's age. I said probably fortyish, with whom she interacts on a regular basis. She's given me three possibilities. One is a librarian at her college, one is a hairdresser and the third works in a baker's shop. She thinks that last one is too old, but she's friendly and interested in what Mischa does. Before you ask, she's alone at home most of the day today. Father, Grandfather and sainted brother have gone out and don't expect to be back 'til much later. They haven't discussed anything of use to us in front of her."

"I wasn't going to ask," Maggie replied. "I'm assuming you're telling her to take great care of her safety and security. Did she know about Timothy Redland?"

"No, I don't think so. She said her father got a phone call, shoved her out of the room and left in a hurry with the others. She may find out from them later and it has to come as a surprise to her. I didn't say anything about it."

"Good. What else have you arranged with her?" Nick asked.

"I told her about the photo and the face ageing software and I said we'd let her see the outcome tomorrow. We haven't arranged anything specific, said I'd text her when we have it."

"Back to the coalface," Maggie said. "What next? We can't sit around waiting for Louisa Ryan to get back to us."

"I think we should go back to the question of Adolphus Quinn, to get the most accurate picture of the man and his veracity," Nick said. "He gave three stories; three versions of why he left Ireland and where he went before pitching up in Newport. He wasn't on the 1881 census in Newport, but could he or Martin be recorded anywhere else?"

"I did check that, but I was looking for Quinn, not Ryan." She brought up the daily activity log on which they recorded everything they had done at the end of each day. "Yes, I looked them up under the name of Quinn and there wasn't anything. I'll check Ryan now."

"And wasn't there an Adolphus Quinn in County Clare?" Zelah asked. "I vaguely remember you saying there was but that he was the wrong age."

"Hang on; yes, there was but he was born in 1874, so ten years younger than Thomas Ryan. What connection can there have been?"

"Possibly none, but this was the right name in the same County. Worth a check, if only to definitely rule him out. We should go back and examine each of the Adolphus Anyones born from, I'd say about 1860 to 1880. How many were there with that first name?"

"Six," Maggie replied. "Like I said before, it wasn't a

popular name plus they're spread around the country. None match our Thomas Ryan's year of birth. A couple are either side. We keep coming back to the fact that the only one with the exact name is the Adolphus Quinn born in Ennis in County Clare in 1874."

"Let's take two each," Nick suggested.

"Morning all," a yawning voice said from the doorway. Jack stood there in his pyjamas. "Any lunch?"

"No, probably dinner later but we're working. Are you going to join us?"

"Yep, I'll just get something to eat then I'll get dressed. Anything special for me to do?"

"Yes," Maggie replied, "we're investigating every possible Adolphus Anybody. You can join in, quicker if we spread it out between four of us. Well, go on then, get fed and dressed."

He was back in ten minutes with his laptop.

"We'll take one each," Maggie said. "Depending how we get on whoever reaches a dead end first can start on the next one. Jack, you take the Adolphus Quinn born in 1874. He's the only one with the right name. He's the least likely but we have to rule him out."

"Great, where do I start, mum?"

"Births, marriages and deaths. Use the national site and if that doesn't produce anything use Roots Ireland. Then you can try the available census records. If he was still there at the turn of the century then he can be written up as not our man. And after that you can try the BNA."

"Newspapers, yeh?"

Maggie nodded, "British Newspaper Archives. Right, let's go."

It was almost an hour later, when Maggie had rejected her first two Adolphus candidates, who were from Dublin and had remained there, and was well into her third when Jack

146

interrupted her.

"Mum?" He waited but she didn't answer. He leaned over and shook her arm. "Mum."

"What, sorry, have you found something?"

"I think so."

"Enough that we all need to stop?"

"I think so." His voice was shaky.

By now Zelah and Nick had already stopped. "Tell us what you've seen Jack," Zelah said. "Don't be hesitant, tell it as you've found it."

He nodded, biting his lips. "This was the Adolphus Quinn born in 1874. He died in 1881." He paused and took in a deep breath. "He was murdered when he was seven years old."

"Is he the one from Ennis?" Zelah asked. "Same place as Thomas Ryan?"

"Yes," Jack replied.

Maggie saw that his hands were shaking slightly, making his pen rattle on the desk. She reached out and put her hand over his. "Do you want me to take over?"

"No," he replied, "no, I'll carry on." Another deep breath, "I've only checked one newspaper report so far, but it was in lots of the papers. He was found in a wood, not far from his home. He had been tortured by being burned on parts of his body and he had deep wounds. He died by strangulation. He was found," he had to pause, his voice shaking, "he was found clutching his toy soldiers that had been a present made by his father for his birthday."

Maggie stood up and put her arms around his shoulders. "That's a horrible story Jack." She turned to the others, "let's take breather now, shall we? We'll go outside."

Zelah and Nick left them to it.

**

At the end of the garden they stepped over the wire fence,

147

crossed the footbridge onto the canal path and walked in the direction of Newport. It was early afternoon, the sun high overhead. Jack walked slowly, with Maggie matching his pace. Occasionally he stopped to kick at a loose piece of earth or a stone, sending it shooting into the turgid water, where it caused a few ripples before the water closed in again. He turned to Maggie. "Why would someone do that to a kid?"

"I don't know, son. Bob might be able to better explain the mind of someone who could do it, I can't."

"Could it have been Thomas Ryan?"

"Well, it bears similarities to the attacks on the women in Newport."

They stood, looking into the water. A man walking his dog on a lead came around the bend ahead of them and passed them with a 'good afternoon'. Maggie nodded and the man walked on, pulling at the dog, who wanted to pay closer attention to Jack but was dragged reluctantly away.

Jack was still staring into the water, as if expecting it to do something. Maggie didn't interrupt. Whatever he was processing needed time and she was prepared to stand there for as long as it took. Jack's reflection was staring back at him from the stagnant black water. It reminded her of the quote from Nietzsche that 'if you gaze long enough into an abyss, the abyss will gaze back into you', or something like that. She must have made an unconscious huff at the thought, as Jack looked round.

"Let's go back," he said. They turned around and walked back up the path, over the footbridge and the fence into the garden. Nick and Zelah were waiting on the patio.

"That was a tough one," Nick began.

"We'll understand if you want to back off Jack," Zelah said, uncharacteristically quietly.

"I don't want to back off," he replied, "I just needed a bit of time. What's next?"

"Good boy," Zelah replied. "We need to find out more about what happened to this child. There's bound to be more in the papers, crimes like that tend to ignite a whole country."

"Hold on," Nick said as she went to stand, "we need a plan here."

"You have one?"

"I do. We need to see if we can establish a link between this child Adolphus Quinn and Thomas Ryan. All we have so far is that they lived in the same town. There may be something in the newspapers. In fact, that's the only place we're likely to find anything at such short notice, so they'll need careful examination. If he was a suspect that might have been mentioned."

"I could work on that," Jack offered.

"And another thing," Nick said. "If Thomas Ryan, potentially alias Adolphus Quinn, did commit this murder, it's likely that there were more. One of his stories was that he moved from Dublin to Liverpool. I'd like to look at the newspaper archives to see if there were any murders committed there of similar nature to those in Newport."

"Under what name?" Zelah asked.

"What do you mean?"

How are you going to establish, if there were similar crimes that Thomas Ryan was in the area at the time?"

"Prize fighting," Nick replied.

"What's that got to do with anything?" Zelah retorted.

"Remember the description of his injuries? To me, they suggested prize fighting. I know it's a vague chance, but if he was making his way as a boxer, his name might have been mentioned in sports pages. I know, it's just a long shot."

"It's a good thought and worth pursuing," Zelah said. "Will you do that, if we concentrate on the child murder in Ennis?"

"Yes, I thought I would," Nick replied, "Maggie you're

quiet. What are you thinking, Maggie?"

She had been oblivious to the discussion for the last couple of minutes, her mind wandering as she gazed up at the mountain. As she followed its contours along the skyline she had been thinking about her children. The one sitting next to her had outstripped her in height some time ago. She still thought of him as a child although he was taking giant steps towards adulthood. What he had just learned would sear his mind for some time to come, probably for ever, but that was part of growing up. She could not and should not try to protect him from the 'bad stuff', as much as it was her instinct to do so. If he didn't learn, with some basic protection, how could he face and deal with such things when no-ne had his back? The other one, a teenager but still oblivious to much of the world. Alice still needed someone to watch out for her and would do for a long time to come. Most kids at their ages wouldn't need to worry that their mother's job would endanger them. She had on occasion felt disturbed, especially after the showdown in Ireland. That had been resolved, well almost; Emer McCarthy Miller was still out there. Was she prepared to give up this work that she loved so much and go back to corporate hell? The mountain stared back at her.

"Maggie!"

"What? Sorry, I was miles away."

Nick gestured to Zelah and Jack to go back into the house and sat again. "Still worrying about putting them in danger?"

"Yes."

"Have you thought about asking them?"

"Of course not, they're just children. It's my responsibility to keep them safe."

"This time next year Jack will be on the point of departure to a university somewhere in the UK. He'll be almost nineteen and Alice will be fourteen."

"Your point?"

"They have to keep themselves safe, it's their responsibility too."

"She leaned forward, staring into his face. "That's all well and good, fine words, but you've never been a parent, have you?" As the words came spitting out she regretted them. She wasn't expecting what came next.

"Yes, Maggie, I have, I am."

Maggie opened her mouth to speak, then closed it again. Nick too was sitting forward in his chair, fists on his knees, staring down at the table top.

"You... have a child?"

"I have a son."

"I don't know what to say."

"His name is Max. He's eighteen, nineteen in a few days. I don't know where he is."

She opened her mouth to respond but changed her mind, unable to think where to start. What was the right question?

"Why don't you know where he is?"

"Because his mother disappeared with him, suddenly when he was ten. We were living in India. I've searched everywhere, ever since I'm still searching."

She reached out to touch his arm, but he pulled away from her, still not looking.

"Please don't ask me any more questions, Maggie. And don't tell anyone else."

"Does anyone else know?"

"Only Stella; that's how I want to keep it.

"Can't I tell Bob? It's going to be tough to keep this a secret."

"If you tell Bob I'll have to tell Zelah. I don't want to discuss anything about it. Don't press me." He stood and walked into the house. In the doorway he stopped, turned to look at her, paused for a moment, shook his head and disappeared into the house.

Maggie's brain was in a fury of thoughts. She might had been on the point of saying that she was going to give up, end her association with Maze, again. Nick's bombshell had overloaded her ability to process anything. She sat on, in the hot sun, staring out over the landscape, trying to pull a coherent thought together, but failing to grasp any one as they whizzed around and passed beyond her grasp. She came to when she realised that she had been seized by the shoulder and was being vigorously shaken.

"Mum! What is the matter with you? I've been calling you. Is there something wrong? Speak to me!" Jack's voice was at yelling pitch. She looked up at him and shook her head.

"Sorry. Deep in thought."

"Deep fugue, more like. What happened to you?"

The terrified look on his face brought her round. "Sorry," she said again. "Lost inside my own head. Wouldn't have thought there was enough room, would you," she added, hoping that he would accept the joke and move on. No chance. He took her elbow and manoeuvred her up out of her seat. "Come on old lady, back to the coalface and stop worrying about us; and thinking you might quit," he added as they walked. "We can look after ourselves, more than you give us credit for."

She knew he was trying to cheer her up. She smiled and went with him, enough to convince him that she was OK.

Chapter 22

Outside the A&E department of the Royal Gwent Hospital, Bob Pugh and his sergeant hunkered down in their unmarked car, waiting for the Quinns to leave.

The heat had increased and Bob was in shirt sleeves. From where they sat they had a good view of one exit. There were two further exits from the hospital and an unmarked police car was parked close to each. The Quinns could not get away without being followed.

Bob was drumming his fingers in a fast beat on the steering wheel. He and his sergeant had run out of conversation. They had worked together for many years, knew each other's thoughts and disposition and had collaborated on the Quinn investigation for the past eighteen months. They were good friends, but Bob drew a line when Sergeant Eric Moreton pulled out a bag of sandwiches from the glove compartment and began to eat.

"For fuck's sake Eric, not tuna; the car stinks for days."

Moreton grinned and continued to munch, as Bob wound down the window. Seconds later the sandwich went out of the window, as the automatic doors at the A&E exit opened and Rufus Quinn came out. He was followed by a small group close behind him, heads down, expressions grim.

Eric Moreton grabbed his camera and started shooting rapid fire pictures of each of them.

"Who's the girl?" Bob said, looking at a tall, auburn haired woman who looked to be in her late twenties. She was clutching Kennet Quinn's arm and crying. "Did she go in with them?"

"Don't think so," Eric replied, "must have already been in there. Relative of Timothy Redland? Girlfriend?"

"Not seen her before," Bob said. "Send her picture back, get them started on checking her out. Tell them to get someone in there, find out if the hospital knows if she's a relative."

As they watched, a Mercedes pulled up and the group climbed in. The car was driven by Stephen Dawes, with Damyan Kostov in the front passenger seat. Rufus, Kennet and the girl got into the back seats.

Bob pulled away at a safe distance behind them as Eric Moreton issued instructions back to their office.

"Fred and Jane at Entrance Two are going to go in to find out who the girl is," he said as they followed the Mercedes out of the carpark and away from the town. "Looks like they're heading back to the Quinn house," he added as the car turned right and headed up towards St Woolos Cathedral."

Instead of stopping at the house the car continued around the cathedral and halted in one of the parking spaces, where Kennet and the girl got out. Bob pulled in quickly, hoping they hadn't seen him. Kennet Quinn kissed the girl on the cheek and she walked away down towards Stow Hill.

"Damn! Eric, get out and follow her. I'll make sure the others are going back to the house. Keep me informed."

Eric Moreton jumped out of the car once the Mercedes had pulled away and walked after the girl. Bob started his car again and slowly drove around the cathedral, just catching sight of the Quinn car turning into their road. They drove into the garage and the automatic shutter closed behind them. Bob pulled up again and settled down for another wait. Ten minutes later his phone rang.

"The girl's not a family member, boss. Gave her name as Anne Smith, a friend. Next of Kin is his mother, but the hospital hasn't been able to contact her. Asked us to try."

"OK." He hit the button to end the call but hadn't put it down before it rang again. Eric Moreton.

"I've lost her."

Bob banged his free hand on the steering wheel. "Where? What happened? Did she clock you?"

"No, I don't think so. She went to the bus station and jumped on a bus just as it was leaving. I didn't have time to get on." Eric told Bob which bus. "I've called it in, a car should be catching up with it. Hopefully, she won't have got off before they get there."

"Tell them to keep their distance. If they stop every time the bus stops someone's going to notice. Get back here, now. I'm outside the house."

He ended the call and began again drumming his fingers rhythmically on the wheel as he thought about what to do next. He was sure that the Quinns were not going to let Timothy Redland's death go easily. They would want someone to blame. The investigation was showing all the signs of it being an accident. There had been no-one up on the scaffolding when the brick fell. It had definitely fallen, the trajectory confirmed that it hadn't been thrown. As much as he wanted to get Kennet Quinn, he couldn't much longer justify sitting in a car waiting for whatever came next.

Waiting for Eric Moreton to get back, he thought over Maggie's situation. He knew that she loved her job, was one hundred percent engaged in it, as he was with his. But he expected to face dangerous situations. Neither she nor Zelah nor Nick, nor anyone associated with them should expect to be constantly looking over their shoulder for fear of someone like Kennet Quinn. He dismissed Rufus Quinn as a serious threat. The old man had become a blusterer and a drunk. He could shout and threaten but there was no action behind the fury. Kennet was a different matter. The man had tried to have him killed. He had tried to intimidate the Maze investigators, all to no avail, as they were not so easily scared. Now he wondered if that was still true. He had seen the signs growing in Maggie in recent days. She was fearful, for her team and for her children. For himself he desperately wanted to put Kennet Quinn away. The man was abominable, but cunning and clever enough to keep himself one step removed from trouble. He glanced over at the house; nothing moving. How he would love to know what was going on in there. There was no chance he would get permission for a phone tap or any kind of surveillance device, not enough direct evidence. The only chance he had was the connection Maggie and Zelah had made with Mischa Quinn. The girl detested her family, true enough but she was only nineteen. If Zelah or Maggie asked her to give them information, and Kennet found out? Given what he had done to his wife Bob had no difficulty believing that Kennet would do something similar to his daughter. This was still the best lead they had in this case, on the one hand… but, on the other hand…

His thoughts were interrupted by a tap on the window. He let Eric Moreton into the car.

"Anything moving, guv? Any news?"

Bob shook his head but as he did so his phone rang. He answered the call, grunted a few times, and ended the call with, "OK, get back to the station." He turned to Eric Moreton. "They caught up with the bus but it had already stopped a few times. She didn't get off at any of the stops before it reached the terminus at Cwmbran centre, so she must have got off at one of the earlier stops. Shit." He went to say something else when the phone rang again and he answered it with a terse "Pugh. What?"

This time he listened intently, then said, "Thanks and keep me posted. That was Smithy at the hospital. "Whoever told them that Timothy Redland's mother was his next of kin was lying. His mother's been dead for years, as has his father.

They're trying to find out who it really is."

"We're staying here for a while, then?"

"Yeh, see if any of them come out again. We don't have much else to go on for now." He sat back and rested his head against the window. His brain was still occupied with Mischa Quinn and if there was any chance that she could be of use, and if so, how he could square that with Maggie and Zelah.

Chapter 23

Following Nick's plan, they had separated the Irish newspapers that were publishing in the late 19th century into three groups, one each for Maggie, Zelah and Jack. They had selected a time period from the day after the discovery of the little boy's body to three months after the event, by which point they assumed public interest would have died down. There were only six papers, – two each, but some published daily, others weekly. It was going to be a long job. They agreed to work for two hours without any discussion, but printing out anything they found relating to the case.

It didn't take as long as they had expected and by mid-afternoon they had a good selection of reports on every aspect of the crime and its aftermath.

Zelah suggested that once they had all of the printouts, one of them should take them all and read them. They should make notes and pull together a bullet point report of each individual fact that came out as the story progressed. Jack volunteered.

"Remember to include and highlight any family names that you come across, and anything that the family said," Maggie told him. "It may or may not be factual, but their opinions at the time may well include something relevant. We can't afford to ignore what they had to say to the press."

Jack nodded.

"Include anything about the other children," Zelah added. "Any names, particularly of any member of the Ryan family, and their neighbours."

"Yep, got it," he said.

"What angle can we look at next?" Maggie asked Zelah. "Got any ideas?"

"Yes, I think we should look at the Quinn family, the real Quinn family. Find what brothers and sisters the real Adolphus Quinn had and see if we can trace any of them to living descendants."

"You know, we are putting all of our eggs into one basket," Maggie said. "The fact that the Ryans and the Quinns both lived in Ennis and might have known each other could be no more than co-incidence. The fact that little Adolphus Quinn was murdered could also be co-incidental"

"Yes we are," Zelah conceded. "But it's the best lead we have." She paused for a moment. "We have to carry on and if it's wrong, let it go. The evidence is leading us in this direction. Going back to the drawing board at this point means we'll almost certainly not get the information we need in time for Thursday's Council meeting. It's a risk, but we have to take it."

"It was always a demanding timetable," Maggie replied. "Let's see what we can get then. As much as we want to prove what kind of man Adolphus Quinn really was, and stick one on Kennet and Rufus Quinn," Maggie said, to which Zelah grinned and nodded, "we can't just make the story fit. We have to believe in it one hundred percent."

"When have we ever done anything else?" Zelah replied, turning back to her computer. "We carry Maze's reputation with this. Ironic, isn't it. If we're right and we win, we'll get nothing out of it. If we're wrong and we lose, Kennet Quinn will make sure that every client we've ever had knows how we messed up. We will have handed him the keys to our own professional obliteration." She strummed her fingers on her keyboard. "Right, you take the Irish Government website, I'll take Roots Ireland."

For the rest of the afternoon they continued in silence. Once, Nick left the room and came back with the whole biscuit jar but no-one commented.

It was the sound of the front door slamming that made them all look up suddenly and Maggie saw that it was already five o'clock. Bob walked into the office and glanced around.

"You all look busy."

"I'm ready to report now," Jack said.

"Me, too," Nick added.

"I've found a potential lead for a member of the Quinn family, so this is a good time to stop. Anyway, I'm thirsty," Maggie said, spinning her chair around so that it met the table.

"Then I'll make us all some tea whilst you lot get yourselves together," Bob replied.

When they all settled at the table with Bob's tea, they were deciding where to start when Maggie's phone pinged. It was an incoming email. She turned back to check on her computer.

"It's a response from Louisa Ryan," she said, opening up the document. "Seems like a good place to start," and she read it out.

"Hello Maze Investigations, I was interested to read your message. I can confirm that my father Liam Ryan is the grandson of Sean Ryan, who I believe did have a brother called Martin. But I don't know about a Thomas. I was only interested in my DNA from my mother's family. The person to ask is my Great-Aunt Celia. I spoke to her when I saw your message and she says take a look at her tree. It's on Ancestry—"

"That's the one I found, but with Thomas missing," Nick interrupted. Zelah went on reading.

"She would be happy to talk to you and can probably give you much more information than I can. I was puzzled why my DNA hints came up with a close match called Mischa Quinn (presuming that's your client?), but I haven't explored any further. Celia lives in Ennis. Do give her a call. She loves researching our family tree and would be interested in what you have to say. Please let me know what you find out. Best wishes, Louisa Ryan."

"I love it when we get a positive response. Has she given us

160

the phone number?" Maggie asked.

"Yes," Zelah replied, "I think we should call, agreed?" They all nodded enthusiastically, but Nick held up a hand.

"How much are we going to tell her?"

"Nothing about the present-day Quinn family," Bob interjected. "The fewer people who know, the better."

"Fair enough," Maggie said. "We'll have to ask Louisa for her agreement to keep this confidential too. We need to guide the conversation towards Thomas Ryan and why – if we've got this right – he isn't on the tree. I think, let's not talk about Mischa. We should continue to treat her as a client and maintain her confidentiality. Yes?" Again they all nodded in agreement. "Right, I'll start the call, but if anyone thinks they should add something, just raise a hand and ask whatever it is." She leaned over to the conference phone in the centre of the table and dialled the number. Bob sat down at one of the spare chairs and took out a notebook, pen and phone, and they all leaned forward in anticipation.

The phone rang out and within a few seconds it was answered with a "Hello?"

The voice was high and reedy in tone, the indication of an older person.

"Good afternoon, Miss Ryan. I am speaking to Miss Celia Ryan?"

"Who wants to know?" If the voice was reedy, it was also firm.

"My name is Maggie Gilbert and I'm a genealogy researcher with a company called Maze Investigations. I and my colleagues, who are also here with me, were given your number by your great-niece, Louisa Ryan. I'm not sure how much she told you about our enquiries?"

"She said you'd be calling so I checked out your website. Fascinating stuff. You do a fine job and look nicely professional.

Louisa said you have a puzzle about one of those DNA test things."

"That's right," Maggie replied, "I'm glad you checked us out first. I hope that means you think we're trustworthy. May I tell you the story?"

"Yes, please. I like a puzzle."

Maggie smiled. "We have a client who did a DNA test too, and Louisa came up as a close relative. The thing is, the client hasn't got anyone called Ryan in her family history as far as she's been able to find out. She asked us to investigate and we've found that she might have had a three times great-uncle called Martin Ryan, who was born in Ennis in 1870. Our first task has been to check that we are talking about the same man as the Martin Ryan on your tree."

"Possibly. My grandfather was Sean Ryan and he had a brother called Martin."

"I can see from your tree that you don't have any information about Martin's descendants. Do you know what happened to him?"

There was silence on the other end. Zelah, Bob, Nick and Jack stared transfixed at the phone. It crackled slightly.

"No, I have no idea what happened to him."

"Well, we haven't been able to find that he died, so we were wondering if, in fact, he left Ennis at some point?"

"I suppose he must have done."

The answers were just too short and clipped for Maggie to believe that they were entirely true. Celia Ryan knew something, but how to draw it out of her? She decided it was time to bring in Thomas Ryan, see what Celia's reaction was.

"We found an anomaly in your family history too, Celia. We found another brother, who doesn't appear on your tree. His name was Thomas Ryan and he was born in 1864." She stopped and waited.

Zelah was blowing out a long breath in the silence that again followed Maggie's statement. Jack went to say something, then changed his mind. Maggie let the silence go on, until she could see that Zelah was at breaking point.

"Thomas Ryan is not on our family tree because our family did not, does not, want him there."

They all exhaled at the same time.

"Can I put something to you, Celia, that I think may save us all some time?"

"Please do, otherwise we'll still be dancing around each other this time tomorrow."

"Good, thank you. First of all a question. Do you know a local family called Quinn and would I be right to say that the reason you don't want Thomas Ryan on your family tree is something to do with the Quinn family?"

"Yes," the answer came back immediately. Then, "It's a long-standing thing and before you ask, I don't know the full story."

"Could you tell us what you do know, Celia?"

"I am prepared to do that, but I want a fair exchange of information. I want you to tell me what you know, I'm guessing you know something or we wouldn't be having this call at such short notice."

Maggie glanced around the room and they all nodded agreement, but Bob again whispered about protecting Mischa's identity.

"Right, Celia. As I said, we have a client. She's young. She believed her mother died when she was a child, but that has proven not to be the case. In an effort to trace some of her mother's relatives she took a DNA test. What that test brought back was a close relationship to the Ryan family. This is not her surname nor, to her knowledge, is there anyone else in her family called Ryan. She asked us to investigate the connection.

We began tracing the history of her father's side of the family and arrived at Martin. " She paused for a moment, "We also suspect we may have found Thomas Ryan. We think he appeared in South Wales around the early 1890s, but under a different name. Because we were able to track down his brother, we are fairly sure that the family of our client is descended from the Ryan family. We also believe that there was some connection to the Quinn family. We found this out from some newspaper reports." She stopped there. This last part wasn't true as far as she knew but it was worth a try.

"Why do you care about a connection to the Quinn family? That can't be of any interest to your client."

"She's a sharp old bird," Zelah whispered.

"I have good hearing too," came down the phone.

Maggie laughed out loud. "Give us a minute, please, Celia. I'm going to put you on hold if that's OK?"

"Just for a minute, yes, I'll be timing you, now."

Nick leaned forward and hit the 'mute' button. "You'll have to tell her about the name that Thomas Ryan chose to live under," he said. "Don't see how you can avoid it, if we're going to be honest and fair."

"You still can't tell her about Mischa, that wouldn't be fair," Jack said.

"No, I agree," Maggie replied. "Let's tell her about Adolphus Quinn and see how she reacts."

She unmuted the phone, "Celia, you still there?"

"Of course."

"Here's what I can tell you, but before I do, I must ask for your agreement to keep this information confidential. That's fundamentally important, to us and to our client."

"There's nothing illegal, is there?" Celia asked.

"No, absolutely nothing," Maggie assured her. "The reason we ask is because this is a complex case and it could cause embarrassment to certain people if this information was made public."

"Well, I wouldn't want that, now."

"Good, then I can tell you that we believe Thomas Ryan left Ennis and moved over to the mainland. He ended up in South Wales. The name he used and lived under was Adolphus Quinn."

There was a sharp intake of breath at the other end. "The bastard, the evil bastard! Did he think he would never be found out? I suppose he must have done. How could he, how dare he?"

Celia Ryan had become so excited that she had to pause for breath.

"Celia, are you OK, you sound distressed?"

"Yes, yes, I'm fine. Right here's what I know. My brother Edward was much older than me, ten years older. I am the only child of Sean Ryan's second marriage. I was born in 1930 when daddy was fifty-five years old. I was something of a surprise, I believe. I'm almost ninety years old now. I have never married. My sweetheart was killed at the end of the war. I never met anyone else after him I thought I could love, even though I was only sixteen when he died. I became interested in my family history about thirty or so years ago. An old maid's interest, some might say. My daddy, Sean was still alive when I was a young woman. He died in the 1960s. When I began to research the family I found out some information at the archives in Dublin and I went to speak to my eldest living half-brother, Eddie. I asked him what he knew about the family and I showed him a list of names. Right away he told me to remove Thomas Ryan, daddy's brother, from the list. He told me the family had disowned him and no-one ever talked about him, nor should they." She stopped and took a few deep breaths.

"I asked him why not? He told me that there had been a

terrible incident, of murder, and that Tommy Ryan had been involved. That's what he said: "*involved.*" I didn't know what it meant. I asked and he shouted at me to let it go. So I left it, I kept Tommy Ryan off the family tree. Then some years ago, Eddie was dying and I went to see him, several times. At the end he was wandering in his mind. He started to talk about 'brother Tommy', kept saying he wouldn't tell. I asked him what wouldn't he tell. He just kept repeating 'we won't tell, Tommy, we won't.' The last time I saw him, we thought he was unable to speak. I had been sat with him a couple of hours, waiting for the end. Suddenly he grabbed my hand and, in a whisper but perfectly clear, he said: 'Father forgive me, I should have told, and Mrs Mag. We should have told. Saw him, saw Tommy doing it.' He cried, then he said, 'the soldiers, poor little doll, daddy's best friend. "Soon after that, he took his last breath."

She stopped there, and for a moment nothing happened. They had all been caught up in the story, imagining the deathbed scene.

"Celia, are you still there?"

"Yes, I am. There now, I've told you. I think you'll be able to work it out, as I have done. There's clues in the newspaper reports."

"We have them printed out ready to search through. I don't think we have any more questions. This has been emotional and I thank you for telling us."

"I have a question," Zelah interrupted. "Celia, do you know anything about the soldiers?"

"No, not really. There's some stuff in the papers at the time about them, why?"

"I'm not sure," Zelah replied. "Something is scratching away at the back of my head. It may come to me. Thank you, we are so grateful for what you've told us."

"Will anything good come out of it?"

"Yes, definitely, but at the moment I can't say what. As soon as it's safe, we'll tell you," Maggie said.

"Sorry just one more question," Nick interjected. "Celia, did the Quinn family believe that Thomas Ryan was involved"?

"Oh yes, they were sure of it, but I don't know why. You'll have to ask them. I found that there's always been a discord between our families. I've never approached them."

"We will do that, Celia, and from all of us, thank you so much. This is vital information. We can relay it back to our client and, as I said, as soon as I know it's OK, I will tell you the full story."

"Well you'd better not take too long, I'm turning ninety next week."

"I'll keep that in mind," Maggie replied with a smile and ended the call.

Chapter 24

They all sat back in their chairs, except for Bob who was still head down over his notebook.

Zelah spoke first. "That explains the final part of the Isobel's message, the doll. Pet name for Adolphus Quinn, the real one."

"I was going to tell you, that's in one of the newspaper reports," Jack added. "One of the family said it. The called him 'our little doll'."

"Let's take a few minutes break, then we should review Jack's report and make notes of our new information," Maggie said. "We need to clear our heads after that." She glanced at her watch. "Almost six o'clock, back in fifteen minutes?"

Assuming rather than hearing they all agreed, she left the room and wandered out into the garden. At the bottom of the path down by the canal she glanced up to see that the sun had almost reached the mountain top. The man with the dog that she and Jack had passed earlier on the towpath, was walking past, the dog still pulling against the lead. He waved and she waved back.

"Who was that?" She hadn't noticed Bob walk up and stand beside her.

"No-one I know, just a man who was on the path earlier with his dog, when I was there with Jack."

"Have you ever seen him before?"

"I haven't ever noticed, why… oh no, you don't think?"

"I don't know but if he's suddenly appeared…"

"Stop right there, I can't live suspecting everyone who walks along the path just because I haven't seen them before. He's probably just a man with a dog."

"Yes he is, or then again, perhaps he isn't. This is how it has to be, for now."

"OK, I'll ask anyone I see walking past for ID, does that work for you?"

He folded his arms across his chest, then unfolded them and had begun to wag a finger when Jack came running down the garden. He stopped when he saw them both in confrontational poses, Maggie hands on hips, Bob's pointed finger.

"I've got a text from Alex. He's already done the photo of Michelle, do you want to see it?"

"Saved by the bell," Maggie muttered as she turned away from Bob and walked back up the garden.

**

Back in the office they gathered around Jack's laptop and he selected the enhanced photo of the young Michelle Morgan.

"He's done a great job," Zelah said. "That's really clear. Now Jack, apply the app, to age her to around forty years."

He picked up his phone, transferred the enhanced photo onto it, then downloaded the app and applied it to the picture. As he worked on it, the woman's face changed and morphed into a mature woman. Although he had retained her hair colour the shape of her face had altered and lines had appeared.

"Fascinating," Nick remarked as the photo transferred back to the laptop screen. "I know we all change as we age but this is so interesting. However there's something I'd like to see first." He turned to Maggie. "Do you have a picture of yourself at around sixteen, seventeen that we could use on the app? I'd like to see how it represents you now and compare it to how you actually look. If that's OK with you?" he added, seeing her raised eyebrows.

"You want to see how accurately I've aged," she said. "Nick, don't look so concerned. I'm just teasing. It's a good point, give me a couple of minutes."

Ten minutes later she returned with an A5 photo. "This is

probably the clearest one I have in colour." She handed it over to Jack.

"Wow, you were really skinny, mum," he said. "What happened?" There was a snort of laughter from Zelah. Nick and Bob bit back their grins.

"You happened, son and then your sister."

"Oh. Right." He turned to the printer and put the photo in, selected the 'scan' option and waited whilst the machine hummed, not looking up. "It's done," He copied the photo to his phone and selected the app again. Within a few seconds he put the new image on his laptop.

"Here it is."

"Well, it looks like me now, but thinner. I guess you can't select a realistic weight."

"No, that's not an option, yet." He still wasn't looking at her.

"What are we going to do with this?" Zelah asked. "I've been thinking, whilst you've been embarrassing each other. I would prefer to meet up with Mischa rather than send this to her phone. Someone needs to be there when she sees it. Remember, she's never seen a photo of her mother, at any age."

"I agree," Maggie replied, "It's a sensitive issue."

"I'll message her now." Zelah said.

"If they're going to meet, can I go with Zelah?" Jack asked. "Perhaps Mischa might like someone her own age there, you know, for support?"

"I don't see why not," Maggie said. "Let's see what her response is, then we can decide."

"She's replied," Zelah said, looking up from her phone. "She wants to meet tomorrow afternoon around 2-ish."

"How will you organise it?" Bob asked.

"I'll pick her up again, she doesn't drive. Jack, I'm OK for you to come with us. We'll go to that same café in Caerleon.

It'll be quiet after lunch."

"We should get back around the table and report what we've found; it's important information, at least mine is," Nick said and sat down in front of his notes. They all followed suit.

"Jack, the newspapers."

Jack put up his set of bullet point notes. "Most of what I found was covered by the phone call and what I told you about earlier, but there is something that makes more sense now. Adolphus Quinn was seven years old. He was found in a wood on the outskirts of Ennis, after he had been missing for two days. He had been tortured with a knife and burns, before being strangled. He was found holding his soldiers that his dad had made for him."

"Is there anything else about the soldiers?" Zelah asked.

"Yeh, there is, just a minute..." He ruffled through the papers. "Yes, his dad made and painted six soldiers for his birthday. There was one of each rank. One of his sisters said he was a generous boy and he let other children play with them. One of the other kids wanted to keep the set for a while, said he would return them the next day. She said 'Doll didn't like that, he always slept with them next to his bed, all lined up, like real soldiers. There was a bit of a spat about it, but the other kids helped him get them back. They all liked Dolly.' Could it have been...?"

"Yes," Zelah said. "Thomas Ryan. Couldn't get what he wanted. That could be when he started, lured the boy into the wood and tortured and killed him."

"You don't know that Zelah. A possibility, yes, but you can't say it with any certainty."

"She can say it with a strong degree of possibility," Bob said. "Think about what Celia Ryan just told us, about when her brother died. About 'not telling', I'm putting two and two together here, with some added conjecture, OK. I think Edward

Ryan, when he died, was repeating what his father Sean had confessed to him. Remember, he said 'daddy's best friend'? Tells me that Sean Ryan was Adolphus Quinn's best friend. If you check their dates of birth you'll probably find that they were about the same age. Sean wasn't alone. He said 'we' wouldn't tell. I suspect Sean Ryan finally 'told', when he was dying. He told his son, Edward, but by the time of his own death Edward was too far gone to tell the story in its correct context to Celia. And remember Celia said that the words Edward used were 'Father, forgive me.' I think he thought he was talking to a priest, confessing what he knew and had withheld for so long. There's another lead in there, too. Who was Mrs Mag?"

"Who?" Maggie asked.

"Celia said that Edward Ryan said the name. He said, 'and Mrs Mag'. He wouldn't have said that if it wasn't significant in the context of the story."

"You've put two and two together and come up with some almighty guesswork, Bob. What's your hypothesis?" Nick asked.

"I suspect that when Thomas Ryan lured Adolphus Quinn into the woods he had his brothers with him. I think the 'we' were himself, Sean and Martin. When Thomas eventually ran, which I think he must have done, he took Martin with him. Martin was eleven, he could travel and work. Sean was only a little boy, same as Adolphus. He would have been a burden to Thomas, so he left him behind, but made sure he understood that he was never, ever to tell. God knows what Thomas frightened him with, so much so that he only repeated it on his deathbed, to his son."

"A monster," Maggie murmured. She turned to Nick. "You have something to share, too?"

"I do, and I'm going to make it quick. Stella's just finished and wants to know if I can go over for a drink."

"Go on then," Zelah said.

"My theory about Thomas Ryan being a boxer was right. There are a couple of accounts in a Liverpool newspaper that name him. Not as Thomas Ryan, but as Tommy the Irish Terror. The description matches the descriptions we've had His nose was broken by an opponent. He had a few fights there over a couple of months, then disappeared. Then Tommy the Irish Terror appears in Manchester and again in Birmingham. He was a feared opponent. That takes up most of a year or more, then there isn't any more."

"What about deaths of women in those places?" Maggie asked, are there any similarities

"Haven't had time to look yet."

"Leave that to me," Bob said. "I have access to databases that you don't have. I'll see what I can find tomorrow. Nick, let me have the dates of the newspaper reports in each place."

Maggie turned to Zelah. "Anything to add?"

"No, not to add, but something is bustling around tapping on the inside of my skull. It's like having a woodpecker in your head and it's driving me crazy. It's important, though, I think." she stood up, "I'm leaving now. A sit down and a glass of wine may help me locate it. Jack, I'll pick you up at half one tomorrow."

"I'll check out where the Quinns are and let you know if you need an escort," Bob said. "I'm coming after you now, don't object."

"Wasn't going to," Zelah replied.

Nick left with them. Jack hung around in the office as Maggie tidied up, watching her.

"Something on your mind?" Maggie asked, after five minutes.

"I wasn't being rude, honest."

She reached out her hand and took his. "Of course I know that, it was funny though. Now, mind, if Bob had said it…" she

173

let her words hang in the air as Jack laughed.

"I'd like to work on a bit, if that's OK with you," he said.

"No problem, I'm going to cobble something together for dinner for when Bob gets back. An interesting day, eh. What are you going to look at?"

"Mrs Mag, whoever she was. See if there's any mention of her in the papers. She must have been local to them, mustn't she? Otherwise they wouldn't have used her name like that, shortened. It must have been shortened, don't you think?"

"Yes, I guess so, good call. Probably something like McGuire, or McGuinness. It's a bit of a needle in a haystack but give it a go. Jack…"

He was sitting at his laptop, but he turned towards her.

"I'm really sorry we had to cancel the girls coming here. This would have been quite something for you all to get into. If it hadn't been for, you know…"

"I understand mum, honestly. I think they might have been upset and horrified at what we've found out. It turned out to be just as well."

"Thanks, right, I'll be in the kitchen. Give me a shout if you find anything."

**

"Did you find out anything about Mrs Mag?" Maggie asked Jack later as they sat down to the all-day breakfast she had pulled together.

He shook his head. "Not really, there was a woman called Norah Maginnis who died in a house fire in Ennis not long after Adolphus Quinn was killed, but it was an accident. According to the report she had a habit of getting drunk and leaving the coals burning, that's all I could find in the papers."

"Did any of you get any addresses for the Quinns and the Ryans, in Ennis?" Bob asked.

"Yes," Jack replied, "they both lived in… Salt House Lane, I think it was called."

"And was that where Mrs Maginnis lived?"

"No, it was a different street. Does it matter?"

"It might do. We'll have a look at a map tomorrow," Bob said. "I've been to County Clare and I spent a day in Ennis. I remember the streets around the centre being narrow and crowded. This was where the poorer people lived. They might have known each other; it's just a thought."

"Are you thinking that there might be a connection between this woman and Thomas Ryan?" Maggie asked.

"There must have been something for her name to have been mentioned by Sean Ryan to his son. She seemed to be a part of the 'don't tell'. I'll do some investigating with Jack."

"Knock yourself out," Maggie replied. "Are you around tomorrow?"

"I'm due to meet with Zelah tomorrow around one fifteen to come over here. I'll have someone check on the whereabouts of the Quinns, and we'll be calling by the Manor for Nick. I'll follow her into Newport to pick up Mischa. I've arranged for my sergeant to follow her out to Caerleon. I have to be in work. He'll wait for them to come back, I presume you aren't going out tomorrow?"

"No, we were supposed to be going to the archives in Cardiff, but it turns out they aren't open to the public tomorrow. I'll have to talk to Zelah to see where we're at and if we can go first thing Tuesday. We still need to check out the baptism for Ada Blackstock's son, see if we can identify his father. We need to know why the brooch was so important to her."

"Couldn't you do that by phone, pay someone to do the research for you?"

"Yes, it's an option, I suppose. We can decide tomorrow." She yawned, "I'm going to bed. I'm knackered. What are you doing Jack?"

"Think I'll play some games with the guys, I need some relaxation after today."

"See you in the morning. What about you?" she said to Bob.

"I want to check in with work, I'll be up later."

"Something we need to talk about."

"She's not thinking about shutting all of this down is she?" Jack asked Bob after Maggie had left the room.

"She's been on edge for days now," Bob replied as they stacked the dishwasher. "I'm just hoping if there's enough evidence, the Quinns won't want it to get out and that will be enough to keep them away from all of you."

"Do you really think they will stay away?"

"Let's hope so," Bob replied.

**

When he finally reached the bedroom Maggie had fallen asleep with a book in her hand. He was just taking it from her and trying to gently remove her glasses when she opened her eyes.

"I've got something to tell you."

"Out with it, whatever it is."

"Nick told me today that he has a son, aged eighteen, and he hasn't seen him since he was ten. He's spent years trying to track him down; he and his mother."

Bob sank down on the bed. "Well I didn't see that one coming. He's a dark horse."

"He's never been one to share. He agreed I could tell you and he's going to tell Zelah. But that's all the information he wants anyone to have, for now."

"A day full of surprises," Bob said as he got into bed. "It's all moving fast now."

"We can't let up. We've delved too far into this case to stop, I realised that today. Tomorrow should bring some interesting news."

He was quiet for a few moments. "Depends on your interpretation of 'interesting', doesn't it?" he replied.

When he didn't get a reply he turned around. Maggie was asleep. He reached out and turned the light out. Whatever tomorrow was going to bring, he was sure that his interpretation of 'interesting' was not something any of them would enjoy.

Chapter 25

On Monday morning Maggie decided to apply herself to a new search. She had puzzled over what to do next and decided to look for a current member of the Quinn family. Before starting, she tried to speak to both Nick and Zelah but neither were picking up. She guessed Nick had stayed with Stella the previous evening but Zelah should have been in her flat. Why wasn't she answering either of her phones? She was just deciding whether to mention this to Bob when he appeared in the office.

"What's up?" he asked.

"I can't raise Zelah by phone, not on her landline or mobile."

He frowned. "Give me five minutes." It took ten, before he returned, his expression worried. "There was a patrol car in the vicinity of her flat, I asked them to go check her building. They got in and went up to her door. No reply, and her car's gone, she isn't there." He paced around the office, rubbing his hand over his stubbled head, then turned to Maggie.

"Would she have gone out on her own?"

"Can't rule it out," she replied, "you know what she's like. She hasn't taken kindly to being followed."

"Damn the woman," he muttered.

"Let me text her, I haven't tried that yet." Maggie sent a quick text. They both waited in silence, but not for long, before her phone pinged an incoming message. "It's her," Maggie said with a sigh of relief. "She's in a meeting. She'll come straight back here, in about half an hour."

His expression told her not to say anything further. She had rarely seen Bob lose his temper. Zelah was going to get an earbashing when she turned up, and serve her right. But when Zelah arrived an hour later there was no shouting.

Zelah had been expecting words and began to speak before she had taken her coat off, but Bob held up a hand to stop her. "Don't bother, Zelah, I don't want to know. If you're determined to take risks with your own life, so be it, but you will not – NOT – endanger anyone else. Don't you dare leave this house later with Maggie's son without telling me, is that clear?"

She didn't confirm, instead, countering with "what I've been thinking is, they aren't going to do anything so obvious to any of us, in the middle of this situation. It's afterwards we should be concerned about, which will be in subtle ways, not obvious ones." She put her hands on her hips, "Kennet Quinn is not going to have our fingernails pulled out, or hit us with iron bars, or anything so straightforwardly brutal. Be honest, is he?"

Bob ignored her.

"Fine, don't speak to me but I'm right. They shot you when you were alone and in the dark, because you were close to bringing down their business. We aren't."

"I wasn't alone, I was with two colleagues. Do you think that makes you safe?"

"For now, yes but I won't risk either Jack or Mischa Quinn's safety, OK?"

He turned and walked out of the room, slamming the door so hard, all of the windows on the ground floor rattled. Zelah turned back to Maggie. "I'm sorry, I truly am; I do think he's overdoing it."

"If anyone gets hurt, Zelah, it will be down to you."

"That's not fair," she retorted, "I don't want an escort everywhere, the rest of you can please yourselves."

"Well, on behalf of my children, I'm not risking them."

"Fine," Zelah muttered, taking off her coat and sitting at her desk. "What are we doing this morning?"

"I don't know about you, but I'm going to see if I can find a member of the Quinn family to speak to."

"Good," after a short pause, "do you want to know where I was this morning?"

"Is it relevant?"

"Of course it is. I went to see the Mayor."

"What!" Maggie jumped up. "You did that without speaking to any of us?"

"Just sit down and listen," she said. "I spent a long time last night thinking. I made a decision, yes on my own without consulting you, because I know politics better than any of you. Leaving it until we have definite evidence was going to be too late. I needed to get the ball rolling. The Mayor is a friend, she's a good woman and a good Councillor. It wouldn't have been fair or right to spring it on her at the very last minute. I've told her, in strictest confidence, about our investigation into Adolphus Quinn. We have enough to prove that he wasn't Adolphus Quinn, but Thomas Ryan and was involved in the death of a child. I told her that it was looking more and more likely that the man was a psychotic murderer."

"Told who?" Jack asked from the doorway. Zelah flapped an arm at him and pointed to the settee. "Sit, listen, I realised last night how close we are to the Council meeting and if she's going to take it off the agenda she would need time. Rufus Quinn is someone she can't upset, after all. He'd find a way to turn the blame back on Gwentshire County Council. We already agreed that this wouldn't be made public. So I sent her a text last night and asked to meet this morning."

"How did she take it?" Maggie asked.

"Who are we talking about?" Jack interrupted.

"The bloody Mayor," Zelah snapped. "She was horrified,

but had the sense not to ask. She's a canny political animal."

"Ask what?" Jack interrupted again.

This time Maggie answered. "The obvious question: does Rufus Quinn know the truth about his ancestor, in whose honour he has petitioned for a statue?"

"But why wouldn't the Mayor want to know, I don't get it?"

"That's because you have a long way to go in understanding the workings of the world, and the business of politics. If you don't already know or might not like the answer, don't ask the question," Zelah replied. "This way she can claim ignorance of any wrongdoing or underhand behaviour and find a way to reject the statue, without making an enemy of Rufus Quinn. She needs time to think. It turns out it's not as straightforward as we hoped."

"Seems crazy to me," Jack replied. "If he's a bad person, why care about getting on the wrong side of him?"

Zelah sighed. "Because he has a reputation and a name to be protected and he will do whatever it takes to ensure that protection. From what we know of the family, they won't care who they destroy to keep their good name intact in the greater business community and beyond."

Jack shook his head. "Anyway, does that mean we stop researching?"

"Absolutely not," Zelah said. "You never know when the subject of the statue might come back up and the information needs to be available should that ever happen. For ourselves, we need to keep going, because we need to keep the Quinns as far away from us as possible. I want to weaponise our knowledge against them. Therefore the more concrete proof we have, the better."

Jack glanced at his watch, "I said it was ok for my mate Jules to come over this morning, for a couple of hours. It is OK, isn't it? His dad's bringing him."

"Yes, of course," Maggie replied, as the doorbell rang. "If that's him go and let him in. You have to be ready, just after one, to go out with Zelah," she called out after him. Turning back to Zelah she asked, "Why isn't it straightforward?"

"Politics," Zelah replied. "It's been through two committees where the funding has been approved. All that's left is for the full County Council to approve the minutes of the committees. If someone stands up and says that this funding is going to be reconsidered, the opposition might seize on it and ask questions. They might think that there's some financial shenanigans or mal-administration, as is their right to question. Their questions have to be answered honestly and truthfully. If they are seen to be even slightly fudging the truth, the opposition will home in and want to know why. They won't suspect the truth, but this could bring it out. Causing embarrassment to the administration is a good tactic for oppositions, but it's not what we want. The Mayor will not lie, even for a good cause."

"That's a bummer. We can't ask her to ignore her responsibilities or question her integrity, I get that. What's she proposing to do then?"

"She wanted time to think about it. She's going to call me when she has a proposal. Right, what are we going to do this morning?" Zelah asked.

"I'm still looking for a Quinn family member. And another thing – I can't see that we have enough time to get to the Cardiff archives to find a baptism record for Ada Blackstock's son. They aren't officially open today but they may take a phone call. How about you call them and see if there's anyone there we can pay to look for us?"

"Good idea, I'll do it now," Zelah got out her phone and left the room.

Maggie decided to start on public family trees on the

182

Ancestry site, to see if there was any mention of Adolphus Quinn, now that she could enter his date of birth and of death. She came up trumps immediately, the tree had been put on the site by a woman called Jennifer Quinn. She named her grandfather, great-grandfather and two times great-grandfather, who was a Michael Quinn, and brother of Adolphus Quinn. There was a chance that Michael could be the youngest child of the Quinn family, as he was born in 1881, the same year in which Adolphus had died. She noted that Michael's parents were called Bernard and Leonora. She needed a quick confirmation that this was the correct family Quinn. It was looking good, but…

"Jack!" she yelled up the stairs, "come here a moment would you please. I need some information from you."

He poked his head around his bedroom door. "Is it urgent?"

"Can you remember the names of the real Adolphus Quinn's parents from any of those newspaper reports?"

He screwed up his eyes and looked up at the ceiling. "Um, just a minute. I think it was Bernard and… what was it… Laura, no, it began with an L, give me a minute. Lena, Leah? Leonora: that was it. There was a sister called Caitlin too, I put it all in the log."

"That's it, brilliant, thanks. You can go back to your games now."

So, Jennifer Quinn, what might she know? Zelah was walking back into the room,

"They can do it this afternoon, I've paid for a couple of hours. We might get it back late this afternoon, but if not, before lunchtime tomorrow at the latest. Maggie, are you listening to me?"

"Yes, but I've just located a member of the Quinn family and I'm thinking about what to say to her. Come and look at the family tree."

Zelah went to look over Maggie's shoulder. "Looks promising; it's the same parents' names. Jennifer Quinn last checked in yesterday, so if we message her today there's a good chance she'll see it. What are we going to say?"

"I was just thinking about that," Maggie replied, "something similar to what we told Louisa Ryan, to get us started. No naming Mischa, but asking about the story of Adolphus Quinn. What does she know about it and, more importantly, did the family believe that the culprit might have been Thomas Ryan."

"All that in one go?"

"No, of course not. I'll just start by introducing ourselves. I'd prefer to have a call with her, if she's willing. I'll try to give her enough to tempt her into a quick reply."

Zelah watched as Maggie composed and sent the message. "I doubt we'll get an answer before this evening. She's young enough to be at work today."

Zelah glanced at her watch, "Half eleven, Bob will be here at one. What can we do in the meantime?"

Maggie sat back, "I can't think of anything new. It's always a good idea to go back over what we've done, see if there's anything more that could be followed up. How about we re-read the newspaper reports? I'd still like to see if there's anything else we can find about Mrs Mag."

"You do the reading, I'll go back to Mrs Mag," Zelah said.

Chapter 26

They stopped just before one. Jack's friend had already left, and Jack was ready to go. He had made an effort to look smart, in dark trousers and a shirt and appeared carrying his best jacket. He had also splashed on some aftershave.

"It's not a date," Zelah remarked as he joined them in the office. He blushed beetroot red. "Shall I wash it off?"

"No, she'll like it." He blushed deeper.

"Let me do the talking, to begin with," Zelah said to him. "You can join in when it's time to show her the picture. We'll discuss some of what we've found, but nothing about how the real Adolphus Quinn died."

"Can we say that the ancestor killed him and took his name?"

Zelah thought for a moment. "Yes we can, she needs to know the purpose behind stopping the statue. Say nothing, absolutely nothing, about what Kennet did to her mother to make her leave. If we find her mother it will be up to her to give Mischa the details, or not."

Jack looked puzzled, then looked up at the window. "Bob's here."

"Then let's go, better not keep him waiting."

"Good luck," Maggie said, walking to the door with them. "Text me when you're done Jack."

She could see the excitement in his eyes as he gave her a quick hug. "Be careful and aware of what's around you." He nodded, but she knew that he was so caught up in the moment, he wouldn't have seen a grizzly bear approaching at ten feet.

**

This time Zelah was driving her new, new car, a Porsche

Cayenne, sleek dark grey with blacked out windows. Jack luxuriated in the front seat, dreaming of owning one. He was still puzzled by what Zelah had said earlier, about what Kennet had done to Michelle. Maybe she had forgotten he didn't know anything about that, but he wasn't going to ask, not right now. When they reached the cathedral they parked on the lower side. Bob jumped out of his car, walked over to them and climbed into the back seat of the Porsche.

I've had a message to say that they are all at the house, including Gerry Quinn. My sergeant is over there," he indicated a black BMW about twenty yards away. "He'll be behind you all the way there and back, then back to Maggie's house." He stepped out, slamming the door behind him.

Zelah and Jack looked at each other and grimaced.

"He bears grudges," Zelah said.

"No, I don't think so, he's OK with you, most of the time."

She opened her mouth to reply, but paused as Mischa appeared, running down the hill. She saw them, waved, which made Zelah wince and hopped into the back seat. "This one's pretty good, too, what is it?"

"It's a Porsche," Zelah replied. "Let's go."

Zelah introduced Jack who went quiet but had a soppy grin on his face throughout the journey. At the café in Caerleon they chose the same table, in the corner away from the other diners. There were only two other occupied tables, one with a couple of women with pushchairs containing sleeping infants and one with a young woman sitting alone, looking at her phone and texting. This time, Zelah ordered a bottle of sparkling water.

"You get to drive Zelah's cars," Mischa said to Jack as they waited for their drinks to arrive. "Lucky you."

"Sometimes," he mumbled.

When the drinks had been delivered Zelah checked around. No-one else had come in.

"Come on then," Mischa said, "I want to see these photos."

"Jack has two to show you," Zelah said. "The first is a picture of your mother when she was in school. A friend of his had it enhanced so he could use an ageing app. Show her the first one."

Jack brought up the picture of Michelle, now just her face without her school friends around her, and handed the phone over to Mischa. The girl gazed at it, a puzzled expression on her face…Zelah and Jack waited.

"I don't look much like her, do I? How old was she then?"

"About seventeen," Zelah replied. "Are you ready?" Mischa nodded, her face serious. She handed the phone back to Jack, who brought up the 'aged' photo. As soon as she saw it Mischa looked surprised, which changed to perplexed. "I don't understand," she said, staring at the photo.

"Does it look familiar?" Zelah asked.

"Sort of, it looks like the woman in the bakery. I told you about her but she's much older than my mother. I reckon she must be at least sixty. I think my mother would be about forty? This doesn't make sense." She continued to examine the picture.

"Could she be a relative of your mother?" Jack said.

"Maybe," she replied. "Maybe my grandmother?"

"Are you sure the woman in the bakery is over sixty? What makes you think so, Mischa?" Zelah asked.

"Well she has white hair, in an old-fashioned style. She has something about her, the way she stands, I don't know. A bit worn out, if you know what I mean? Lots of wrinkles and scabby skin."

"What about her voice?" Zelah asked. "Is it the voice of an old woman? The voice changes as you get older. It can be a bit thinner, a bit more breathy and sometimes deeper."

Mischa considered this, "I wouldn't say that she has a

187

particularly old voice, but I don't really know what that means."

Zelah thought for a moment. "Hands," she said. She held up the backs of hers. "I'm in my sixties and I've got these lines and liver spots." She indicated the small brown dots on her skin. "You only get these as you get old, bit like cracked parchment."

"I wouldn't know what her hands look like. She always has gloves on."

"Always, even when she's handling money? I can understand when she's handling food, but doesn't she ever take them off? What do the gloves look like?" Zelah, feeling a prickling in the hairs on the back of her neck, sat up and leant forward.

"Um… they're like, white cotton and no, I've *never* seen her take them off. She must have arthritis or something, because a couple of times I've seen her wince and rub the joints."

Jack frowned but said nothing.

"How about Maggie and I go to speak to this woman, see if she might be related?" Zelah said, "It's worth a try."

"I suppose so. It's a bit disappointing though, isn't it? I thought this might be her."

"Never mind," Zelah said, standing up. "Let's go, lots to do." She walked towards the exit.

"What's up with her?" Mischa whispered to Jack.

"Oh, she's always like this. Once she gets something in her head she wants to check out she'd swat bulldozers out of her way. You get used to it."

Zelah drove back to Newport breaking the speed limit most of the way, which told Jack that something had happened, but he had no idea what. He hoped she hadn't forgotten they were being tailed by an unmarked police car. She practically threw Mischa out of the car back at the cathedral.

"I might call you later," she said to the departing girl. "Will you be able to speak to me?"

"Sure, I'll find a quiet place in the house." She sounded puzzled and rather hurt, but stepped out of the car and walked around the cathedral and out of sight. Zelah set off again immediately, at great speed.

"What's going on, Zelah?" Jack asked, clinging onto the arm rest with both hands.

"Tell you when we get back. Call your mother and tell her we have a breakthrough."

**

They found Maggie on the doorstep. She followed Zelah and a confounded looking Jack into the office.

"Definitely her?" she asked.

"I'm pretty sure," Zelah replied.

"How can you possibly know?" Jack demanded, as he paced around the room. "Nothing fits. That woman is much too old

"The hands," Zelah replied.

"There's something you don't know," Maggie said, "I haven't told you because it's another horror story. I'll tell you now, sit down."

He threw himself into a chair, looking mutinous.

"On Christmas morning, when Mischa was four years old and her brother Gerard was three, Kennet Quinn poured boiling water over Michelle's hands. We don't know why, it was something to do with the way that she was preparing lunch. There was probably some violence before that but this time she ended up in hospital. Her hands are most likely terribly scarred and she'll have trouble moving them. She went from the hospital to a women's refuge in Cardiff where she stayed for a couple of weeks. Then she disappeared and hasn't been seen since. You see, Kennet has always told his children that their mother was dead."

Chapter 27

As she told the story Jack's face took on an expression of incredulity. When she finished he put his head in his hands. "She doesn't know?" he mumbled.

"No, we haven't told her, we didn't think we should. If this really is Michelle, then it will be up to her whether or not Mischa learns the truth."

He nodded his head but didn't take his hands away, "What are you going to do now?"

"I think we need to go to see this woman now, this afternoon," Zelah said. "There's just about enough time." She glanced out of the window. The black BMW was still there. "I'm going out to tell PC Plod that he needs to come with us again."

Maggie went to grab a coat. "You'd better come with us in the car," she said to Jack. "I don't want to leave you here on your own."

During the ten-minute drive back down to Newport, none of them spoke. The café was a short walk from the new university building and the student digs that bordered the river Usk, close to the centre of town; a convenient place for students to get drinks and snacks.

As they reached the building Maggie was relieved to see that there were no customers. The woman who might be Michelle was finishing up, cleaning down empty shelves that had held the hot food of the day. She looked old, dilapidated and tired, round-shouldered, with a careworn expression. Her face bore the lines of old age, her white hair cut in an unflattering bob. Her clothes hung loosely on her stick thin frame.

"Sorry, we're just about to close," she said glancing up, but something stopped her. She put down the cloth she had in her gloved hands and straightened up, motionless, eyes alert.

"Who are you? What do you want?"

"Are you Michelle Quinn, formerly Michelle Morgan?" Zelah asked. The woman didn't reply. She glanced around at the back of the café, where there was an open door leading to an exit and took a step back. Maggie took a step forward. "Please don't run, it's not what you think."

"Kennet is looking for you. We've managed to get here ahead of him," Zelah said. "We need to talk to you, it's about your daughter."

Michelle Quinn put her hands onto the glass counter and pressed down hard, staring at them. "I don't know what you're talking about."

"Yes you do," Zelah replied. "We don't have time to pussyfoot around. We are not the bad people. We're trying to help Mischa, who has found out that you aren't dead. She's seen your picture today, or at least a picture of what you should look like. Here it is."

She held out her phone to show Michelle the picture of herself, 'aged' by the app.

The woman stared at it for a few seconds. "Not flattering, is it?" she said.

"It's good enough to see that it's you. Mischa wasn't sure, though. She expected you to look younger. It was when she told me about the gloves, I knew it was you," Zelah said.

"What do you want from me?"

"Well," Maggie replied, "it's also about what you want. Your daughter wants to find her mother. Do you want her to know it's you? Plus we have something we need from you." She stopped and took a deep breath. "Look Michelle, I can understand your fear. We've met your ex-husband. He's gunning for us now. My partner is a policeman. He was shot six months ago and he believes Kennet Quinn was behind it. My business partner," she indicated Zelah, "and I run a company called Maze Investigations. We were investigating something concerning the Quinns – Rufus to start with – when Mischa heard us in her father's house and followed us out. She had been trying to find you and had done a DNA test, the results of which are a whole new story. If you're willing to hear us out, I think – I hope – we can convince you that we're OK but we need your help. The situation with Mischa, well, it's up to you. Zelah realised today that you are Michelle Quinn. We're happy to tell you the whole story. We haven't told Mischa yet that we know it's you; we just came straight here to talk to you. What do you say?"

The woman had listened in silence, without moving, barely breathing. Now, she took her hands away from the glass counter and folded her arms. "I haven't trusted anyone for the best part of fifteen years, so why should I trust you now, when you just walk in off the street like this? I am Michelle Morgan. I gave up being Quinn years ago. So what?"

Zelah stepped in, "I don't know what we can do to make you trust us, except come and listen to what we have to say. Will you come back to our office? My car's outside. Maggie's son is there. He met Mischa this morning. There's another car with us; a police car. The driver can show you his ID. He's following us to make sure that your ex-husband can't get at us. We only have a couple of days left. Please."

A silence... then, "I want to see his ID."

"I'll go out and ask him to come in." Maggie stepped out. Zelah waited. She didn't see much point in saying anything more until Michelle made a decision.

Maggie came back in with Sergeant Eric Moreton and Jack.

"This is my son, Jack. Sergeant, will you please show this lady your warrant card?"

He did so without asking any questions. He looked quizzically at Maggie who nodded and he went back to his car.

Inside the café Michelle Morgan stared at them, then looked around, then back at them. Then she said, "Where's your office?"

"In my house, on the outskirts of Cwmbran."

"I'll go with you and listen to your story; that's all, for now." Then she hesitated. "How do you know that Kennet or one of his people aren't outside, watching?"

"They're being tracked by the police, but keep your head down. It's impossible to see in through the windows of Zelah's car. We can park right outside my house and Eric will follow us. When we get there we'll go straight into the office. I'll just get my bag and my keys, I have to lock up."

By the time she reached the front door to lock it Zelah was already in her car, with the engine running. Michelle did as she was told, put her head down and walked quickly to the back of the car, where she got in next to Maggie.

They were back at the house in less than ten minutes. Maggie told Eric Moreton that they were going to be at least an hour, after which they'd have to take Michelle home. He radioed in and received a message back to wait.

"Nice house," Michelle said, as she walked through the hall and into the office.

"It's my home," Maggie said, "and we work out of here. We don't usually bring clients back, but under the circumstances, we consider you an exception. Sit yourself down, what can I get you to drink?"

Michelle shook her head. "Let's get on with it."

"Yes, let's. I'm going to tell you the story of how we arrived here, including how Mischa came to ask us to help her find you."

It took Maggie almost twenty minutes to run through the

whole story. She stopped a couple of times to see if Zelah wanted to add anything, but she didn't. "You're doing fine," she said to Maggie, "keep going."

Just once Maggie saw Michelle's eyes widen, which was exactly where she hoped it would be. She included their knowledge of Adolphus Quinn's crimes, the fact that they believed he had stolen a child's identity and the connection with the Ryan family. She told her about their meeting with Rufus and Kennet Quinn and the unease with which they were all now living. When she had finished she sat back and said, "I have told you everything about our case. I've done so because, if you are going to trust us, it has to be mutual. Some of what I've just told you can never be revealed outside this room."

The woman sat forward, leaned her elbows on the table and put her hands together, fingers clasped, covering her mouth.

"I'm going to tell you my story, which will take a while." Michelle sat upright and folded her arms. "First of all, he's not my ex-husband. We're still married. I met Kenny – that's what I've always called him – when I was seventeen. I was happily obsessed and believed I was madly in love. No, I was madly in love. We married when I was twenty and I had Mischa when I was twenty-one. At first it was idyllic, he couldn't do enough for me. Then I started to notice that he was less and less interested in Mischa. He said looking after a baby was a woman's job. I believed that too, so it didn't seem odd, not back then." She stopped and took a deep breath, "I'd like a glass of water." Jack stood up and went to get one for her. She drank half the glass in one go, then spoke again, without looking at any of them, instead gazing into space, with a look of fierce concentration.

"Then I became pregnant again and this time it was a boy. Kenny was over the moon. He did everything for the baby. 'My son', 'my boy', that's how he always referred to him. Rarely by

194

his name, Gerard, after his own grandfather. He stopped my feeding Gerard before long, changed to a bottle and did the feeds himself. By this time he was making nasty remarks about Mischa who, was almost two. I made a joke about it. That was the first time he hit me, and kicked me. It wasn't the last. I learned to keep quiet and look after Mischa and she learned to not get in her father's line of sight."

She stopped and sighed, drank more water.

"He isolated me from my family, made me think it was my fault. The beatings continued. He blamed me for any little thing that wasn't perfect. I knew it was getting worse, but I kept going. Then came that Christmas morning. Mischa was just turned four, Gerard was three." She paused... "You know what happened?"

They nodded, Michelle stretched her neck from side to side, back and forward and licked her lips.

"I was in hospital for almost a week, I can't describe the pain. I've never spoken of it. He told the doctors I'd done it myself, that I was clumsy. He said he was concerned about my co-ordination and my mental health, he feared it needed to be investigated. He sounded like such a caring, loving husband. When we were alone, he told me that I should expect more of the same. Lying there, day after day, I knew I had to get away. I knew he would harm me or get rid of me, he didn't need me. He didn't need Mischa, either. He had 'his boy' and I'd been nothing more than a delivery vessel. I summoned up the courage to ask him to let me go, to take Mischa and go away. He laughed at me, '*I can't have that happen*' he said, '*what would people think?*' I knew I was being condemned to a short life of misery that would culminate in my death through my own so-called clumsiness. Or I would be sectioned, for which he was preparing the way. When I was being discharged from hospital I called a friend who came and took me away to the refuge. Of course, he came looking for me, but he met his match in the women at the refuge. He threatened to harm Mischa if I didn't come back. Then…" she stopped, taking a shuddering breath. "I had to protect her," she said, looking directly at Maggie. "I sent him a message that if he so much as harmed a hair on Mischa's head, I would kill his son."

"Wow," Maggie whispered. "Do you need a break?"

"I could do with stretching my legs." She stood up. "Do you have a garden?"

"Don't go out there," Zelah interjected, "we know that Kennet is having us watched and possibly followed. Better if we can keep you indoors."

"Come with me into the kitchen," Maggie said, "and I'll close the blinds." She glanced over at Zelah and shot her a puzzled look.

"Man with dog," Zelah muttered, "well, he could be right."

"You really do have a nice house," Michelle remarked, glancing into the living room as they walked past and into the kitchen.

"My great-grandfather built this house," Maggie explained as she shut the blinds. "It's a strange story, a bit eerie. I'll tell you sometime."

"Does Maze Investigations do a lot of eerie?"

"Yes we're all a bit odd. We have another partner called Nick. He's odd too." She smiled and filled another glass of cold water from the American-style double fridge.

"I've always wanted one of those," Michelle said, her eyes narrowing, taking the glass.

"If this all works out, your life might change."

Michelle gave her an 'as if' look with a *tsking* sound and walked back to the office.

"Let's keep going. I stayed with friends for a while, until my hands improved. The hospital wanted me to have plastic surgery, but I couldn't risk it. He would have found out, somehow. I went away. My friends gave me some money and I went to London. I thought I could get a job, make a life for myself, and then somehow come back and at least get Mischa out of there. How stupid was that?" She stopped, laughed and shook her head. "I couldn't hold down a job; kept getting fired. Then I fell in with a bad crowd, turned to alcohol, then drugs." Her hands shook and one of her feet was tapping out an inharmonious rhythm on the floor. "I was homeless after that. I lived on the streets for a couple of years, feeding my habit by stealing. I was caught stealing one time too often and sent to prison." Her shoulders sagged. "For two years."

"Just for theft?" Zelah asked.

"No, for mugging the old man that I stole from. I'd hit rock bottom. I was ashamed of who I had become.

"But it gave me the chance to get off the drugs. Not easy. Not easy at all. But I did it. I slowly pulled my life back together. Found a job when I came out. Then I decided to come back to Newport, see what had happened to my family, my children."

Maggie put her hand on Michelle's arm, but Michelle pulled away. "I don't need your pity."

"Sympathy not pity," Maggie replied. "We're not judging you."

She glanced at Maggie from under lowered lids. "Once I'd tracked Mischa down, I've been watching her, from a distance, for the last two years. I was delighted when she went to the local college. I found the job at the bakery; lots of the students come there. That's it. What now?"

"That ball is in your court," Zelah replied. "If you want to meet Mischa we can arrange that. When she came to us for help, she was giving you the benefit of the doubt. She has no respect for her father. It's been a lonely life for her, without anyone caring for or about her. But she's remarkably resilient. She knows now that you left, chose to leave her and her brother. She isn't judging you, either, but she will want answers. Up to you if you want to face her and tell her what you've told us."

Michelle cocked her head to one side, gave Zelah a probing look. "I don't know, I'll have to think about it." She stood up and started for the door.

"Don't take too long," Zelah said. "The first person through your bakery door tomorrow morning may be your husband, who isn't going to listen to what you have to say, about anything."

"Only if you tell him where I am."

"Oh for fuck's sake," Zelah said, "we told you he's watching us. He doesn't know that we're even looking for you. We want him out of our lives and the only way we're going to get that is for you to help us."

"So this is just all about you? I thought as much. You're just a selfish bunch of self-interested…"

"Oh no we're not," Zelah interrupted. "We need something from you, yes. Maggie caught the look when she mentioned it and I did too, but it's also about Mischa." She paused for a moment. "Michelle, I'm not a person for being careful in what I say or trying to find the right words. With me it just comes out, so here it is. Everything has changed; everything. Kennet is looking for you. Mischa knows that you are not dead and are possibly close by. I like your daughter. Personally, I would tell her everything, but we have no right to interfere in your relationship with her. If you choose to meet her, that's up to you. The danger is all about Kennet. We need a plan, all of us."

Michelle stopped and ran a gloved hand through her hair, making it stand up on end.

"You want the brooch," she said without turning around.

"Exactly, yes, we do. It's the best, the only real solid piece of evidence we have to stop Rufus Quinn getting the statue put up. You do still have it?"

Michelle turned around to face them. "Yes, I have it, I don't know why. I could have sold it years ago but somehow I never did. I tried, but each time something stopped me. On that Christmas morning, Mischa called it my sparkly shiny fairy brooch. She probably doesn't remember. It was the only thing I had that in any way connected me with her. I couldn't let it go, no matter how bad things were." She walked back to the table and sat down again. "If you are sure that it can stop Kenny, then you can have it. But that isn't enough, is it?"

"If you mean stopping the statue, then there's another piece of evidence we could do with," Zelah said. "The one that Kennet stole, or arranged to have stolen from the archives. There's something else potentially," Maggie raised her eyebrows with a surprised look towards Zelah. Ignoring this Zelah went on, "if you mean about you and Mischa, as I said, everything has changed. You can never go back to how it was. If you give us the brooch and we use it, he will know it came from you. If you don't give us the brooch but you do tell Mischa that you're her mother, he is bound to find out. He will hunt you down because he wants the brooch. If you choose to walk away… well, he's going to find you, sooner rather than later. There are any number of scenarios. Although you don't come out well in any of them, there is something I can offer you."

"What's the quid pro quo? You want to help me out of the goodness of your heart?"

Zelah smiled. "My friends and colleagues will tell you, if there is any goodness in my heart it's never on display. I don't wear my heart on my sleeve. I'm a tough woman. Don't think you're the only one who's had a hard life. My hard times were just as bad as yours. Now, I have a lot of money and I do have both a conscience and some morals. I will help you evade Kennet, whatever your decision. You have to decide whether to believe me and you have to decide now. We're out of time."

Michelle looked slowly from one to the other, examining them, weighing them up. Looking, so Maggie thought, for signs of deception and lying. They all stared back.

"I have been self-reliant for so long it's hard to trust anyone who appears out of the blue, offering hope, and perhaps redemption. I need time." She held up her hands, "I accept that's a luxury I don't have. I need a bit of space."

Chapter 28

She stood up and paced, first around the room, then into the kitchen and back again. As she walked, she moved her hands in time with the conversation in her head, her lips moving silently. She stopped, paused, then started pacing again. After five minutes she came back into the office, where no-one had spoken since she started pacing.

Facing them cross the table she said "As I see it, there are just two options now. One, I walk away. You said you'll protect me. This is the easiest and the most selfish option. If I take it, I have to accept I will never see my daughter again. I have already given up hope of reconciling with my son, but my daughter…" She breathed in heavily. "Two, I reveal myself and I must tell her everything. I have to risk her rejection in which case I will lose her anyway." Maggie opened her mouth to speak but Zelah kicked her under the table.

"OK, I have to take that chance. I don't know why I'm trusting you, probably because I think Mischa trusts you?"

"Yes, she does," Zelah replied.

"She's young and given how she's been treated by her father, I think it's a miracle that she trusts anyone."

"She's also tough and an optimist," Zelah replied. "Those are the reasons I like her. I've said a few harsh things to her but she hasn't judged me."

"It's not the same."

"No, it's not. But anyway."

"How do we do this, and when?"

"As soon as possible," Maggie said. "Best to get on with it. Not give yourself time to change your mind. Tomorrow morning?"

"I start work at ten. Can we do it before that?"

"I have to see Mischa first," Zelah said, "to prepare her. No, before you argue, we won't tell her anything personal about you; that's your decision. All she needs to know is she's about to meet you."

Michelle nodded.

"I'll text her this evening, to tell her that we need to speak to her first thing tomorrow. I'll say there's been a development, we have a lead and someone for her to meet. I'll arrange to pick her up in the usual place and I'll book a room at a hotel, probably the Celtic Manor. When she's settled I'll leave her with Maggie and come to get you. What happens after that? We'll have to wait and see. That's as much as we can arrange for now."

"Good. I need to go home now. I need some time alone."

"Our escort is still outside. Let's go." Zelah stood up, giving Maggie no time to say anything, and headed out to her car.

"Thank you," Michelle said to Maggie. "Although I'm not sure that I'm going to stay grateful to you."

Maggie went back into the office and flopped down on the settee next to Jack.

"This is not a normal day," she said,

"Couldn't do this all the time. Why do you think she decided to not walk away? I thought she was going to at one point."

"Me too. She was treated like property, not like a human, then discarded when no longer wanted, like an old settee. She's been through hell. Look at her, she's only thirty-eight or thirty-nine."

"No way, she looks older than Zelah."

"Like she said, drugs, alcohol, abuse, prison; but she still has a tough carapace."

"A what?"

"An outer shell, external skeleton, impenetrable, like a tortoise. Nothing gets through, except something just did. She loves her daughter and she seems prepared to take this risk."

"That's brave."

"She might turn out to be a brave woman."

"Who might?" The voice made them jump. "I just saw Zelah leaving with Eric. Is she going home?" Bob half sat on the table in front of them, arms crossed.

"Yes but she's taking someone home first."

"There was someone else in the car? Who?"

"That was Michelle Quinn, in the back. The dark windows work."

He rubbed his chin. "You found her. Well done, I have to admit. Did you get what you wanted?"

"Sort of, we're getting the brooch, so we're a step closer to stopping the Quinns and their benighted statue. She's going to meet Mischa in the morning." She stood up. "We're going to need your help."

"Of course," he replied immediately. "Just because Zelah can be a bloody reckless fool, doesn't mean I'm not going to keep you safe. Come on, let's get a beer for the boys and a G&T for you. We'll go outside and enjoy the last bit of sun."

It spoke volumes for Maggie's fuddled brain that she didn't object to Jack drinking alcohol.

**

Bob ordered a takeaway to be delivered, and whilst they were waiting a text arrived from Zelah.

"She's going straight home," Maggie read. "She wants to know if I can get over to her in the morning so we can pick Michelle up and take her to the hotel."

"I'll take you," Bob said, "and I have some good news, for me at least. We've got another lead from a tenant who's been threatened. I'm setting up a meet some time tomorrow. I'll sort someone else to stay at the hotel with you and get you back home."

Another text pinged.

"She'd sent a message to Mischa, who's up for it. So it's all go. God, I hope we're doing the right thing."

Before she could say any more the phone rang. "Alice. I'll take this inside."

The food arrived while she was on the phone and Bob organised them ready to eat. Maggie returned with a rueful grin.

Bob paused in uncovering cardboard dishes. "What now?"

"Her friend Matthew, who she spent the weekend with. His parents have a villa in the Dordogne and they've invited the same group to spend a month with them in the summer. Alice is desperate to go. The latest obsession is the Lascaux caves and pre-history. She says all of the others have permission from their parents to go."

She plonked herself down in front of the food. "What do you think? Will it be safe? What?" Bob kept his head down, as he dished himself up spoonfuls of rice and noodles. "Bob?" she asked again, more forcefully.

"She'll be as well protected there as anywhere else, probably better. His father is… someone in my line of work but much higher up. A different branch, if get my meaning. Don't ask me anymore, I can't tell you. I recognised the name when you told me who she was spending the weekend with. I expect the place in the Dordogne is like a fortress. Believe me, if Kennet Quinn were to try anything, he's likely to end up in the Tower. Now don't give me that look, it's only been a couple of days since I knew and we've been busy with other stuff. Alice will be safe," he said as he shovelled food into his mouth.

Maggie sat back, thinking, "I'll trust you on this one. It's a relief to know. I suppose I have to say, 'yes' now."

"When's she going?" Jack asked.

204

"I'll be picking her up Friday when school finishes. She'll go with them on the following Monday morning. They'll pick her up from here and head down to the ferry for Monday night."

"Nice for her," Jack said non-commitally. Maggie was about to reply when Bob interrupted.

"Given me a thought," he said. "How about a plan for once this is all over? When Alice is safely in the Dordogne we can take my camper van, the three of us, and head down there too? We could all do with a break, but of course, it depends on how my whistle-blower works out."

"Great," Jack replied, "Just what I was thinking."

"I'll think about it," Maggie said, smiling. "We've only just come back from a holiday but I'm always ready for a new adventure, of the right kind."

"Roll on tomorrow," Jack said, beaming at them.

Maggie rolled her eyes up to the slowly fading blue sky.

**

She woke at 5am and knew that there would be no more sleep. She lay awake for a while thinking about where they were, with just two days left before the Council meeting. Zelah hadn't heard back yet from the Mayor so they didn't know what her proposal for stopping the statue might be. They had to keep gathering information and evidence for their own sakes.

They could prove through the DNA results that Adolphus Quinn was really Thomas Ryan but that meant exposing Mischa's involvement. They had the information from Celia Ryan that the Ryan family believed that Thomas Ryan had been involved in the death of the real Adolphus Quinn, though this was only hearsay. They had, or would soon have, the brooch taken from Ada Blackstock. They had a copy of the letter from her family that described it well enough to prove it was hers. What they didn't have was the letter left by Thomas Bale, with the supposedly more solid police information. There was no way to get their hands on the original, if Kennet Quinn hadn't already burned it. There had been nothing from Jennifer Quinn in response to their enquiry.

They were so close now, but what more was there that she could do? She hated having nothing more to follow up. The only matter outstanding was the response from Jennifer Quinn; if there was going to be one. And the information from the Glamorgan Archives needed a follow up, although it was unlikely to reveal anything useful. Why would Ada Blackstock put something on a church record that she hadn't put on her son's birth certificate? Maggie knew that for the legal record, the father had to be present to give his consent to being named as the father on the birth certificate. This was why, following the birth of a child to a single female, it was either the mother or another female relative who often registered the birth. Usually the father had no wish to be associated with his illegitimate child. The church didn't ask for such proof. Maggie had only known of one case they had investigated where the records were different. This had been where the mother had registered the birth without the father's name. Following this, she and her husband, who had known that the real father was his own brother, had gone to church and named themselves as the parents. In that case they had given the child immediately to a maiden aunt to bring up, then moved away. Therefore no-one else in the family – except the real father – had even known that the child existed. They would have been horrified to know that that revealer of dark secrets – the internet – would one day expose their sham respectability. She didn't judge them. They had been creatures of their own time, trapped by Victorian two-faced morality and respectability.

Back to the present. She could check to see if there were responses to either enquiry.

Bob had been working a night shift and wasn't due home

until around eight. He was going to take Maggie down to Newport to meet up with Zelah, who would then pick up Michelle, and drive to the hotel. Another member of his team would then take over. She knew, too, that he couldn't keep this up, couldn't justify the cost, for much longer. The pressure was on everywhere.

Eventually she got up, showered and dressed ready to go out. There was still enough time to check her computer, where she was delighted to find that there were responses from both parties awaiting her.

She decided to start with the Glamorgan Archives. They had found, scanned and sent the information on the baptism to Maze. A quick first glance showed that there was no father listed, as expected. She scanned through the other information available. Not much there. Just the date, the mother's name and address and the son's given name. What she saw next caused her to jump out of her seat.

She was standing in front of the computer screen, mouth open, when Bob came in from work and saw her.

"Come on, we have to go, we're meeting Zelah in twenty minutes."

She nodded, "I'm ready" and grabbed her coat. "I have something to tell her that's going to shake this case to its foundations."

Chapter 29

She didn't get a chance to talk to Zelah until they reached the hotel.

It was a five minute journey from Zelah's flat to the bedsit, where Michelle lived. She was hovering inside the door waiting for them. In the car the discussion was about what Zelah was going to say to Mischa. Again, it was barely a five minute journey onwards to the hotel.

Zelah drove behind Maggie and Bob into the underground carpark. She had already cleared a way to check in without speaking to reception. Money spoke louder than regulations and she wasn't unknown at the hotel. Michelle pulled on a floppy hat and dark glasses, as they took great care to get her out of the car and into the lift in seconds. The lift took them up to the third floor, where Zelah had booked a suite. Michelle did a double take when she saw the suite.

As Michelle looked around Maggie whispered to Zelah, "Who does Mischa think she's coming to meet?"

"I told her it's the woman from the bakery."

"Does she suspect this might be her mother?"

"No. It isn't my place to tell her. She thinks the woman is a relative."

She went back to her car and left to fetch Mischa, as Michelle gazed around at the opulence and luxury.

"Nice way to live," she said to Maggie. "Where's the coffee machine? I need some. I haven't slept well."

Maggie found the machine, made coffee for Michelle and tea for herself. Zelah had also ensured that there was a supply of pastries, so they wouldn't have to call room service and have any staff see them. Michelle took a plateful and sat down in front of the TV screen that filled half of the wall.

Apart from the CCTV no-one had seen them come in and hopefully no-one would see them leave.

**

At the Quinn house Mischa was hopping with anticipation. She had positioned herself in the kitchen, where no-one was likely to see her, waiting for Zelah's text to say that she was outside the cathedral. Gerry had appeared for a few minutes, too hung over to notice his sister's mood, ignored her, made coffee and left. She stuck her tongue out at his back, as the text arrived. Running up the stairs from the basement and into the hall, she paused for a moment, to compose herself, in case anyone appeared from one of the other rooms. She knew that her father was about by his light, quick tread; Rufus rarely surfaced before eleven.

As she was about to set off the doorbell rang. She stopped. Kennet appeared from his office, ignored and walked past her to the front door. He opened it to a young red-headed woman. Mischa decided to wait until he and the woman had passed. Her father hadn't asked where she was going, as he usually did when she was dressed in her full Goth look. Today she had settled for the clothes, but not the makeup.

She gave the young woman what she hoped was a disinterested look as she and her father passed by. She didn't make eye contact with her father. As she hoped, Kennet took no notice, but the woman paused for a brief second to look at her, then walked on.

As soon as the office door closed Mischa ran to the front door, let herself out and closed it with a bang behind her. Banging the door loudly was one of her trademarks. No need to alert Pa by behaving any differently.

Zelah was waiting at the bottom end of the cathedral, Bob a few yards away. No-one had followed the girl. She jumped into

209

Zelah's car and they set off.

**

Back at the Quinn house Kennet sat in one armchair in front of the unlit fire. The young woman took the other and he poured coffee for both of them.

As he handed it to her, she asked "Who was that girl in the hallway?"

"My daughter," Kennet replied, his cup to his lips. He sipped lightly at the coffee, "why do you ask Helen?"

Helen Redland rubbed her cup across her bottom lip. "I've seen her before, recently. I have a good memory for faces. Where was it?" She leaned forward to put the cup back on its saucer, took out her phone and scanned through it… "Oh, yes, I remember."

**

Zelah gave Mischa the information they had agreed. Nearing the hotel the girl, who had so far talked non-stop, went quiet as it came into the view. As they entered the underground car park Zelah could see Mischa's hands shaking. She pulled the car into a parking slot as close to the lifts as she could, turned off the engine, then leaned over and put her hands on Mischa's.

"It will be OK, just give it a chance and listen. I know I'm not a great one for taking my own advice, but just be as calm as you can, OK?"

"I'm scared."

"Of what?"

"I dunno, of what I'll find out, I guess."

"The truth is always easier than whatever's in your imagination. Remember that."

The girl nodded and the lift arrived. As it started to move Mischa turned to Zelah and gave her a quick hug. "Thank you for… whatever."

Zelah felt herself hugging back.

210

The lift reached the third floor and they stepped out. Mischa was shaking so much that Zelah had to put an arm on her back and guide her down the corridor to the suite. She rang the bell and Maggie opened the door, stood back and ushered them in.

Michelle had turned off the TV and was sitting on one of the settees. Mischa stopped dead when she saw her. "You," she said in a deadpan voice, "you know my mother?"

Michelle stood up, rocking from leg to leg. Twice she opened her mouth then closed it again. After several agonising seconds she jerked her head and spat out the words. "Yes. No. I am your mother, Mischa. Sorry."

**

Kennet Quinn stood up and walked over to the window. He stayed there for a few minutes, staring down at the beautifully groomed garden, in which he never sat. Helen Redland didn't move.

After slowly moving his head from side to side like a rocking cradle he turned back to her.

"Thank you for that information. It's interesting. We should go now."

Helen jumped up, picked up her coat and bag and made her way to the door, followed by Kennet. As they reached the front door he stopped he said, "wait a moment please," and turned to the stairs. Rufus and Gerard were on their way down from their rooms on the first floor, arguing good naturedly about a Welsh football player who had missed an open goal. They stopped midway when they saw Kennet.

"Helen and I are going to meet the undertaker to arrange Timothy's funeral. Mischa has gone out. She should be back some time this morning. Please inform me immediately she returns."

"Shall we tell her you're looking for her," Gerry asked, a

malicious smile on his face, knowing his sister was never wanted in person for anything good.

"Tell her nothing," Kennet replied as he ushered Helen through the front door.

The two men looked at each other and shrugged, then continued their discussion as they made their way down to the kitchen.

**

Mischa Quinn took a step backwards and Zelah put a hand at her back to steady her. She sensed that the step was due to shock rather than a deliberate movement away from Michelle, but Michelle had seen the backwards motion. She turned away and walked to the window, hugging herself, staring out at the view of the Bristol Channel across to Somerset.

"Why don't you both sit down?" Maggie said. "It might help."

Zelah leaned over to Mischa. "Your mother has a story to tell you. Whatever the outcome, you should listen." She gave the girl a gentle push towards an armchair and walked over to the window, led Michelle to the settee and sat her down. She took the second armchair next to Mischa and indicated to Maggie to sit next to Michelle.

When all four were facing each other she said, "This is it. This is the one chance that both of you are going to get. Make the most of it. Mischa, you probably can't think of Michelle as your mother yet. Which is understandable. Michelle, you must understand that you've been chatting to Mischa knowing that she was your daughter. She must be feeling deceived right now." She glanced at Mischa, who nodded. "The path you've both had to take to get to this point has been one on which the majority of people would have fallen and never got back up. The fact that you are both here is testament to your strength and resilience. I don't often say anything that nice about

212

anyone," this time looking at Maggie who nodded emphatically. "I am asking you both to set aside whatever your feelings are right now and listen to what each other has to say. Be open and answer each other's questions honestly. Don't hold back. I believe that honesty always brings you to the best place, no matter how hard it is." She sat back. "Who wants to go first?"

"I will," said Michelle, "if that's OK with you Mischa?" The girl nodded. "Can I have a glass of water first?"

Maggie jumped up and poured one, put it on the table in front of Michelle and sat down next to her.

"I'm going to tell you everything. You're not a child any more, and I haven't been able to protect you from whatever you've undergone at the hands of your father. So I am going to be brutally honest. And some of what you're going to hear will be brutal."

She spoke, slowly and hesitantly. She began to describe, in painstaking detail, the story of her life from her childhood to the present day. Her voice was monotone, she didn't ask for pity, understanding or comment. Some of the time she looked down at the table, but mostly she looked at Mischa. A couple of times Zelah noticed that Mischa shuddered. When Michelle talked about what had happened to her hands the girl's expression was murderous. When Michelle had finished she said, "that's it," and sat back on the settee. She leaned forward to pick up her glass of water but couldn't hold it steady.

Zelah jumped in. "Leave that, we'll get you a hot drink, you need one. Now, does anyone need a break?" No-one spoke. "Mischa, what do you want to do next? Do you want to tell Michelle your story or do you want to ask her anything about what's she's just said?"

"I can talk about what it's been like for me."

"Good, do you need a drink?"

"No."

"Off you go then."

Chapter 30

Mischa's description of her life was much shorter. She talked about how lonely her childhood had been, no friends allowed back to her house and how other children stopped inviting her to parties because she never had one herself. She talked about how no-one had been interested in what she had achieved at school, how there was never any praise for her, not even when she passed eleven GCSEs all at A and A* grades, or when she achieved her four A Levels again with top star grades. She told Michelle that she had gone to college to try to make friends there. Older kids were more understanding about difficult parents, so no-one judged her. And she explained how chatting to Michelle in the bakery store was the first chance she had to talk about herself and her ambitions. "You were encouraging," she said, "I liked that. I told you that I wanted to go to university and you encouraged me to have a go, but when I explained that my father wouldn't have it you never said anything. Why not?"

"I'm sorry," Michelle replied. "I was boiling, seething inside, but I couldn't show it. I was so proud of you, though.

"I felt that a bit. It seemed odd, you know, coming from a stranger." She smiled.

Then she talked about how she had overheard Kennet saying that he was looking for her, that he needed something. That was when she had knew for definite that Michelle really wasn't dead. She had suspicions already, but assumed there had been something dodgy about Michelle's death; suicide perhaps. Then Zelah and Maggie came to visit and she heard them tell Kennet they knew that Michelle wasn't dead. She asked them to help and they had.

As each woman spoke, the tense atmosphere lifted a fraction. They had both been as stiff as dress shop dummies when they began, but as they listened and spoke they began to move, leaning at times towards each other. Maggie felt a glimmer of hope that they might come to accept each other after all, which had seemed unlikely at the start of this strange meeting.

As Mischa finished speaking Michelle had leaned down to her handbag, reached in and taken something out, wrapped in tissue paper. She handed it to Maggie, who opened it.

"I've kept it in good condition, taken care of it." She turned to her daughter, who stood, walked across and knelt next to Maggie.

"I remember this," she whispered and looked up at Michelle, "your fairy badge."

Tears glistened in Michelle's eyes. She wiped them away with the back of her sleeve. She reached out to touch Mischa's head, but changed her mind and pulled her arm back.

Mischa didn't see it.

"Let me see." Zelah put her hand out and Maggie passed over the brooch. It was just as the letter from Ada Blackstock's sister had described. Small, with exquisite and intricate gold filigree, rectangular in shape and interlaid with tiny amber stones.

"We can keep this?" she asked Michelle.

"Yes, put it to good use."

Mischa returned to her seat. "Why does Pa want it so badly?"

"Because it belonged to one of the women Adolphus Quinn murdered, a woman called Ada Blackstock," Zelah replied. "We believe he took it from her. He took trophies." She paused for a moment, frowning. "This was an odd one. She was an odd one. Before her he'd only killed prostitutes, so it's difficult to understand why he picked Ada. She was respectable, apart from being a single mother, which was not considered decent back then. Victorians were sanctimonious hypocrites, but Ada was a respected medium and well known. It was probably just a random chance, that he came upon her close to the place where he'd taken some of the women to torture and kill them."

"Not random chance, actually."

Zelah's head snapped up to look at Maggie. "What?"

"It came this morning, the report from the Glamorgan Archives. They found the baptism details."

"You mean it does name the father?" Zelah turned to Michelle and Mischa. "Maggie and I need to talk about this, but it's just detail and you don't have to listen. We'll go into the bedroom and talk. You can stay here and talk to each other," and she went to get up, but Michelle stopped her.

"No way, I want to hear it. They told me the whole story yesterday," she said to Mischa. "I get why your father wanted the brooch so badly and I want to hear if there's something new."

"Me too," Mischa added eyes shining. "If it screws Pa even further, I want to hear it."

Michelle laughed.

"OK with me," Zelah replied. "Maggie?"

"Yep, OK" She got her tablet out of her bag, hit the start button and accessed her emails. "Prepare to be shocked and awed. We thought it was random he came across Ada that night. Maybe it was, maybe it wasn't, but his motivation wasn't murder. It was the brooch. Remember the letter from Ada's family, her sister, to the police? It's the one that asked for the brooch to be returned, as it had sentimental value, with a connection for her son. We thought that meant that it was given to Ada by the father?"

"Although she didn't name the father on the birth

certificate. Don't tell me she put his name on the baptism register?" Zelah said.

"No, and yes."

"Oh for fuck's sake, explain!"

Maggie glanced at Michelle and Mischa, but their expressions mirrored Zelah's.

"There were various types of baptismal records, some basic, some with more detail. This church used the type with good detail, similar to the birth certificate. The father's name is blank, with only Ada recorded as a parent. Where it differs from the birth certificate is that on the birth certificate she named her son as Henry George Blackstock. On the baptism record he's Henry Adolphus Blackstock."

Zelah jumped up from her chair, snatched the tablet from Maggie and glared at the contents of the email and the copy of the baptismal entry.

"Fuck's sake. Adolphus Quinn was the father. He came across her wearing the brooch, realised he'd made a huge mistake and took it back."

"Exactly what I thought," Maggie said. "Speculation, but it's a definite possibility, as Bob would say. Ironically, the missing brooch was never made public, an enormous error by the police. The family's letter gave them the information and a good description. If it was a commissioned piece, a jeweller might have recognised it. Perhaps Adolphus had been thinking the same. He might have known that she was attending a séance that evening and set up the meeting, we don't know. We also don't know if Ada's family ever knew who he was, but what they did know was the brooch was a connection to baby Henry's father. The policeman in charge, Inspector Freeman, should have picked that up."

"It explains why Adolphus picked such a different woman to kill. He made it look like all of the others but it wasn't. Do you think he knew that she had given his name at the baptism?" Zelah said.

"Could it have been a co-incidence, giving the baby that name?" Michelle asked.

"I don't think so," Maggie replied. "If it had been on the birth certificate as well it might have been co-incidence; but different names on two documents? No, I would say she knew what she was doing."

"I agree," Zelah replied, "I'm wondering how they met?"

"I have an idea about that," Maggie said. She turned to Mischa. "Your father is a superstitious man, isn't he?"

"Pa? Yeh, he's obsessed with spirits and all that. He thinks there are witches and demons and stuff." She turned to Zelah. "He probably thinks you're one, after you made that door slam."

"I'd forgotten all that," Michelle said. "I remember once he slammed my head into the wall because I put a pair of shoes on the table. Apparently, it's a guarantee of bad luck."

"Well he is paranoid," Zelah replied.

"You remember, Zelah, in one of those newspaper articles, Adolphus Quinn talked about evil in the world and never going out on Halloween or Beltane Eve?"

"No, don't think I saw that one."

"I read them all," Maggie said. "Again, we can only speculate now, but the Victorians were fixated with the spirit world. He might have attended a séance, perhaps one of Ada's, and they hit it off. He was a charming and attractive man, after all."

"When he wasn't being a psycho murderer, and what's Beltane eve?" Mischa interjected.

"Exactly, and Beltane is the equivalent of May Day. The Eve of Beltane has similarities with Halloween, spooky things. All old Celtic and pagan traditions, look it up. Anyway, it's all conjecture now. It does look like Adolphus was Henry Blackstock's father, doesn't it." Zelah stopped and slapped her forehead. "That also means that Isobel is related to the Quinns." She turned to Maggie. "Do you think she has any idea?"

"Probably not," Maggie replied, "and we aren't going to tell her."

"Fair enough, she's on her own with this one. Isobel started all of this," she said to Michelle and Mischa. "For now, we have to decide what to do next. I think you two might like some more time to talk to each other. You both realise that everything has changed, right? Mischa, I don't even know if it's safe for you to go home. As soon as Kennet finds out we have the brooch, he'll know we've found Michelle." She stood up and walked around the room.

"He's not interested in me," Mischa said, "he won't notice if I'm there or not. I meant to tell you, I know where that other letter is, the one you said was stolen from the archives, the police letter. It's in his desk drawer in a file and I think I can get it out. He'll never know it was me."

"Of course he'll know," Zelah snapped. "Think about it, how many people have access to his office?"

"I could copy it, there's a photocopier in there."

"No Mischa," Maggie said, "it's too dangerous. I agree with Zelah. She's right, it may even be too dangerous for you to stay at home, now. Just one slip of the tongue… we have to get you out."

"I'm going to suggest something to both of you, for you to take away and think about," Zelah said. "It will mean a complete change of life. I have a friend in Canada. In the first instance I can take you there. We'll need to give you new names when you get there. We can talk to Bob about how that can happen, there will be a way. Then, I have a place in Ireland.

You can stay there longer. It's a lovely house and it's being used as an education centre for children, with lots of horses and plenty to do. It has security, good security. Don't say anything now. Think about it."

"I'll have to think about it," Michelle replied. "It's a lot to take in. Mischa?"

The girl looked around at them. "It's a big thing," she said. "I'd need to get some stuff from home. I'll go back, grab a few things and leave again. I don't have a passport. Will that matter?"

"Oh, me neither," Michelle added. "Might be a problem with my criminal background."

"You will be able to get one. They can be done quickly," Zelah said. "We will have to check if Canada will let you in. It should be OK, if we say it's just for a holiday."

She turned to Maggie. "I don't think there's any harm in Mischa going home, for a couple of hours. Kennet doesn't know anything about her knowing us."

"Not that we know," Maggie said. "I don't like it, Mischa. Don't even think about trying to get that police report. Go in, get your stuff and let Zelah know as soon you can leave safely. Whatever you both decide, you need to talk about it. Perhaps they could stay here tonight, Zelah? This suite has two bedrooms. They can talk it over, decide what they want to do. It's not up to us, is it?"

"I have it booked for two days; you would be safe."

Mischa nodded, but Michelle looked wary.

"Anyway, we're done for now. Let's go. We'll drop Michelle off at her bedsit, then take Mischa back to the cathedral car park. We have some work to do, too."

"There's also a reply from Jennifer Quinn," Maggie said, "that I haven't even opened yet."

At the cathedral, before Mischa was out of the car, Zelah

said to her "Call me as soon as possible and don't do anything stupid."

Mischa gave her a wry smile and jumped down from the car. "Don't worry so much, I'm invisible in that house and at last that's a good thing. It'll be OK."

**

Back at Maggie's house, before they tackled the response from Jennifer Quinn they gave themselves time to talk over what had happened that morning.

"I think Kennet knew about the brooch and its significance. It stands to reason. Could Kennet himself have been 'Mr Smith'?" Maggie said. "If he found the letter from Ada's family he would have recognised the description and known that it was the brooch, handed down in the family that he had given to Michelle. This also means that he and Rufus knew everything about the man they still call Adolphus Quinn, and what he was responsible for."

Zelah shook her head. "Why didn't he take that letter too? It doesn't make sense, maybe he didn't think through the significance of it until later? No, he's not that careless; something stopped him. Could someone have come along, seen him and he had to put the letter back? No, he could have asked for a photocopy. Oh, I don't know. I'll talk to Ben at the archives. As for Rufus, if he wants a knighthood, that ambition has overridden every moral or principle he ever had. If he ever had any."

"Doesn't it make you sick to your stomach," Maggie said, "that they were prepared to cover it all up? Do you think they found out before Rufus got the statue approved at the sub-committee, or after?"

"Difficult to say, there aren't any clues for either option, are there?"

"I haven't thought about it 'til now. Let's catch up with

whatever Jennifer Quinn is bringing to the party."

Chapter 31

Jennifer Quinn's email turned out to be usefully informative. She knew the history of Adolphus Quinn, her whole family did. Without having been asked she said that the family believed they knew the identity of the killer, but it was never proved. She was working until three but happy to speak to them after that, to discuss the case further. Her family had always said they would welcome any information that shed light on this aspect of their history and she gave her phone number.

Maggie checked her watch. "Three thirty. We should call now. Let's not lose the momentum if she's willing to speak."

They dialled the number and it was answered on the first ring. "Jennifer Quinn."

"Jennifer, hello, this is Maggie Gilbert of Maze Investigations. Thanks for getting back to us so quickly. I'm here with my colleague, Zelah Trevear. May we talk to you about your ancestor, Adolphus Quinn?"

"Please do, Mrs Gilbert, I looked up your website when I had your email - it's impressive." Jennifer's voice had the soft melodic Irish open-vowel tone of the west coast.

"Thank you, please call me Maggie and my colleague is Zelah. I can see from your tree that your two times great-grandfather was Michael Quinn, the youngest brother of Adolphus. But I'm thinking that he never knew him, as he was born in the year that Adolphus died?"

"That's correct," Jennifer replied. "Though he did know the story of Adolphus' death, which was terrible, as it had been passed down through the family. I heard it from my grandfather Cillian Quinn. My dad isn't too interested, but he knows the story too."

224

"Is Cillian still alive?"

"Oh, yes, he certainly is, he's seventy-nine, he'll be eighty next year. He remembers his grandfather Michael. Michael lived into his eighties, too, he died in the nineteen sixties. We're a healthy long-lived family, the Quinns."

"That's good for you then. So, what do you know about Adolphus?"

"Before I answer that, can I ask you a question?"

Maggie looked at Zelah, who nodded, "Of course."

"I am presuming that your client has some information about Adolphus' death. Who is your client and what does he or she know?"

"I can't tell you the name of our client, Jennifer. I can tell you it's a 'she', and she asked us to help when she got a DNA test that gave her some interesting and unexpected family information. From that information we uncovered the story of Adolphus' murder."

"Has whatever you have uncovered told you anything about who might have killed him?"

Again, Maggie checked for a confirmatory nod from Zelah, about what she was thinking. "Yes, it does. We have a name. I'm guessing you have a name too. Shall we tell each other that family name?"

"You go first," Jennifer Quinn said.

"OK, the name we have is Thomas Ryan."

There was a long expelled breath on the other end of the phone.

"Yes, that's the name we have too."

"Is there a story behind how you know this name?" Zelah asked.

"Yes, I'll tell you now. Remember though, my great-great-grandfather Michael wasn't there. He was told this by his eldest sister, Caitlin, who was thirteen at the time. The children were

225

playing out in the street. Dolly, that's what they called Adolphus, was playing with his soldiers. His father, Bernard made them for him; he was a carpenter. Anyway, the Doll and his best friend…"

Zelah interrupted with, "Sorry, the Doll?"

"Yes, that's how he was known too. He was said to have been a beautiful little boy, like a painted doll, black hair, blue eyes, and a lovely nature. His sisters all adored him. Why do you ask?"

"We were told about the Doll, but we didn't really understand. I had supposed it was a kind of nickname, but just checking, for confirmation, please carry on."

"Well, these soldiers were something special. Dolly and Sean Ryan – that was his best friend, the same age – were playing with the soldiers with some other children. Along came Sean's big brother Thomas, and another brother Martin. Thomas wanted to see the soldiers, to hold them but Dolly said no. No-one liked Thomas Ryan. He was about fourteen or fifteen and had a reputation as a bully. He tried to take the soldiers off Dolly, but the little lad hung onto them. Thomas hit him but he hadn't reckoned with Dolly's sister Caitlin Quinn. The story is that she launched herself at him, jumped on his back and clawed at his face, and bit a lump out of his ear."

Zelah punched the air, silently mouthing, 'Yes'!

"That was brave of her," Maggie said.

"Wasn't it just. Two other sisters and their mother heard the noise and came out to see what was going on. They pulled Thomas Ryan off and sent him on his way. Dolly had been hugging his soldiers, the same way he was still hugging them when his little body was found two weeks later."

She paused and Maggie thought that she caught the sound of a sob.

"Are you OK, Jennifer?"

226

"Yes sorry, yes, every time I think of what happened to that poor little boy I get upset. How he was dragged away, how terrified he must have been, and how much pain he must have suffered before he died. Sorry, that must sound silly, eh? Almost a hundred and twenty years ago, what's there to be upset about, indeed?"

"Of course you're upset," Maggie said. "The death of a child is horrible. What happened to little Adolphus, knowing the story; what you've just described has given me a lump in my throat."

"You said 'dragged away', I think," Zelah interjected. "Do you know that's what happened or are you just guessing?"

"That's the next part of the story," Jennifer replied. "There was a woman called Norah Maginnis."

Zelah punched the air again.

"She lived at the end of the toll road and next to her cottage was a lane that led to the woods where Dolly was found. She wouldn't tell the police anything, but if she had, I believe Thomas Ryan would have been arrested and probably hanged."

"Would have been better for many people if he had been," Zelah muttered. "What did she know?"

"Sounds like you have something to tell me," Jennifer Quinn said. Maggie scowled at Zelah.

"Let me rewind. There was a funeral for Dolly, of course and the Ryans all attended. Thomas Ryan approached Dolly's mother, crying and said how sorry he was. He hadn't intended any harm to the boy when he wanted to look at the soldiers. It was just that no-one had ever done anything so great for him and he had been jealous. He was ashamed now and would do anything to help find out who had killed Adolphus."

"And she believed him?" Zelah asked.

"Yes, she did. Apparently he was a clean cut, handsome boy and seemed sincere. The other kids hated him, mind you, but

227

Mrs Quinn took comfort from what he said. What a bastard he must have been. Anyway, a couple of weeks after the funeral Mrs Maginnis' cottage caught fire. There was evidence of arson they found out later, although at first they thought that she had been asleep and had left coals burning, when she was drunk, which they say she often was. She was brought out, but was in a bad way, and agitated. Her face had been burned and she could hardly speak, but she managed a few words before she died. I know them off by heart. They were, 'Four of them dragged him, down the lane. Soldiers, soldiers. I heard."

"Thomas Ryan and his two brothers, not four soldiers," Maggie said. "I think he would have had to drag Sean too but not Martin. Is there anything else we need to know?"

"Well, the search was concentrated on looking for four members of the local regiment and other soldiers in Clare. Some of them were a disreputable lot, but no-one could think why they would kill a child. Dolly had nothing for them. There was a suggestion of a sexual assault, he was a lovely looking boy… but they never found anyone for it. And that was the end of it, case closed."

"We read that he was found with his soldiers?" Zelah said.

"Yes, that's right, most of them."

"Some were missing, were they found?"

"There was evidence that one or two had been burned, plus there were burn marks on another. I believe that Thomas Ryan deliberately burned them in front of Dolly. He didn't stop there…" again she had to stop and breathe deeply.

"We know," Maggie said, "you don't have to tell us anymore."

"I have another question," Zelah said. "Did Thomas Ryan stay around?"

"Disappeared, him and his brother Martin. The family said that they had gone away to Dublin to find work. Now, you

228

have something to tell me, I think."

"Just one more bit of information, for detail. How many soldiers were there? Can't have been many for a little boy to clutch them all."

"Six, I think. His father had made them one for each rank and painted them individually. What was left were buried with him. Now, you have something to tell me, I think? Fair exchange of information as we agreed?"

"Right," Maggie said. "We believe that Thomas Ryan and Martin his brother didn't go to Dublin but to Liverpool, then moved around England and ended up in Wales."

"I hope he died a horrible death."

"He was murdered," Maggie said.

"Good. Do you know anything about it?"

"His death, you mean? No, not yet but we're hoping to find out at some point. Jennifer, I have something to ask you now. It's important and essential, for our client's safety. We need to ask you to bear with us for a while. I can't say for how long at the moment. We are getting more and more information and getting closer to the time when we can reveal what happened. But this is absolutely not the time. You see, Thomas Ryan had a family. We will eventually tell you all about it, but not at the moment. The health and safety of two women, one younger than you, is compromised by this story and if it gets out now they will both be in some difficulty. So we need secrecy from you and I promise we will tell you everything and hopefully give your family some measure of closure, after all this time. Until we can do that, I am asking you to keep this story secret from everyone in your family. Can you do that?"

For a few seconds there was silence on the end of the phone. Jennifer Quinn was weighing up her options.

"The person who would most like to know is my granddad. Can I tell him there's a lead?"

"Only if that's all you tell him," Zelah said, "but you can promise him that he will get the full story… soon."

"Yes, I can agree to that, will you please keep in touch?"

"Most definitely," Maggie replied, "and thank you, this hasn't been easy for you."

"Not at all, I'll look forward to hearing from you." She ended the call.

Maggie turned to Zelah. "It never fails to amaze me how much people relate so compassionately to their ancestors. Even after so much time has passed, old wrongs need to be righted."

"I might be able to get them all together, when this is over, at Rosscarbery," Zelah mused.

"Rosscarbery House is safe enough, Zelah?" Maggie's concern, that the house Zelah had inherited from her recently discovered Irish relatives would be easily discoverable by the Quinns, was its security.

"Of course it is," Zelah replied. "My nephews have made sure of that. They've installed additional safety measures. Their mad cousin won't get near the place without them knowing."

Maggie shook her head. Their all-too-recent history with the McCarthy Miller family, Zelah's niece Emer McCarthy Miller, who was on the run from the police, was still raw. But, she had to trust Zelah's judgement.

Zelah looked at her watch and frowned. "I haven't heard from Mischa. She should have got her stuff together by now."

"Maybe she can't get out at the moment, nor do we know how much she wants to bring. She might need to wait until the house is empty."

Zelah shrugged and walked off into the kitchen.

Another hour passed and there was still no word from Mischa. Maggie was starting to get twitchy. Jack offered to try to contact her, but they said no, they had to leave it up to her to get in touch. Michelle had called a couple of times and was also anxious but there was nothing any of them could do, only wait.

Chapter 32

Mischa arrived back at the Quinn house and had to pause on the doorstep to dial down her excitement. She still wasn't sure about how her relationship with Michelle would work out but she was willing to try. The fact that she was going away with somewhere to go, was the best thing that had happened to her for as long as she could remember. She approached the front door, put a dour, bored look on her face, just in case anyone was in the hall and entered as quietly as she could. She stood for a few minutes, listening, but the house was silent. She decided to pack her important stuff and crept up the stairs into her room. She hadn't noticed that her brother Gerry was sitting quietly in the lounge. Gerry was never normally quiet for any length of time. He usually behaved like an over-excited five year old and couldn't move around without making a lot of noise. He waited until she went upstairs, then took his phone out of his pocket and dialled.

Up in her room Mischa selected the biggest rucksack she could find and a smaller overnight bag. There wasn't much to choose from. She had few mementos, nothing worth taking with her. She had never been gifted with expensive or sentimental presents. She didn't want her Goth clothes; that was a look she could put behind her. She chose some practical clothes and her toiletries and stuffed them into the bags. Checking for noises from any of the bedrooms and hearing none, she walked out, closed her bedroom door and crept back down the stairs. Still no noise from the ground floor. She had moved quietly in case Grandpa was asleep somewhere. At the bottom of the stairs she had only to go through the hall to the front door and out. It was an exhilarating feeling that she would never return to this miserable excuse of a home again. She turned to the front door but noticed that the door to the office was open. The police letter. She knew it was in the desk drawer. Zelah needed it and she was the only one who could get it. Zelah and Maggie had both said no, leave it, they would be OK without it but this could be her big contribution to screwing her father. She paused, hesitated, then put her bags down next to the stairs and went into the office.

The desk drawer wasn't locked. She opened it and saw the file sitting at the top. She grabbed it out, opened it on the desk and found the letter. The original copy, bastard. He had stolen it or had one of his idiots steal it. She took out her phone, then thought again, and dug deep into the secret pocket of her coat, where she kept Zelah's second phone. Best do it on that one. She quickly snapped the picture a couple of times, then tucked the phone back. She picked up her own phone and was about to put it away when she was alerted to the creak of… something. Damn, there was someone around. She went to put the file back in the drawer, but not quickly enough. The office door was flung opened and Kennet strolled into the room, followed by Rufus, Gerry and the red-headed girl. Mischa tried to stuff the file back into the drawer but her hands were shaking too much.

Kennet quietly closed the door behind him. "What do we have here?" he smiled as the others fanned out around him. Mischa judged whether she would be able to reach the door. She flung the file back down as if she didn't care and went to put her phone in her outside pocket. Kennet was too quick for her.

"I'll take that," he said as he whipped across the room and held up her arm to grab the phone. All she had left now was bravado.

"That's mine, none of your business." She tried to sound

outraged and grab the phone back but he held it out of her reach, and her voice squeaked with fear.

"I think it is my business, isn't it?" His free hand took hold of her hair and dragged her to the centre of the room.

"Let me go, that hurts you moron," she screamed.

"You're going to hurt more before I'm finished."

As she thrashed around she saw her grandfather look away. Gerry, on the other hand, was displaying a grin that almost split his face in half. The redhead looked both interested and puzzled.

He threw her onto her knees and looked at her phone. It was locked. "Open it," he said. She sat on the carpet, hugging her knees. "No", she replied without looking up.

He grabbed her right hand and forced her thumb onto the unlock button. Nothing happened. "Which finger?" he said.

Mischa didn't answer him.

"I will take each finger and break it until I get the right one."

She thought '*he really would*' and held up her left thumb. He grabbed it and jabbed it onto the phone, which opened. He checked through the contacts.

"What name are they under?"

"Don't know what you are talking about. I've only got a few contacts. I don't have friends, thanks to you," she spat at him.

"Don't lie to me," he said in a bored voice and kicked her in the back. She screamed as she arched her back to get away from the pain and rolled on the floor. The redhead raised her eyebrows and went to sit in one of the armchairs, where she sat checking over her groomed nails.

Rufus Quinn took a step forward towards Mischa, but a look from Kennet stopped him. Gerry continued to fold his arms and grin, leaning up against the door.

"I know you are lying," he said to the prone, shaking figure on the floor, bending down close to her head level. "Helen there – she's Tim's sister, by the way – saw you in a café in Caerleon, where she lives. You were with the witch and the Gilbert boy."

Mischa screwed up her eyes and cried. "I don't know what you mean. Leave me alone, please, Pa."

He hauled her back up to her knees and hit her this time, a solid punch in the gut. Mischa thought she was suffocating. "You're going to tell me. Helen wants to know why you were with the person who killed her brother and I want to know why you are helping them."

"My mother," she said, through gritted teeth, "they are helping me find my mother."

Gerry laughed out loud. "You silly cow, she died years ago. Who's the witch, Pa? How did she kill Tim?"

"Later," Kennet said not looking up. "Tell me what you were doing with that file."

No reply. The pain in Mischa's back was so intense she could barely hear him and she began to shake all over. He stood up and walked to the desk where he took out the file. On the top was the police letter, "I see. They need this." He picked up a cigarette lighter, went back to her and stood in front of her. "Look at me." She didn't move, "I said, look at me." He grabbed her chin and forced her head up. He lit the flame and set light to the paper. "A hundred years of history, up in flames, shame."

"Now you are going to tell me everything you know but no-one else needs to watch." He turned to Gerry. "Open the door." The boy jumped to obey. Kennet took Mischa by the hair again and dragged her through the door into the hall, where he dropped her, then closed the door behind him.

Inside the room Rufus sat in the second armchair, his legs shaking and unable to hold himself upright for a second longer. Gerry wandered over to the window and looked out. Helen

Redland continued to examine her nails. For the next five minutes none of them spoke as the intermingled thuds of boot on flesh and screaming began, then slowly died to a whimper until they could no longer hear anything. Then a shout from the hall made them all jump.

"Steve, get up here." Footsteps ran up from the kitchen. Take this," he nudged Mischa body with his toe "down to A&E. Drop it off outside. Don't go in."

"Won't the CCTV pick up the car?"

"The cameras cover the entrance. Just throw it out of the boot close by. You're supposed to be the professional, get on with it. Take these," he said pointing to Mischa's bags. He turned his back and walked into the office.

**

By seven Zelah was pacing around the living room. "Something is wrong, I can feel it."

Nick and Stella had arrived earlier and Nick told them that he had received some news about his son. "He's back in the UK, I believe without his mother. We don't know where he is. I wonder if he'll try to find me."

Maggie thought he looked more animated than she had ever seen him but cautioned him to manage his expectations.

"You don't know where he's come from or what he's been through. You may need to give him some time and space. He's just eighteen."

"Exactly, he'll need somewhere to go and I'm the obvious choice."

Maggie smiled but thought that whatever reason Max's mother had used to take him away, she would have continued to use as the narrative of their lives, to her son. Max's feelings about his father were unlikely to be positive. However, this was not the time to have that discussion.

Instead she asked, "How did you find out he was back?"

"I have a friend with access to… the right information," he replied. "Max arrived last week."

She thought for a moment. "How did he get a passport Nick? His old childhood one that took him and his mother out of the country must have expired."

"I don't know," he replied, "good question, I guess she sorted it out for him."

"Then he must still be in touch with her."

"Could he be staying with relatives of hers?"

"She's Spanish, there aren't any relatives in the UK."

"Oh, well, wait and hope, eh?" She brought him up to speed on the Adolphus Quinn case and why Zelah was pacing around, as Bob arrived.

"I've had a thought about another aspect of this case" Nick said. "About how he died, no, about who might have killed him. I'd like to hear your take on this, Bob." He sat down in one of the armchairs that Zelah was walking around and went to talk again, when Zelah's phone rang. She looked at it, shook her head to indicate that it wasn't Mischa and answered the call. As soon as whoever it was began to speak, Zelah's eyes widened. She held onto the back of the armchair. Her responses were "yes" and "I see, thank you" and "yes, I'll be there."

At the end of the call she swayed briefly then flopped down onto the closest chair.

"That was the A&E in Newport. Mischa Quinn was brought in earlier this afternoon, unconscious. She has received a severe beating. She came round sufficiently to indicate a phone, buried in her pocket, on which I am the only contact. They've only just found it," she put her hand to her mouth and sobbed, once. She stood up again, her legs firmer now.

"I'm going to the hospital, I'll pick up Michelle on route."

"Has she been able to say who did it?" Bob asked.

"I think we can guess," Zelah replied. "We all thought of

protecting ourselves but no-one protected her." She turned to leave.

"I'm coming with you," Bob said.

"No need."

"This isn't about you, this time, Zelah. We're all assuming it was Kennet or one of his people, which is probably right and if so she'll need a police presence. I'm anticipating the hospital has already called us in, but if they couldn't identify her they won't know what they're dealing with. I'll need to find out what the situation is and organise something. I'll see you there".

"Do you want me or any of us to come with you?" Maggie asked.

"No, ring Michelle and tell her I'm on my way and there's been a development. I'll tell her more in the car."

"I will," Maggie walked up to Zelah and put her hands on Zelah's arms. "Please let us know how she is, Zelah."

She nodded, picked up her coat and left.

Chapter 33

On the journey to the hospital Michelle had been hysterical. She sobbed, cried, blamed herself and spewed out all of the terrible things that might have happened until Zelah, outwardly passive and in control, snapped at her to shut up.

"We don't know anything, so just shut the fuck up and wait until we get there."

Michelle was shocked into silence for a few minutes. She spent the rest of the journey rocking back and fore, as far as the seat belt would allow, head in her hands, muttering words that Zelah neither could nor wanted to hear.

When they reached A&E Zelah introduced them both. They were shown into the relatives' room, where a doctor would join them. As they waited, Zelah spotted Bob and a uniformed woman with the staff. He was talking intently to them, jabbing arms and fingers, laying down the law about something. She thought he was probably telling them that Mischa's father shouldn't be allowed in. They would be arguing, for the time being they had no reason to do otherwise.

The doctor arrived and Zelah introduced them both. She then offered to leave Michelle to talk to alone, but Michelle clung onto Zelah's arm.

"No, please stay, I hate this place and I won't remember anything I hear. I need you here, you're the only friend I have."

They all sat and the doctor addressed herself to Michelle.

"Your daughter has sustained severe injuries. Not life threatening." Michelle let out a small cry as the doctor continued, "but potentially life changing. We don't know yet. Her face is damaged, she has a fractured lower jaw that will need surgery, but at present is too swollen for us to operate. She has several broken ribs and we're concerned about her kidneys. It looks like someone has kicked her repeatedly in the back in the area of both kidneys. She's had X-rays and a CT scan and we're going to observe her for now. The damage to her kidneys is of concern and she may lose her spleen. There's evidence of internal bleeding. There were also some serious blows to her head but there's no fracture of the skull. We need to monitor her closely over the next few days."

"What happens next?" Zelah asked.

"We're sending her up to the intensive care unit. She will probably be placed in an induced coma until the swelling goes down and the monitoring shows no further danger. Then the need for surgery can be assessed."

"Is she conscious now?"

"Yes." The doctor gave Zelah a puzzled look. "She's been asking for you, not her mother."

"She and her mother have only just met; they've been separated for a long time. She just knows me a little better, now can we see her, please?"

"Yes, I'll take you through." She stood to leave, expecting them to follow, but Michelle stayed in her seat, shaking her head.

"I'll stay here, you go. I can't cope with this."

Zelah took her by the arm. "If you want any chance to have a relationship with her, you need to come now. You've managed your own injuries, you know what it's like," and she yanked Michelle up out of the seat.

Feeling the trembling and shaking that had overtaken Michelle, for a moment Zelah felt a rush of pity. This must be bringing back all those years ago when she was here, her hands agonised and ruined. She straightened up and steeled herself. This was not the time to think about the past, they had to toughen up, no choice, now.

240

When they entered the resuscitation room Zelah was surprised to see Bob there, but she made no comment and walked over to the bedside. She gripped her fists in tight balls to brace herself not to react when she saw Mischa.

The girls was unrecognisable. The left side of her face was bloody and swollen and she had clumps of hair missing. Her nose looked like it could be broken and her right eye was closed. She was able to see Zelah and raised her hand, which Zelah took hold of as Mischa muttered something unintelligible.

"Don't try to talk," she said, leaning down, "your jaw is fractured. You're going to be alright, it's going to take a while but we will take care of you. Your mother is here." As she tried to stand aside Mischa gripped her hand and pulled her downwards.

Zelah bent over and thought she heard the word 'phone'.

"You want me to look at your phone?"

Mischa's head nodded slightly, Zelah turned to the doctor. "Where's her phone?"

The doctor brought it over from the nursing station. Zelah turned it on, saw that it was unlocked, and opened it.

"I told you to put a lock on this, anyway, what am I looking for?"

Another grunt.

"Photo?"

A nod.

She opened up the camera to find two photos, both of the letter from the archives.

"You took this when you got home?"

Nod.

"I need to give this to the police, it will have a date and time stamp on it but first I'm going to send it to myself."

After she had done so, she handed the phone over to Bob.

"We told you to leave this. Did he catch you?"

Nod.

"Silly, silly girl," she said. "In future, do what the grown-ups tell you." She leaned in and gave Mischa a gentle hug, for several seconds. "You're going to be alright, I'll make sure you have everything you need, to get better and be safe. Now, your mother will sit with you for a while because I need to go and sort out some things."

She grabbed a crying Michelle and guided her down in the chair next to the bed. "I'll be back," she said, in her best Terminator impression, and signalled to Bob to follow her.

They walked out into the artificially bright corridor, where other groups of people pressed themselves against the whitewashed walls, some arguing, one crying.

"Kennet did this, either himself or had someone else do it," Zelah growled at him.

"He did it himself; she told me, before you arrived. I need to get some security organised for her, so the staff don't let him anywhere near her, should he have the bloody nerve to show up here before I can arrest him and take him in for questioning."

"If he shows up here, I'll kill him," Zelah said, matter-of-factly.

"No you won't, not your job. Its mine and I need evidence, so I need to get on with it. Are you OK to stay here with Michelle?"

She was about to reply when the automatic doors at the end of the corridor wooshed opened. They both glanced up, and saw Kennet Quinn ambling along the corridor towards them, followed by Stephen Dawes.

He strolled up to them,

"I'm here to see my daughter. I understand she's had an accident?" he said in a mocking tone.

Bob called on his radio for the officer who was with Mischa. She came running out as he took Kennet by the arm and said

"Kennet Quinn, I'm arresting you on suspicion of grievous bodily harm. You do not have to say anything…" as he continued Zelah stared in disbelief at Kennet, who was smiling. Bob finished the caution and told the officer to call for more support. He marched Kennet Quinn to the door, without resistance. Instead Kennet called to Dawes, "Get on the blower, I want Kennedy at the station, and I want him there before me."

Stephen Dawes took out his mobile and began to dial. Zelah snapped back to attention and grabbed the phone out of his hand, making him yell in rage and try, unsuccessfully, to snatch it back.

Two more police cars had just pulled up outside beyond the automatic doors. Bob pushed Kennet Quinn into one of them, told the two men to take him to the station and put him in a cell to await his arrival.

When he got back to Zelah, Stephen Dawes was pinned against the corridor wall, seemingly unable to get away, still shouting about his phone.

"He gave it to me," Zelah said, "no idea why."

"You'd better give it back, then. We can't have him saying that we tried to prevent his brief from seeing him."

She handed the phone across the corridor and Dawes fell off the wall, grabbed the phone and ran out.

"You shouldn't have done that," Bob said, his expression varying between surprise and laughter.

"He won't make a complaint, he couldn't explain it in a way that anyone would believe."

"Hmm, Ok, I have to get to the station. I'll call Maggie later to let you all know what's happening."

Zelah went back into the Resus room to find that Mischa was being wheeled out. She was moaning and muttering incoherently, which the nurse explained was the painkilling

243

drugs and not to worry. As soon as she saw Zelah she held out her hand and tried to say something.

"Of course I'll come with you," Zelah said. "Michelle and I are going to stay." She turned to Michelle, who looked as if she had taken root.

"Come on," Zelah hissed, "she needs you."

"No, she needs you, I'm going home. You can call me later, let me know how she's getting on." She walked out of the Resus into the corridor that led to the exit.

For a moment Zelah couldn't speak or move. A sharp call from the nurse brought her back to the present and she followed the bed trolley out of the room and towards the lift that would take them up to the intensive care unit, the WPC alert and following.

**

Zelah got back to Maggie's house in the early hours of the morning to find the lights blazing, and Maggie, Nick and Jack all waiting. They jumped up when they heard her key in the door and called her into the sitting room.

Zelah walked in and sank down into an armchair.

"She's going to be OK," she said, "but it's going to be a long haul; he did a job on her."

"Drink?" Nick asked.

"Whisky please, with a splash of water, I need it."

"What are her injuries?" Maggie asked, also sitting now.

"She has a fractured jaw. One eye is severely swollen. They are looking at whether or not there will be permanent damage to her sight. She has a couple of broken ribs and one of her kidneys got a bad kicking, not sure about that yet. There's also some swelling on her brain. She will be put into an induced coma for a couple of days. I think it depends on how they assess the rest of the injuries, which ones need intervention right away and which can wait a bit longer."

Jack, who had sat next to Maggie, jumped up and walked out of the room, to join Nick in the kitchen. He returned with him a few minutes later.

"Jack's just told me what Kennet Quinn did," Nick said. He handed the glass to Zelah, who snatched at it and almost missed. Steadying herself she took a gulp, drew a deep breath then put the glass down on the arm of the chair.

"What can we do?" Maggie asked.

"Not much at the moment, except ensure that Kennet Quinn and any other of his family involved, get what they deserve." She picked up the glass in a shaky hand and drained it in one gulp. "At the moment you wouldn't recognise Mischa." She put the glass back, missed the armchair and watched it fall and bounce on the carpet. "Good job that's empty," she said to Maggie with a low laugh, "would have made a stink on your carpet."

"Sod the carpet," Maggie said, ignoring the glass. "I haven't heard from Bob, any idea where he is?"

"At the station. Kennet Quinn turned up at the hospital, just strolled in wanting to see his daughter who he heard had been in an accident. Bob arrested him there and then. Mischa had already told him her father had done it."

"I presume Michelle is still there?"

Zelah gave another long, low belt of a laugh. "You presume wrong, she went home. Couldn't deal with it."

Maggie stared at her for a few seconds then said, "Shocking but not surprising. Did Kennet see her?"

"No, Bob whisked him straight off. He had one of his thugs with him who he told to get their lawyer down to the station… shit, I'm tired."

Maggie stood up. "You can't drive home, especially not after that whisky. I made up a bed for you, just in case and Nick's staying. It's too late to plan anything, so I'm thinking we all try to sleep and re-group in the morning, as early as possible? Hopefully, Bob will have let us know by then what's happening."

Zelah nodded. "The hospital will call if anything changes." She felt too drained to say anymore. She was secretly shocked at her feelings; her desperation to protect Mischa, her feelings of contempt at Michelle's behaviour, all this in addition to her all-consuming hatred of Kennet Quinn. These were not her normal, well-controlled emotions. Needing some quiet and privacy she got up and made her way up to the bedroom that Maggie had prepared for her. Without undressing, she laid down on the bed and almost immediately fell asleep.

**

Bob Pugh arrived just before seven. He tried to sneak in and grab a few hours' sleep, but found Maggie on the settee in the living room, still awake.

"Is Zelah here?" he asked.

She nodded.

"I have some news and she isn't going to like it."

Maggie's stomach lurched. "Mischa?"

"No, Kennet Quinn, we had to let him go, he's on the loose again."

Chapter 34

Maggie thought Zelah was going to have a meltdown when they assembled and Bob passed on his news. It didn't happen, instead she sat thoughtfully, not commenting, until they all stopped talking and looked at her.

"What?"

"Don't you have anything to say?"

"Not right now. The way he came sauntering into the hospital with that smug look on his face, told me something wasn't quite right. From what Bob's just said, I suspect Kennet had spent the day lining up his alibi, which sounds watertight - right Bob?"

"Must have done, only way he could have pulled it all together. The lawyer arrived at the station with the same smug expression."

"You said how many signed statements?"

"Seven," Bob replied, "his father and son, and the woman Helen Redland. Steven Dawes, of course, who says he drove Kennet to Birmingham, and three people who said they were present at a meeting in a house in the West Midlands with him."

"Are you checking them out?" Jack asked. "What does he say about Mischa? What about forensic evidence?"

"Of course," Bob replied, "including looking for the car he says he was in, to and from the Midlands at the times Dawes said they were driving. Still it wasn't enough so we have to let him go while we're checking. Don't hold your breath that we can break through any of this, quickly or easily, if at all. He knows what he's doing, he's acting the concerned father. As for the forensics, she was checked over, as far as it was possible but they live in the same house and mainly he kicked her. We're going to look for shoes and it at least gets us into the house, although I suspect he's well prepared."

Zelah nodded, then stood up, "I have things to do. This isn't going to be sorted directly or straightforwardly."

Bob moved to block her exit. "I've warned you Zelah, don't do anything that might need my attention. I will not protect you."

"I just said it can't be sorted directly or straightforwardly. I'm not stupid, I'm not going to put myself in any danger of being arrested and I'm not going to hurt him. I need to think and I have to go back to the hospital to see what's happened. Plus, I have someone I need to speak to, and a visit to make."

"And are you going to share any of this with your colleagues?" Nick's tone was almost angry.

"Yes," she replied, "soon."

"What about the Mayor," Maggie asked. "The meeting is tomorrow."

"I haven't heard anything, now, I have to go." She glared at Bob, who reluctantly moved aside.

They waited until the front door slammed.

"I have to go, too," Bob said, kissing Maggie. He looked around at all of them, "I meant what I said. If she tries anything, anything at all, I won't protect her."

When he had gone, Maggie said to Nick and Jack, "What are we supposed to do now?"

"I don't think there's anything else we can do on the case until the Mayor tells Zelah her proposal. I suggest we get on with other work, it's not like we haven't got anything else to do." He turned back to his computer, leaving Maggie and Jack on the settee.

"Do you mind if I go back to bed?" Jack asked.

"No, go ahead, I haven't slept at all either. I might try to get an hour in the living room and then help Nick. I have an overdue report to write but I'll do it later. If I try now it won't make any sense."

When she was alone at last, she closed her eyes but sleep wouldn't come. The occasional low hum of Nick's voice in the office on the phone interrupted her efforts to shut herself off, empty her mind and sleep. Giving up, she went to make some strong coffee and joined him.

"I'll get on with some research," she said, yawning.

**

Zelah had plans, as she had said earlier. Sitting next to Mischa in the intensive care unit she had time to work out what she thought was about to happen. Michelle's refusal to come up to the ward, and the fear in her eyes was leading her to believe that the woman wasn't going to come through for her daughter after all. When the crunch moment came, she had collapsed, despite her previous good intention. In one way that appalled Zelah; but somewhere within her was a modicum of pity. However, the girl needed more right now than an insubstantial, unable-to-commit parent. She already had a psychopathic one, what she did need was someone reliable. For the first time in her life Zelah felt that perhaps she might have made a good parent. She and Martin had never had children and although he had expressed regret on the odd occasion, Zelah had never felt sorry. Now, well, this was a strange feeling for her. She liked this kid, this feisty, energetic kid who was exactly what Zelah would have wanted in a daughter. However, this was someone else's daughter, as much as she had asked Zelah to stay with her. As they had reached the Intensive Care Unit Zelah had reached out and taken Mischa's hand and in response the girl had given back a tiny squeeze and a sloppy, drug induced smile. It was enough to tug on Zelah's heartstrings; something she wasn't used to. She loved Maggie's kids and would do whatever it took to protect them. This was a feeling of vulnerability and that startled her as much as it was overwhelmingly compassionate. A lot to take in, and think about.

On leaving the hospital she had driven almost absent-mindedly, and now glanced around, surprised to find herself sitting on the roadside. She had pulled up outside Michelle Morgan's bedsit. This was something else that she had spent time thinking about… she knew what she had to do.

The twitching curtain suggested her arrival had been anticipated. As she walked up the path the door opened and Michelle let her in. Ahead was a set of stairs covered in a threadbare carpet that might once have been beige. Next to the stairs on the left was a door, which was ajar and led into the main living area. Michelle's ground floor bedsit consisted, as far as Zelah could see, of a bedroom-come-living room. Hanging at the bay window were curtains of indeterminate colour and great age. Sitting in the bay was a two-seater settee, probably second hand, covered in sixties brown draylon. A fireplace was blocked up and covered by a one-bar electric fire. A mini TV sat on a coffee table on the opposite side of the fireplace. At the back of the room was a single bed, unmade, a pine wardrobe and matching drawers. On the bedside table sat coffee cups, bottles of pills and other unrecognisable detritus.

"Where do you cook?" Zelah asked.

"Small kitchen, out there," she pointed to another door leading from the bedroom end. "There's a shower and toilet next to it, not much is it?"

"No, it's shit, isn't it?" Zelah replied.

Michelle laughed. "Tell me why you're here so early?"

"You haven't asked me about Mischa."

"Well you're going to tell me, aren't you?"

"She's in the intensive care unit, some of her injuries are sufficiently serious. She'll be closely monitored for the next few days. Thankfully, she's young and strong, unlike you."

"You don't mince your words, do you?"

"I aim for pith. What do you want to do, Michelle?"

"What do you mean?"

"Don't mess me about, Michelle. At the point of need last night you copped out. You missed Kennet by seconds, by the way." She said this deliberately to see the effect it had and wasn't surprised to see immediate terror. "What's more important to you? Your daughter or your freedom?"

"What do you mean?"

Zelah spotted a fold up garden chair next to the settee. She picked it up, unfolded it and sat, indicating to Michelle to sit on the settee, sat back and crossed one elegantly shod leg over the other, taking in Michelle's grimace of envy.

"You have choices. If you choose to stay with Mischa, there will, for some time to come, be a concern about Kennet finding you. I can hide you both away, once she's out of hospital, then he has to be dealt with. There is a risk that he will track you down. If you choose not to stay, I will give you enough money to get away completely. You can get some plastic surgery for your hands, and for your face if you want to change what you look like. If you go, you can't come back. Ever."

Michelle looked away, rubbed her gloved hands together.

"She hardly knows me," she said, as much to herself as to Zelah.

"Not yet, but she can get to know you if you give her the chance."

"What if she doesn't like me?"

"Oh for fuck's sake woman, why should she not like you? You're her mother."

"No, I'm not, not really, I abandoned her and her brother. I could have gone back, taken her away."

"Why didn't you, if you're saying now that you could have

251

done. Why didn't you go back for her?"

Michelle looked directly at Zelah, her eyes blazing for a second. "Because I was more scared of him than I was concerned for her and I still am, I know that now."

Zelah put her hand up to her forehead and pinched the bridge of her nose.

"How much?"

"What?" Zelah blinked for a second.

"I said how much, how much will you give me to go away?"

"Is this your decision?"

"I think so. How much?"

"One hundred thousand pounds."

Michelle gasped. "Are you serious?"

"Deadly. I said it would be enough to get yourself fixed physically. I can't do anything about what's inside your head."

"If I did get myself fixed, could I come back, one day?"

"If you leave her now, in this state, what do you think?"

Michelle shook her head. "She won't forgive me, will she?"

Zelah didn't answer and Michelle stood up, arms folded.

"When can you get me the money?"

"By the end of the day. Are you sure this is what you want? There won't be a second chance"

"I'm never going to be sure but I think it's the right thing to do."

Zelah stood to face her. "Give me your bank account details. I'll get it done and I'll give you the phone number of a lawyer who can help you with whatever decision you make about what you're going to do." She paused. "Are you going to see her again before you leave?"

Michelle shook her head. "Best not but please tell her I love her. Tell her this is for the best, I'm not good enough for her."

Zelah took the paper with the bank account details that Michelle had scribbled out. She also gave Zelah a phone number and said, "I'd like to know how she gets on; will you let me know? And I need the number of that solicitor."

Zelah wrote down the name and number.

Handing it over she said "There is one caveat to this money. You know the whole Adolphus Quinn story. We trusted you with it. You can never tell anyone. If I find out that you have, for whatever reason, I will find you and I will take back every penny I have given you and I will ruin you. Understand?"

Michelle nodded violently.

Zelah turned and walked to the door. Without saying goodbye, she let herself out and got into her car. Glancing round before she drove away, she saw Michelle standing next to the curtain.

"Poor pathetic woman," she muttered, and drove back to the hospital.

**

There was a uniformed policeman on the door of the ICU, arguing with a young man who was trying to get in.

"Get out of my way, you fucking pig! I'm going to see my sister." He tried to push past but was held back and shoved into a side room, with help from another policewoman who had come running up the corridor. Zelah recognised her as the one who had been in the A&E with them the previous evening.

A few minutes later the young man departed and Zelah followed him down the corridor, catching up with him at the lift.

"Are you Gerry Quinn?"

"Who wants to know," he growled, spinning round, raising his fists.

"A friend of your sister. Your mother sends her regards."

"What are you talking about? My mother died."

"No, Gerry, she isn't, I've just left her, very much alive. Your father has been lying to you all your life. You should leave

253

off the steroids, not good for you." She turned around and marched off down the corridor towards the intensive care unit, hoping that she had set something going that would have a substantial ripple effect. Time would tell.

In the intensive care ward Mischa was still unconscious, a mass of tubes and wires. Zelah had been in this environment before so wasn't surprised at the amount of light and noise. People who hadn't experienced ICU expected it to be quiet, low lit and sensitive. It was anything but. Nurses walked briskly albeit quietly, checking the constantly buzzing and beeping machines under bright lights. Looking around, she saw that the other five beds were taken, each with two silent visitors.

She sat for an hour, during which time a doctor came and went, telling Zelah that Mischa was doing well but it was still early days. She didn't want to ask any more detailed questions, not yet.

After the hour was up she went outside, called Maggie to let her know how things were going, and made another phone call. This call was quick and brisk, during which she made an appointment then went back in for a further hour. Then it was time to go, to add the next piece to the almost finished jigsaw of the Quinn family story. She squeezed Mischa's hand and said, "I'll be back later. I have an important visit now."

Chapter 35

Claire Lewis sat next to the open French windows of her ground floor flat in Penarth, breathing in the scents from her garden.

She had once lived in the Manor house of which this flat had become an extension. She had sold the Manor house when her husband Ted had died, five years previously and had renovated and moved into what had been the old wash house. There was too much furniture and far too many curios and other odd collectibles, but Claire couldn't bear to part with any of them, so they crowded the flat, ensuring that anyone who visited her had to follow a zig-zag path to get anywhere. Yet no-one who visited here ever felt constricted by the lack of open space. Its irregular shape, with two open box-like areas off the main living space areas that served as dining area and kitchen, gave it eye-catching interest.

Beyond the old-fashioned, multi-paned French windows that stretched across the living area and gave the room so much light, was a sizeable walled garden, the product of many years' work. A central circular lawn was surrounded by trees, shrubs and plants, many of which were either in flower or close to opening up their summer buds. Surrounded by a high wall, some might have thought it claustrophobic but Claire loved its privacy and quiet. She was one road further on from the cliff side, at the bottom of which was the sea. She couldn't see it, but could smell the tidal waters on the breeze most days and hear it roar during the winter storms.

The garden was also south facing and a heat trap, meaning it would be an hour or so yet before she ventured out to make the most of the afternoon warmth. If she went out now she might

255

not hear the doorbell announcing her visitor

She was puzzled about this visitor, who had called her and asked for an urgent appointment. She didn't usually take on new clients without a recommendation. She didn't need more clients but this was about someone she knew. The caller had sounded both harassed and determined to see to her.

She was a little anxious, too, about seeing someone she didn't know, alone. The voice had sounded genuine enough though and the knowledge of a friend in common reassured her that there wouldn't be anything worrying about the meeting.

The doorbell rang and she got up to answer. As soon as she saw the woman waiting on the doorstep, Claire knew that there would not be a problem. There was a deep unspoken sense of mutual recognition and a feeling of shared understanding. She invited the visitor in and took her out into the garden, which she sensed was a good place for them both to feel at ease.

She put cold drinks on the table next to a small fountain.

"Welcome, Mrs Trevear, how can I help you?" The lilt in her voice suggested origins in Scotland.

"Thank you for seeing me at such short notice Mrs Lewis. I would like to talk to you about Isobel Blackstock, with whom I believe you are acquainted through your spiritual society?"

Twenty minutes later Zelah left, thanking Claire Lewis and promising to be back on Friday for a fuller discussion, to which she would bring her colleague, Maggie Gilbert.

**

Zelah needed to head back, but barely felt able to drive, so she made her way down to the sea front. She drove past the pier where people were walking shirt-sleeved in the sunshine and was lucky enough to find a parking spot facing the sea. Having parked the car, she crossed the road and stood at the railings that bordered the high wall above the beach. Along the promenade there were strollers, many walking their dogs, all nodding a polite smile as they passed by. Penarth had always been a refined kind of place. The mid-channel islands of Flat Holme and Steep Holme stood dark and sturdy as the tankers and boats from Cardiff and Newport docks made their way around them down the Channel to the Atlantic

It was high tide and the brown sea waters had reached right up to base of the wall, hiding the rock and mud beach. The sun sparkled on the murky waters of the Bristol Channel, as Zelah stared out to sea. The outline of the opposite coast of Somerset was clear today.

She gripped the rails hard, until her knuckles turned white. What she had just heard was what she had expected to hear, but it didn't make her any less livid. The burning sense of anger made her muscles taut throughout her body and she swore out loud, causing one dog walker to take a wide path around her.

What to do now? It wasn't going to greatly affect the case. They had started and they would follow through. Like each case that began on paper, this one had developed dimensional tentacles that were now reaching out in unexpected directions. So be it, they still had enough proof of Adolphus Quinn's reign of terror during his relatively short life. Was it enough to stop the statue? Probably, but certainty would have been better.

There was one more thing but she still wasn't sure it was real, that she hadn't imagined it. Was she trying to fit a fleeting, at the time, unconnected observation into the deciding factor of this case? The problem was there was no way now of getting back into the Quinn house to check. Damn! Damn! Damn!

She hoped they had enough to convince the Mayor that stopping the funds for the statue, or whatever her plan, was sufficient. She still hadn't heard from her, which was worrying. She checked her watch, time to get back. She wanted to check in at the hospital again, sit for a little while. Then she wanted to go back and speak to Michelle again. Uncomfortable pangs of doubt about what she had said earlier were gnawing. Michelle was Mischa's mother. Had she offered the money too soon?

She let go of the rail, turned and crossed the road back to her car.

**

At the hospital, the nurse in charge of Mischa told Zelah there was a small improvement and they were considering lifting the sedation, probably in the morning. She sat for a half hour then decided to check in on Michelle, before going back to Maggie's house.

At five o' clock she reached Michelle's bedsit, parked and walked up, past the broken gate to the front door. No-one answered her persistent knocking, until a window opened above and a man in a dirty vest leaned out.

"Stop that bloody racket, will you, I'm trying to sleep."

"I'm looking for the woman who lives in the ground floor bedsit."

"Are you Zelah?"

"Yes why, how do you know my name?"

"She's gone, she left something for you, in the hall."

"How exactly am I meant to get my hands on whatever it is?"

"The front door's not locked," he shouted back and slammed the window shut.

In the hallway standing on the first step was a letter addressed to 'Zelar'. It was no more than a brief note, asking her to understand why Michelle decided to leave. She thanked her for the money, begged Zelah to speak well of her to Mischa, to tell her that she just couldn't face it all. And she promised to keep the secret. There was the same mobile contact number, which Zelah suspected was a pay-as-you-go. The woman had made her choice, had chosen to disappear again. Zelah shrugged and put the note in her pocket. When she got

258

back she would put it in the shredder.

**

At Maggie's house, they had had a productive day, although the atmosphere was tense and the usual chat non-existent.

Nick had been particularly frustrated about a case he had been dealing with for some time in which he was still hitting the ubiquitous brick wall. Despite hours on every website he could find and several visits to the archives at Liverpool's magnificent library, he had come to a dead end on the case of William McRoberts, a police constable, who over a period of ten years on the force had become a detective, then disappeared. The McRoberts family had always wanted to know what had happened to him and had commissioned Maze to help them. Nick discovered that Detective McRoberts' wife and children had not passed on anything they knew, although all three of his children had testified their father as being 'deceased' at the time of their marriages. Nick had not been able to find any evidence about how, when, where or why he had died. The present-day family story was that McRoberts had found a significant hoard of treasure in the home of someone to whom it did not belong, and that person had murdered him. Nick knew that if a policeman had been murdered it would have been a story of national interest. The apocryphal story was highly unlikely and, unsurprisingly, there was nothing in the newspapers about the man. Nick shut down his computer with a shake of his head, not for the first time.

"I'm going to have to tell them that we've come to a dead end, pardon the pun. Why on earth didn't his wife or children just say what happened to him?"

"They didn't know, at a guess." Maggie replied. "The only place it says that he was 'deceased' is on the children's marriage certificates, there's no actual proof anywhere else, is there? The same for his wife saying she was a widow in that street directory

259

you found."

"Which is also how she described herself on the census returns from 1891 onwards.

"Pity all of the police records for the time have been destroyed," Nick added. "That would at least have told us if he was still on the force when he died."

"Everything gone?"

"Yep, even the pension records. Their archivist was helpful, but apologetic. Everything before 1890, gone; shredded. We don't even know which force he was serving with as there were several in Liverpool at the time."

Maggie was about to ask more questions, when the slamming front door announced Zelah's return. As soon as they saw her Maggie knew that there was news but not necessarily good news. She brought them up to speed with Mischa's condition first, then told them about Michelle's sudden departure.

Their immediate reaction was silence, then Maggie said, "Zelah, did you pay Michelle to go away?"

Zelah flung her bag and coat on the floor and, hands on hips, faced Maggie and barked, "Why the hell would I do that?"

"'No' would have been a simple answer."

"Well then, no, I did not pay her to go away. Yes, I said I would pay for her to have plastic surgery to fix her hands. She had already made up her mind that she was going, she's too frightened of Kennet. She realised, overnight, how much courage and strength it would take to stay and decided she didn't have enough of either. So, I said I would give her enough money to get away. I'm sorry that you think I would bribe her, because that's what you're saying, isn't it?"

"Just cool down will you, I accept it wasn't a bribe. I do believe though, that part of you wanted her to go, tell me I'm wrong about that."

Zelah put her hands down. "No, not wrong. She wasn't able to do it, I can understand that. I know you think I'm a hard-hearted bitch, Maggie but she would have gone sooner or later. The more Mischa became attached to her, the worse it would have been. So if you're asking am I sorry she's gone? No, I'm not.

"It was too soon, I think." Nick now stood up and faced Zelah. "She needed a chance to say goodbye to her daughter."

"She had that chance. Last night she didn't even come up to the ICU and she practically ran out of the A&E department. I asked her this morning to come with me. She said no." She wasn't going to tell them about the note, nor was she going to tell them that she was the person that the girl clung on to. "I'll find a way to tell Mischa that her mother has gone, in a compassionate way."

It was time for some distraction, so she told them about Gerry Quinn and his reaction to being told, again, that his mother wasn't dead. "Any spanner we can throw into the works for Kennet will give him yet another problem that he can't fix."

Maggie was too tired to ask any more. "He's still a boy, really, in a nightmare situation. How could his own father have sent him out with a gun? Anyway, I think I'm going to have an early night but first, we must talk about tomorrow. How is the meeting going to go, Zelah? It's public, isn't it? Do we need to be there?"

"I think so, I still haven't heard from the Mayor." Her phone rang. "At bloody last, this is her, I'll take it in the kitchen."

When she had gone Maggie and Nick looked at each other and shrugged. "What do you think?" Maggie asked.

"I didn't meet Michelle so I can't really say. Are you surprised?"

Maggie sat back down at the conference table and

considered the question. "I'm surprised she went so quickly, but if she ran from the hospital, I guess she wouldn't have coped for much longer; perhaps it is best she goes now. What's going to become of Mischa?"

"Can't you guess?" he replied, eyebrows raised.

Before she could think about what Nick was suggesting, Zelah came back into the office, phone in hand.

"What's happened?" Maggie asked immediately.

Zelah put her phone down on the table. "She says she can't do anything to stop it going through. It will get passed by the full Council tomorrow night."

Maggie jumped up. "What do you mean it will go through? How can she think that's a good thing?" she shouted.

Zelah lifted her finger and pointed at the settee. "Sit."

"I won't sit, we've put too much into this already, and I want to speak to her myself." She marched around the room and was heading towards Zelah's phone on the table when Jack ran down the stairs.

"What's up? I heard shouting."

"The bloody Mayor isn't going to do anything. She's going to let it through tomorrow night," Maggie yelled.

Jack spun round to Zelah. "You said she was one of the good guys."

"She is," Zelah shouted back. "If you will all sit down and shut up, I'll tell you what I think has happened and why. Then I will tell you what we need to think about next."

Maggie, Nick and Jack sat down, all on the settee, like soldiers in a row, each of them with folded arms. Zelah stood at the far side of the table, leaning over with her hands flat on the table top.

"This is about politics and how the system works. We agreed, did we not, that we wanted the statue stopped but without publicity?"

Only Nick replied. "Yes, we did."

"OK, the procedure at full Council is that the minutes of sub-committees generally go through on the nod. That's because they have been discussed at length and agreed. It's a given that whatever has been agreed, unless it's contentious, will not be challenged; with me so far?"

No reply. She stood up away from the table and paced around the room.

"This statue has not been a contentious issue. The finance has been agreed, Rufus Quinn lobbied well and is due to match the Council's funding with his own money. If it is pulled under the glare and publicity of a full County Council meeting, remembering the press will also be there, that's going to raise its profile a thousand percent. The opposition, who are always keen to get hold of anything that might even smell slightly of a potential issue, never mind a scandal, will want to know why. The Mayor won't lie, she cannot lie; it is illegal for her to lie. That will set both the opposition and the press off on the trail of a story. Once they start digging they won't stop until the whole history becomes public and that's the last thing we want. We will be thrown into the spotlight, we'll have to talk about how and why we investigated the history of Adolphus Quinn. We won't be able to lie either and it will bring Isobel Blackstock into the frame, giving her the publicity we don't want her to have. Most importantly for us, if our story causes the Quinn family public humiliation, embarrassment and ridicule, Kennet Quinn will never leave us alone. In that situation I would fear for our safety, for Michelle's and Mischa's, and anyone and everyone associated with both us and this case."

She paused for a breath and closed her eyes.

"But what happens if it goes through?" Maggie said. "Doesn't that give Rufus Quinn free range to push ahead with it?"

"Just because it's been approved, doesn't mean it will happen. The best thing is that it goes through without any fuss, then gets kicked into the long grass, from which it never re-appears. We hold all the cards now, at last, to ensure that it never happens."

"How are we going to make sure that Rufus Quinn understands that?" Maggie asked.

"We're going to have to go to the Quinn house tomorrow and face them with everything we have. I think there may be one more thing. A clincher. We'll have to convince Rufus and his son that if they ever try to get the statue put up, we will not hesitate to bring out the full true story. It would be an end to his chances of getting knighted."

"But that's terrible," Jack said. "It's underhand. People need to know the truth. They have the right."

"Why?" Zelah said, turning to him. "Why do people have to know the truth, Jack? What right? We are so used to living in an age of instant news in which everyone believes that they should have access to everything. Is that really the case? Really? Will it make any difference if Rufus Quinn gets knighted?"

He didn't reply as he thought about what she was saying.

"This is a political solution but I believe it's the best one for us too. It does mean that Maggie and I, at least, have to face the Quinn family again tomorrow. I don't relish the thought of that, although I was hoping that we could get into that house one more time. Now, if any of you has a better idea, this would be a good time to bring it on. I need some air." She marched out of the room.

After five minutes and some discussion, Maggie volunteered to find her. Zelah had walked to the end of the garden and was standing next to the fence, looking into the canal. Maggie went to stand next to her.

"We see what you're saying. I don't like it. But we agree. We have to do it. Nick and Jack want to talk about what we're going to do. Bob is going to have a hissy fit. I don't like this, I hate deceiving him. But if we are going to do this, I don't think I can tell him. I'm torn."

Zelah turned to her. "I think you should tell him. Of course he won't like it, he'll probably forbid you to go. Maggie, I don't want you to compromise your relationship with him; Kennet Quinn isn't worth it."

"There's something you're not telling us, isn't there, Zelah?"

"Two things, one isn't so relevant right now. The other, as I said, might just clinch it. I could be wrong and if I am we'll have to go in with what we have. If I'm right, though…"

"Let's go back in and start planning then. It's going to have to be our best plan ever. Do you have any ideas yet?"

"Oh yes," Zelah replied, "I certainly do. We're going to need a diversion."

Chapter 36

They spent the rest of the evening planning how the meeting might go, trying to think through every little detail. They critiqued each possible outcome until Bob arrived back at eleven thirty and asked what they were doing.

Nick and Zelah were staying overnight and they quietly made their way up to bed, as did Jack, leaving Maggie to talk to Bob, trying not to listen to the explosive shouting coming from the ground floor, followed by the front door slamming.

When she didn't hear Maggie come upstairs, Zelah made her way back down.

"That went well, then?"

Maggie's white face didn't so much as twitch.

"Is he coming back?" Zelah asked.

"I have no idea, not any time soon. I guess," She looked away from the window at which she had been staring "but he will be outside the Quinn house tomorrow morning."

"All is not completely lost, then?"

"I wouldn't say that, it depends on the context."

Zelah gave Maggie's arm a squeeze, "I sent a message to Rufus Quinn earlier, saying that we intend to call at eleven and asking that he and Kennet be there."

"Did you get a reply?"

"Not yet, he'll see it in the morning, we should sleep now."

"No chance."

Zelah yawned. "Speak for yourself, I've had a long day. See you at eight." She left Maggie alone in the office.

Although Maggie had stood her ground, the conversation with Bob had been brutal. He was the one who had walked out, in the end. She understood his concern, his fear, especially in the light of Mischa's Quinn's beating. Maggie truly believed that Kennet Quinn would not try anything in his own house, especially if he knew that there was a police car sitting outside whose occupants knew that she and Zelah were in there. She thought that Bob believed this too. She hoped he would come round. He had walked out before she explained the detail, how they were going to cause the diversion, and why. Well, that would have to wait until after the event.

With that she went to bed. She hadn't expected to get much sleep, but managed a few hours around dawn. When she went back to the kitchen at eight, she found the others sitting there, drinking coffee in silence. Jack jumped up and poured her a mug.

"I'm going to get on with some work," Nick said and left them.

Jack went back upstairs to play computer games, leaving Maggie and Zelah.

"I don't suppose you've heard from Rufus Quinn?"

"Not yet," Zelah replied, "I hope it won't be long, this plan depends on him being too curious to say no to the meeting."

She was right. Just before nine a text came through from Rufus Quinn saying he and Kennet would see them at eleven.

"Do you think he's feeling confident?" Maggie asked Zelah.

"Probably was, but hopefully that feeling has changed to anxiety. Let's go over the plan one more time."

They were ready to leave at ten thirty and hung about in the office, coats on, Zelah holding a set of papers. Jack was hovering. "Is the story straight in your head, Zelah? Will you remember it when you're there?"

"Yes, and yes. Stop it." She turned to Maggie. "Let's go. We can wait outside the house for five minutes, settle ourselves." She nodded to Nick. "You OK?"

"Absolutely," he said.

Maggie hugged Jack. "You got your phone set and ready, mum?"

She nodded again, then joined Zelah at the door. They drove off without waving goodbye.

When they arrived at the Quinn house Bob was there in a marked police car, with a colleague. He ignored them.

At eleven on the pip of the BBC news Zelah switched off the engine. "Let's do this."

They walked up to the front door but barely had chance to ring the bell. Rufus Quinn had been waiting for them. He greeted them with a sneering grin and closed the door behind them.

"I'm thinking, spider to the fly," Maggie whispered to Zelah, who shrugged.

"Just remember the plan," she whispered back. Rufus opened the office door for them and Zelah, who did a rapid scan of the room, then gave an inaudible sigh of relief. Her greatest fear had been that the meeting would be held in a different room. As they entered the office she glanced over at the fireplace and mouthed an exultant 'yes!' to Maggie, as pre-arranged if she saw what she hoped to see. The plan could now go ahead full throttle. Maggie took out her phone and pressed the send button.

"What's she doing with that phone?" Gerry Quinn said as he walked towards Maggie.

"Checking in," she replied, "on a fixed timetable. If they don't hear they'll break your door down."

Gerry Quinn moved towards her, his hand held out, but his father stopped him with a shake of the head.

Zelah, who had been watching the exchange, turned around into the room and stopped dead. "What the fuck is she doing here?"

Sitting in an armchair at the back of the room, looking at

home and comfortable, was Isobel Ramona Blackstock.

"Darlings," she said, "dear Rufus told me you were coming and I simply had to see you."

Zelah looked at Rufus, then Kennet and exhaled a loud sigh. "I am shocked, but not surprised, Isobel. These are the backers for your new show, I presume?"

Isobel smiled graciously and blew a kiss to Rufus, who shook his head.

"In return for which, let me guess..." she paused to make a theatrical gesture of putting her right index finger up to her tilted head. "You are going to say that you never spoke to us, that the whole story of Ada's message was made up by us. That we've done all of this to get back at you, because of some former affront?"

Kennet, who was standing in the window, acknowledged her with a regal wave. "What message? I don't believe such a message ever existed."

"If you're talking about a message that Isobel here received from Ada, you are right, there was none." She turned to Isobel and began a slow handclap, "because she never received this message, or any other. Isobel Ramona Blackstock is a fraud, a liar and a cheat. She gets her messages from other mediums and passes them off as her own. I met with one of them yesterday, the medium who did get the message from Ada Blackstock." She turned back to face Isobel who had jumped out of her armchair and was flailing her arms around like a demented windmill.

"That is libel. I will sue," she spat.

"It isn't and you won't. If it weren't true it would be slander, which it isn't, as it's true. Claire sends her regards, by the way. No wonder you ran away every time her name was mentioned." Zelah turned back to Kennet. Time to get this back on track which meant getting Kennet away from the window.

"I understand Kennet that you want to keep the family close. You have them all here, and Miss Redland. And of course, Isobel who is also a relative."

She turned again to Isobel. "You got the message wrong, Isobel. If you'd listened properly you would have saved us a lot of time. She said, 'father of my son', not 'father and son'. Which means that you are both a Blackstock and a Quinn; good luck with that."

Isobel Blackstock was now staring at her open-mouthed. Undecided about whether to answer, she flopped back down into her armchair.

"Now, where were we? Tonight is the full Gwentshire County Council meeting when the Committee minutes that include the agreed finance for your statue will be proposed. They will be accepted. Then you," she turned now to Rufus Quinn, "are going to ensure that it goes no further, use your influence to ensure the Committee kicks it into the long grass, from which it never appears again—"

"As if," Rufus Quinn interrupted, sneering.

"Don't interrupt, it's rude, now, here's why you will do exactly that. First of all, Adolphus Quinn was a psychotic murderer. He began when he was a teenager in Ireland. We have the evidence. He continued when he reached the mainland, including his time in Newport. I believe he also killed a young police constable here in Newport. Next, the letter, the original of which I believe is in your desk drawer, proves this."

Kennet smiled, but didn't speak or move.

"Yes, I know you've burned it already. Never mind, I have a copy." She produced a piece of paper, battling inwardly to keep her hands from shaking, from the folder she had carried in. He held out his hand, but Zelah didn't move. Maggie was holding her breath. For a few seconds, no-one moved. Then Kennet Quinn walked around the desk and took the paper from Zelah's hand; she heard Maggie breathe out behind her as he examined the page. She handed him the 'animus' note.

"Don't you want to know how I got it?" She was teasing him now, playing to the audience, building up to the moment.

"I presume it has something to do with my daughter," he replied, not looking up from the paper. "She has paid for this."

Zelah clenched a fist but didn't rise to the bait.

"I also have the one you missed. By the way, was it you or Timothy Redland who stole the police letter from the archives?"

"None of your business" Kennett sounded irritated.

"Whatever, but whoever it was missed another, more crucial letter. Or did they? Perhaps you thought no-one else would see it or ever realise its importance?" His head twitched slightly and Zelah knew the latter was the reason. He had miscalculated; that one should have been taken too. "The one from Ada's family," she went on, "asking for the return of the brooch. They described the piece in detail. Here's a copy, Mr Smith." She passed the next piece of paper to him, which he took and studied and nodded.

"Before you ask, yes we have the brooch, safe and sound. As is your wife, soon to be your ex-wife." Maggie cleared her throat behind Zelah, a warning to not get carried away. She hadn't reckoned with Gerry Quinn's reaction.

"My mother is dead," he growled in a staccato voice from where he had been standing next to the door.

Zelah turned to him and gave a theatrical sigh. "No, your mother is alive and well, as I told you at the hospital Gerard. I'm guessing that Pa has never told you why she left. Allow me. On Christmas Day, when you were three years old, he poured boiling water over her hands. Slowly, so as to cause her agony. After she was discharged from hospital, she ran away. She was wearing the brooch on that day and she kept it. She gave it to us yesterday, here's another picture for your collection." Her voice was taunting as she flung the paper towards him. Kennet Quinn took it and gave all the papers to his father.

"She was a clumsy bitch," he said, "did it herself."

"The police didn't think so. You see," she turned to Gerry again. "If you spill boiling water on your hands yourself, you'll be holding the container with one hand, so the injury will be worse on one hand than on the other. The burns on your mother's hands were identical. What was she holding the pan with, Kennet, her teeth? Or did you help him?"

This was directed at Rufus, who immediately shouted back "No I did not. I wasn't there, it was an accident; she was crazy."

"What about the bruises on her wrists that showed where her hands had been held together?"

Rufus didn't reply.

"She's dead," Gerry whispered again but this time he shot a puzzled look at his father.

'*Enough*' Zelah thought, '*time to move on and keep to the script.*'

"Believe whatever you want, you can check with Pa later. To continue, we have two letters and the brooch and we know the murder of Ada Blackstock was not part of Adolphus Quinn's ongoing killing and torture spree. He probably saw her wearing the brooch and wanted it back. Once he had lured her into the death house, I expect he just couldn't help himself. Rather like you Kennet, when you began to beat your daughter."

Maggie cleared her throat again and Zelah strolled over to the window, glanced out and walked back to stand next to the mantle. As she did so she saw Maggie's eyes widening and her mouth speak a silent 'oh', as she saw what Zelah had seen but not understood, on their previous visit.

"Sorry about your brother, Helen. I'm supposed to say that,

aren't I? But I'm not sorry at all; he deserved what he got."

Helen Redland walked forward, hand raised, but Kennet stepped in front to stop her. "She trying to provoke you Helen."

"You did something," the woman snarled, "his death is down to you." She pulled against Kennet's grip, but couldn't free herself. "Kennet told me about you," she said as she twisted and turned.

"I did nothing, it was an accident Helen. I can do things, if I want to, would you like to see?" She turned to the window as Maggie pressed another button on her phone.

Expecting her to open and close the door again, Rufus turned towards it and Kennet glanced in that direction. They were looking the wrong way. They all jumped, Isobel screamed and Helen Redland stopped dead as a brick came crashing through the window. It shattered the centre window pane into fragments across the desk, rising high towards the ceiling and landed at Kennet's feet.

As they all stared for seconds at the brick Zelah took her chance, stepped closer to the mantle and picked up an object sitting on the end, the painted lump of wood. "Got you," she whispered.

"She just took something off the shelf," Isobel shouted, as the others all looked back to Zelah. Kennet looked around the room, then back at Zelah. He started towards her, then stopped, a puzzled look coming over his face,

"Put that back," Rufus roared, stepping forward, "that's mine, how dare you."

"Let me guess," Zelah said in a mocking voice, holding up the object. "Your grandfather Michael gave it to you. A precious gift to him, from his father Adolphus Quinn, who in turn claimed that his own father had made it for him, it being the only thing of sentiment he ever had to connect him to his family, when he had to leave dear old Ireland."

Rufus, who was now inches from Zelah, stopped in his tracks. "How do you know that?" His voice had become low, his tone wary.

"Keep away from her, Pa," Kennet said quietly to his father.

'*He really does think I'm a witch,*' Zelah thought. Keep going, almost finished.

She stepped around Rufus so her back was to the door, giving them a clear exit. "This," she showed it round, "was taken by the man who called himself Adolphus Quinn, from a child he killed before he had to leave old Ireland. He liked trophies, this was his first. Let me fill in the details for you. Your family name is not Quinn. This little soldier was made by the real Adolphus Quinn's father as a birthday present. Your ancestor took it from him, when he tortured and murdered the little boy, who really was Adolphus Quinn, because he wanted it and the child wouldn't give it to him. The method of the murder was similar to those that came later, although as time went on he refined his technique. Your ancestor's real name was Thomas Ryan. He didn't just take this little soldier, he took Adolphus Quinn's name and his identity. He was a sick, dangerous, evil man."

She paused and scanned each face. They all seemed frozen, stunned. Kennet was looking at her with calculation in his eyes.

"Four separate items of evidence, all of which we can fully prove; some of which you already knew. You knew what he had done." She spat the words out.

"We'll be at the meeting tonight and we'll be watching you, Rufus Quinn. If anything unexpected happens, you can expect to see this story in the national and international news media tomorrow." She turned back to Kennet. "If anything happens to any one of us, my retribution will be immense."

Kennet Quinn gave her a brief acknowledging grimace of a smile. "You will find that I can be subtle in my undertakings,

274

Mrs Trevear."

"You and me both, Kennet." She turned to Maggie. "We'll leave now. Enjoy the rest of your day, sorry about the mess."

With the little carved soldier in a firm grasp she and Maggie marched out of the room. No-one tried to say anything or to stop them. On the front step Maggie acknowledged Bob with a quick affirmative nod, then she and Zelah walked at a brisk pace back to the cathedral, where they jumped into Zelah's car.

They both sat in silence for a full minute, then they burst into hysterical laughter.

Chapter 37

When they reached the house, forewarned by a call from Maggie that they were on their way back, Jack and Nick were hovering near the front door. Although they had been laughing both Maggie and Zelah knew that they had suffered more stress than a turkey at Christmas… nor were their necks off the chopping block, yet.

They all went into the kitchen, where a fresh pot of coffee was waiting. Together they sat around the table, a warm breeze blowing in from the garden.

"What happened? Did I get it right?" Nick asked.

"Perfect timing," Maggie said. "I think they really believed that Zelah had raised that brick up, like a magician's act when the body rises from the table. It was well aimed, too, it hit the ceiling and landed at Kennet's feet, which I know was pure luck, but it really couldn't have gone any better. Well done."

"I haven't run that fast in a long time," he replied. "I couldn't tell from those footpaths how much anyone could see from the window."

"I don't think anything could be seen," Zelah said. "When Mischa told me about her secret escape route she must have known that no-one could see her. That gap in the wall is really well concealed, isn't it Nick?"

"Indeed, took me a few minutes to find it."

"I was concerned but when I checked and saw you'd put the brick on the patio table I knew we were OK. It was just down to your throwing arm."

"All those tedious javelin throwing lessons at school came in useful at last."

"You must have been good at it," said Jack.

"I was, good enough for the County team. Could have gone further if my mother had supported me." He stopped there.

"Well it paid off in gold today," Maggie said, squeezing his arm.

"So tell us the whole story," Jack said.

Maggie was about to start but was interrupted by the sound of the front door slamming.

"Oh dear." She waited until Bob found them in the kitchen. Before he could say anything she said, "come and sit down, I'm about to go through the whole story."

He plonked down into a chair, crossed his arms and stared at the table.

She went through the story in as much detail as she could remember, Zelah adding the occasional piece of information, up to the point where they walked out of the house. Nick and Jack tried to ask a couple of questions but she asked them to wait until she had finished.

"There it is. We have to go to the full Council meeting tonight over at Red Bridge. My feeling as we left is that Rufus Quinn saw enough to believe we have sufficient solid evidence to ruin his reputation. I doubt he will ever try to get the statue brought back onto the agenda. He'll find a way to stop it."

"What was all that about Claire? Who is this woman?" Maggie asked.

"Yes, I never got around to telling you, Zelah said. "Isobel never received any messages, it was a clairvoyant, a genuine practising medium called Claire Lewis. She moves in the same circles as Madame Ramona. She lives in Penarth and I went to see her yesterday. I didn't tell her what Isobel had done, I just asked her about the actual message."

"So that story she spun about how she 'heard' Ada, it was all lies?" Nick asked.

"Yes and no. The facts were more or less correct. She heard

the story from Claire, but she misunderstood a crucial detail. The 'father of my son' bit."

"Like you said, knowing that would have made a difference right from the start," Maggie added.

"Probably; I think she was genuine enough in trying to get the statue stopped. When the Quinns found out that she had contacted us to help her, they first tried to stop her by setting fire to her flat. Then they persuaded her on board. I suspect they offered to repair the damage and to finance her tour. Isobel couldn't resist that."

"If she's a fraud, how does she get, like messages and stuff, really?" asked Jack.

"She doesn't, she makes it all up and relies on others. Somehow I suspect that her tour will run into difficulties, if it happens at all now. Maggie, you and I are going back to see Claire tomorrow. She says there's more to the message, not about Adolphus Quinn, but something else, specific to us."

Maggie shook her head, "I have to pick Alice up from school tomorrow afternoon."

"I knew that, I've arranged to see Claire at nine."

"When did you know that they had the toy soldier?" Nick asked.

"It had been on my mind from the time I heard the story."

"That's why you wanted to know from Jennifer Quinn how many soldiers there were?" Maggie asked.

"Yes, at that first visit I didn't connect the lump of wood with painted eyes, sitting on the mantelpiece, with anything in particular. As you can see, it looks nothing like a soldier now. I did think it was an oddity in that impersonal room, which is why it stayed in my mind. I didn't remember any more detail until Jennifer told her story, I thought 'what if…' I had to check as soon as we came into the room, and as it turned out, I was right."

"What next?" Nick said.

"Nothing, I hope," Zelah replied, "We go to the meeting tonight, see it through, then monitor the Committee to make sure it never makes its way back onto the agenda."

Bob sat up slowly, unfolded his arms and put his hands on the table in front of him. All eyes were on him. "Do you really think, are you naïve enough to believe, that Kennet Quinn thinks this is the end of it? Game over? Congratulations to the winners?"

Maggie went to reply, but he held up a hand. "Let me tell you what happened when you left the house. We, Eric and I, waited for another fifteen minutes in which nothing happened so we were satisfied that no-one was following you. Then the front door opened and Kennet Quinn appeared. He stood on the doorstep smiling at us. He raised his hand, made the shape of a gun and mimicked firing it. At me."

He looked around at their shocked faces. "He will now get more sophisticated in the way that he goes for you. And probably for me. The outcome for the police? We have nothing on him, nothing to stop him, think about that." He stood up and left the house.

"Mum," Jack said with an imploring, helpless look.

It was Zelah who replied. "We are neither naïve nor stupid. Of course Kennet Quinn will want revenge but it isn't like we don't have any weapons. Let's not think about him for now. Nothing will happen quickly, I'm sure of that."

**

The Council meeting passed off smoothly. At one point, when the relevant sub-committee minutes came up, a Councillor stood up to make a point of order. Maggie panicked momentarily but it was about money spent on entertainment at awards events. The Mayor gave him a stunning rebuke. "I can't believe I'm hearing this. We have a sponsor, a benefactor, who gives thousands of pounds to support aspiring young artists throughout South Wales who need funds of any kind to further their careers. And you are arguing about the price of a few pretzels?"

The Councillor huffed and puffed, blustering about whether entertainment was necessary, surely the award itself was enough.

"Do you want to make us look like Scrooge, when we get the credit from these events, at little cost to ourselves? Is anyone else objecting to a few pretzels?"

No-one moved, "I suggest you sit down Councillor." He did.

The minutes were agreed and the agenda moved on. Maggie noticed a tiny, surreptitious nod between the rebuked Councillor and the Mayor, followed by a swift raise of the eyebrows at Zelah.

"What was that?" Maggie leaned over and whispered.

"Diversion. He owed her."

Rufus Quinn ignored them, both during the meeting and in the lobby afterwards. Kennet Quinn was not present.

"I think we're OK for now," Zelah said as they left.

Chapter 38

The following morning, Maggie and Zelah set off for Penarth to meet Claire Lewis. Bob had not returned but he sent a text to say that he had to work and would be back at lunchtime.

"He's sulking," Zelah said.

"The Quinns tried to have him shot, Zelah. He could have died and Kennet Quinn has made it clear he isn't finished."

"Sorry."

"Thank you, he'll tell me later. He's angry because he's concerned for all of us and he thinks we deliberately put ourselves in the firing line."

"We did."

"Yes, so what are we going to hear this morning?"

"Something about more of the message from Ada Blackstock, without the theatricals."

Claire showed them straight into her garden.

"What a lovely place," Maggie said, taking in a deep breath to smell the fragrances that were already releasing themselves from the flowering plants. "I wish I had this much talent; a garden is the best place in the house when you can make it as peaceful and tranquil as this."

"It's the work of about thirty years," Claire said as she sat with them. "My late husband loved it too, we spent most of our spare time out here; and a garden is never finished.

"Thirty years? I feel better now, I've only been at my home for four." Claire smiled. "Much patience is needed for a garden. Now, you're wanting to know about Ada and what she had to say?"

"We understand there was more than just information about Adolphus Quinn?"

"That's right, although that was shocking enough. I read about the statue, is it going ahead?"

"No," Zelah replied.

"Well I am glad to hear that. Now, Ada told me about two other people. One is a policeman called McRoberts, does that mean anything to you?"

"Yes it does," Maggie exclaimed to Zelah. "That's the case Nick has been working on." She turned back to Claire. "He disappeared in the late 1870s, I think. His immediate family started to refer to him as being dead after a year or so, but our colleague Nick Howell hasn't been able to find any evidence of his death. It's been a long-standing mystery. It's a genealogist's brick wall."

"I don't know how much the message will help, but Ada said that this man is lying on fallow ground. No let me think, on a fallow hill, does that mean anything?"

"Not to me," Maggie replied. "Zelah?" Zelah shook her head.

"We'll tell Nick when we get back and the other information?"

"That was about someone who was a friend of Charlie, I believe it has a Scottish connection. There was another phrase too, It sounded like 'low sin to mooch over', I'm sorry it wasn't any clearer than that."

Zelah again shook her head but Maggie was ruminating. "Somebody once told me about a Charlie. I can't remember who, or where or when; perhaps it will come back."

"If there is anything again, I will let you know, I have Zelah's card. Sometimes the spirits return, sometimes not, I can't say."

"Thank you Claire, you've been helpful," Maggie said. They spent a further ten minutes drinking their tea and chatting about the sea and the weather.

**

At home there was no sign of Bob and it was time for Maggie to set off. She told Jack where she was going and messaged Bob to say she was on her way to Hereford.

She and Alice chatted happily in the car during the journey home. Alice was going to miss her friends and was both excited and delighted about being asked to join Matthew's family in France.

"No-one's ever asked me before," she said, innocent of self-pity, but leaving Maggie's heart breaking.

"Well it sounds like you have a good group around you now."

"I like all of them, there isn't anyone at school I don't like. A few are a bit quiet, but that's OK, I think they like me."

"Enough to invite you to stay a month in a beautiful place."

They spent the rest of the journey talking about what Alice would need. She was excited at the prospect of shopping for some new clothes at the weekend, which would be the first mother-and-daughter outing of its kind for which Alice had shown enthusiasm. Previously Maggie had had to drag her out. She listened to Alice's new obsession – prehistoric history. Here Maggie had the advantage, she had already visited the Lascaux caves.

They reached the house in a good mood which for Maggie turned to anxiety at the sight of Bob's car sitting outside. She wondered what she was about to find herself on the receiving end of this time. To her surprise and relief the table in the kitchen was spread with Chinese takeaway dishes for four people and Bob and Jack were sat waiting.

After the exchange of hugs and greetings, they all sat down. "Thanks, Bob," Alice said, beaming. "They serve good wholesome food at school; boy have I missed this." She dived into several of the containers.

Maggie mouthed a 'thanks' across the table, which he returned with a hesitant smile. They would talk later, there would be rebuke, reproach, and guilt-tripping; it wasn't going to be easy.

**

Once dinner was over and both Jack and Alice were gaming, together for once, in Jack's room. Bob and Maggie went into the living room, each with a bottle of beer.

At first they made small talk, Maggie telling him more about the additional messages from Claire Lewis.

"Nick will pick up on Detective McRoberts and I know something about 'Charlie' but I haven't had time to think about it. I expect it will come back to me."

"I can tell you about that," Bob said. "Remember our visit last year to Lluis in Gandesa? He said we should go to find out about Charlie. I already knew the story but we never followed it up."

"Of course, I remember now. Is it interesting?"

"As for Charlie himself, I don't think there's been any progress for some years. It's part of the history around Gandesa, and Charlie is a nickname because no-one knows who he was. His skeleton was found when some civil war bunkers were excavated. They know he was a young man, but no-one has figured out his name or where he was from. He's been the subject of a tug-of-war between the Spanish state and Catalonia as to whose responsibility he is. All that's known is that he was one of the fighters who stayed behind to keep Franco's troops back whilst the rest of the army escaped capture, by being given time to cross the River Ebro. They were a group of International Brigaders who couldn't go home, Italians, and Germans and so on. They stayed to defend a strategically vital hill, knowing that they were going to die. Last I heard Charlie's bones were sitting in a bag on a shelf somewhere in Madrid, I think."

"That's terrible!" Maggie exclaimed. "He should be properly buried."

"It might have been sorted out by now, I don't know."

"We'll get onto it. Would you be interested in going back to Catalonia with me?"

"Of course, it's become an interest since our last trip but you can't afford to get too emotional."

"Why not? What I found out on that trip changed me. We should go back."

"Then I'll come with you. You said there was a message. What was it?"

"You're emotional too, no matter how hard you try to not show it," Maggie said. "The message was something like: 'low sin to mooch over'. It's nonsense to me. Why are you laughing?"

"It's not nonsense, it's Spanish. It sounds like it was probably 'lo siento mucho'. It means: "I'm very sorry.""

"Sounds intriguing. Anyway, we were getting around to elephant in the room. I know how angry you are with me."

"I was angry. I've cooled down, but just a bit. Do you understand what might come next?"

"I can make some guesses. Kennet Quinn is going to spend time trying to work out how to hurt us?"

"You sound flippant," he replied.

"I'm not," she protested, "but I don't see how he can, not without putting himself in the firing line for it."

"Then you're naïve, my Maggie. I could sit here and list ten ways in which he could hurt you physically and get away with it. He's getting away with attempting to destroy his own wife and daughter. He hasn't killed them, he doesn't want that now. He wants to know that they have a huge degree of pain. He gets satisfaction from that." He paused for a moment, to take a swig from the beer bottle. "He probably didn't expect that Zelah would take care of Mischa, but the kid's surplus to requirements now. He'll concentrate on you and Zelah; you personally, your kids, and your business."

"Then perhaps we should go for him first."

The veins in his neck stood out as he clenched his jaw and he banged his bottle down on the table. "So he can arrange to shoot you? Do you think I'm not trying hard enough to stop him?"

"Let's not get nasty with each other, Bob, you know I don't think that." She sat back in the armchair and put her bottle down on the table next to his.

"Have you thought about your security?" he asked.

"Of course, but I don't see how we can…"

"Not you, your business security, are your client files adequately protected?"

"I hadn't thought about it. I'll talk to Zelah first thing." It was her turn to pause, then she said, "I hate the idea that we are going to have to spend time looking over our combined shoulders; I don't want to just sit and wait. If he can work out how to hurt our business, then surely we can figure out how to hurt his."

"Good luck with that. Let me know if you come up with anything useful."

"Now you're being sarcastic but we have to try, starting tomorrow. Take the fight to the enemy."

Bob shook his head. "Just don't consider anything illegal, OK?"

Maggie sat up and directed a fierce stare at him. "As far as I am concerned right now, everything is on the table for consideration."

"That's what I'm afraid of."

Ten Weeks Later

Zelah settled into the deep comfortable armchair in front of a blazing fire, listening to the occasional hammer of the rain on the windows and read the local newspaper. The McCarthy Miller boys had assured her that this was not unusual weather for this part of Ireland at any time of year and it would clear up by the weekend. It wasn't unusual either to have a warm September but Zelah wasn't holding her breath.

This room was reserved for the boys and their family – of which she was the only remaining member they would acknowledge – and their personal guests and friends. Zelah and Mischa had been there for two weeks and would be returning home the following week.

The sound of shouting and laughter from somewhere inside the house paused her reading. She put the paper down; she hadn't really been concentrating on the local news. She sat back and for the umpteenth time thought over events of the past few months.

She continued to marvel over how Mischa had made a remarkable recovery. Surgery had repaired her jaw, her ribs had repaired themselves and her kidneys had returned to their normal function without intervention. There was some damage to her sight in one eye, which would not recover fully but the specialist she had consulted assured her there was hope for further improvement. She would have some vision there, enough to be able to drive, which was her burning ambition.

Whether or not the psychological damage would have a lasting effect was yet to fully show itself. Mischa had at first been depressed when she understood that Michelle had gone, but her early 'training', as Zelah called it, had taught the girl to read people well. She had not been too surprised that it had all been too much for her mother. At the start she blamed herself. If she hadn't looked for her mother would she still be working in the bakery, chatting to Mischa whenever she went in? Zelah had pointed out that the part Mischa had played in stopping the, albeit ignorant, public esteem of a psychopathic murderer was not inconsiderable. She was in a much better place, away from her abusive family, and safe. The situation would have come to a head one way or another and Michelle was never going to have been able to look after her. Mischa agreed, but Zelah thought that sometimes the girl still had moments of self-blame. Time would help to heal, but it was going to take a lot of time.

In the meantime they had talked about her future. She couldn't go back to her college course, which hadn't challenged. Zelah had proposed that she take up some further home study to prepare for going to university. Mischa had been thrilled at the prospect, she wanted to be a doctor. It was a secret wish that she had harboured for many years, without any believable prospect of it happening. Now that it could the question of where she would live in the meantime weighed heavy. She couldn't, and didn't want to, stay in Newport. The next best thing was to stay here at Rosscarbery House in Cork with the McCarthy Miller boys. This made Zelah anxious, it was still too close. She was now thinking that Mischa could go to Canada to spend a couple of months with Rick. She could take her when planned to visit him at the end of September. She would suggest to Mischa that she should accompany her, in the first instance.

They had not heard anything from Kennet Quinn since the night of the Council meeting, at the end of June. Of course, Zelah knew he hadn't gone away, he was just planning his next move… as were they.

There was, however, one big secret she was keeping, that she hadn't even hinted at to Bob, Maggie and Nick. The day before she and Mischa left for Ireland, she had been out shopping in Cardiff where, in the middle of a shopping centre, she had been confronted by Gerry Quinn.

He stomped up to her, blocking her path. "Where's my mother?"

"I have no idea," Zelah replied. "She's long gone. She was too scared of your father, now get out of my way."

He leered at her. "You were lying."

"Oh for God's sake boy, I met her, she worked in the bakery opposite the college in Newport. Check it out for yourself. She went by her maiden name, Michelle Morgan."

He looked hesitant but didn't move.

"I said, get out of my way, or I'll call that security man over there."

"Like I care."

"You're a coward, Gerry Quinn, just like your father and grandfather. You can't shoot me in the middle of a shopping centre in Cardiff, can you sonny."

He laughed then. "I had a knife that night, not a gun, you stupid cow," and he walked away.

Zelah had puzzled many times over that meeting and its implications. She was going to have to tell her colleagues but not yet.

She had kept in touch with the Irish Quinns and Ryans, and had proposed a weekend meeting in the autumn. They had tentatively agreed; remnants of the old feud still causing some reluctance. However, the prospect of a weekend, all expenses paid, at Rosscarbery had its attractions and Zelah felt confident that they would come together.

Maggie, Bob and Jack, having gone to France to meet up with Alice and her friends' families, were now back in work, and Jack and Alice were both back at college and school. Nick had left for America, where there had been news of his son Max and would be back in a few days. He was coming home disappointed, having reached a dead end again in his search for the boy. They all had work to get back to. The Adolphus Quinn story was finished and done. Nick had finally gotten around to revealing his theory about Quinn's death, on a day trip to Barry Island a few days after the Council meeting, which they had decided would do them all good. They had walked the length of the bay in sparkling sunshine then sat at a café underneath the covered end of the promenade.

"Haven't you worked it out yet?" he asked as they tucked into tea and ice-cream.

"You obviously have, so why don't you just tell us?" Zelah replied.

"He had to be stopped. There was only one person who knew the full story, who had been there at the start and could see that, in Newport, it was escalating."

"Are you saying that it was Martin Quinn?" Maggie asked. "He killed his own brother?"

"I am saying just that. And I believe he was the person who attacked and killed after Adolphus' death, in the same manner. He had to make sure his brother couldn't be suspected. It must have been horrendous for him. And finally, I suspect that he told Bridget everything. They married and both took the secret to their graves."

"I didn't come close to guessing that," Maggie said. "Did you ever find any more evidence of deaths as he moved around?"

"Yes, that too. In Liverpool and Manchester. All prostitutes."

"Then he did society a favour," Zelah replied.

They walked back out in the sunshine, reflecting on what

Nick had said, each with their own thoughts.

**

For the remaining summer months Zelah had kept up to speed with her story writing and they had new clients. There were the two cases from the information that had come from Claire via Ada Blackstock. Nick, when told about the policeman McRoberts, had been excited and looking forward to getting back into the case. He didn't understand the fallow hillside but was sure he would work it out. Maggie, now that she knew 'Charlie' meant Catalonia, was making plans to return there in the Spring of next year. Before she and Bob could travel, she had to find out the reference to the 'friend of Charlie'.

It was going to be an absorbing and busy autumn.

**

The End
To be continued in: "The Policeman"

Thanks and Acknowledgements

My grateful thanks and acknowledgements go to my first readers, Rose and Cheryl, who have again given me encouragement, feedback and advice on how to get out of plotholes!

I must also thank Dr Emma Alofs for her advice on psychology and Dr Pauline Cutting, for checking medical matters.

Once again, Ellen Morrow has done a superb job of re-proofreading this latest edition.

My family, as always, give me support and encouragement, technical advice and plenty of tea.

The cover, as for all of my books is designed by Alison Morgan at AliCat Design of Monmouth.

Thank you for reading this book!

If you have enjoyed it, it would be great if you could leave your feedback on Amazon and/or Goodreads. If you have any questions about anything featured within it, please contact me via my website: www.mkjonesauthor.com

As well as the website, there's also a Facebook page (currently Maze Investigations) and an Instagram page @mkjonesauthor.

I also write a newsletter, about my research and writing. You can sign up on the website and as a thanks for signing up, you'll receive two Maze Investigations case file stories:

"The Missing Air Raid Warden 1941"

And

"Murder in the Family 1840"

Following these there will be a new story with each newsletter.

Happy reading!

Have You Tried My New Series?

It's called 'The Curiosity Club of St Foy'.

There are two books in the series and both are available at Amazon, in both Kindle and paperback versions:

Printed in Great Britain
by Amazon